To Helvetica and Back

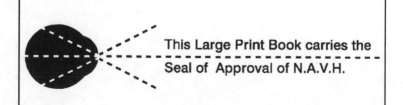

This Large Print Book carries the
Seal of Approval of N.A.V.H.

A DANGEROUS TYPE MYSTERY

To Helvetica and Back

Paige Shelton

WHEELER PUBLISHING
A part of Gale, Cengage Learning

GALE
CENGAGE Learning·

Farmington Hills, Mich • San Francisco • New York • Waterville, Maine
Meriden, Conn • Mason, Ohio • Chicago

GALE
CENGAGE Learning®

LIBRARY OF CONGRESS CATALOGING-IN-PUBLICATION DATA

Names: Shelton, Paige, author.
Title: To Helvetica and back / by Paige Shelton.
Description: Large print edition. | Waterville, Maine : Wheeler Publishing, 2017. | Series: Wheeler Publishing large print cozy mystery | Series: A dangerous type mystery ; #1
Identifiers: LCCN 2016058734| ISBN 9781410498601 (softcover) | ISBN 1410498603 (softcover)
Subjects: LCSH: Large type books. | GSAFD: Mystery fiction.
Classification: LCC PS3619.H45345 T6 2017 | DDC 813/.6—dc23
LC record available at https://lccn.loc.gov/2016058734

Published in 2017 by arrangement with The Berkley Publishing Group, an imprint of Penguin Publishing Group, a division of Penguin Random House LLC

Printed in the United States of America
1 2 3 4 5 6 7 21 20 19 18 17

For all the daydreamers.
You're my people.

ACKNOWLEDGMENTS

Thank you to:

My agent, Jessica Faust, who doesn't believe in giving up.

My editor, Michelle Vega, who also doesn't believe in giving up (I see a good pattern here).

Assistant editor Bethany Blair, copyeditor Courtney Wilhelm Vincento, cover designer Lesley Worrell, publicist Danielle Dill, cover artist Anne Wertheim, interior text designer Kelly Lipovich, and everyone at Berkley Prime Crime who has done such an amazing job with this book.

The Utah State geologists and paleontologist who spent a whole afternoon with me. Jim Davis, Mark Milligan, and James Kirkland — your stories about volcanos and scorpions and dinosaur bones made the day one of the best ever. Your kindness and generosity were above and beyond, and any mistakes I make in the book are because you were all so interesting just to listen to that I slacked when it came to taking good notes.

Ken Sanders, owner of Ken Sanders Rare Books in Salt Lake City, who spent a bunch of time answering my questions and telling me rare book secrets. He's a kind man with a wonderful bookstore.

My dad for his perfectly timed true story about baseball, a garbage truck, and a blind pitcher. His stories are always the best, but this one captured a whole room full of people's attention.

My readers and friends. I'm becoming very attached to you all.

My guys Charlie and Tyler. They save me from rocky rapids and bad hiking decisions, all while making me laugh and love them more and more every day.

A special thanks to an old and new friend Marianne Corbin Liston. I'm so glad we had a chance to know each other in high school *and* when we were all grown up. Your kindness and willingness to lend an ear are so appreciated.

I created Star City, Utah, but if it looks a little like Park City, Utah, that's no accident. When I lived in Utah, Park City was one of my favorite places to visit. I couldn't resist using its location and some of its charm and history to dream up an interesting place for a few murder mysteries. Thanks to all the Park City folks for looking the other way when I let my imagination take over.

1

"The trouble is with the 'L.' Do you have any idea how important an 'L' is?" Mirabelle said as we peered in at the old black Underwood No. 5.

"I do," I said as I wiped one hand over my leather work apron. I didn't think my fingers were dirty, but I usually had ink on me somewhere.

I reached into the back of the old Subaru and pressed down on the "L" key, feeling no pressure and seeing no movement. "It seems that the type bar has detached."

"Can you fix that?" Mirabelle said.

Mirabelle Montgomery was one of our more frequent customers. She'd been one of my grandfather's very first customers when he opened his shop, The Rescued Word, almost fifty-five years earlier. Back then, she'd been wildly independent, writing scandalous stories on her already-half-a-century-old and classic Underwood No. 5

typewriter that she sold to even more scandalous magazines; that is, when she wasn't carving powder on the slopes, taking on moguls and black diamonds like the fearless skier she'd been.

Mirabelle and my grandfather had formed a fast friendship, and though he had also been a fearless and accomplished skier, he often stated that he'd never been as good as Mirabelle. Chester, my grandfather's name and what he wanted everyone including his grandchildren and great-grandchild to call him, had started his career by fixing typewriters. Back in 1960 when he'd just turned twenty-two and was already a father of two, he'd known he had to find a way to earn an income, so he started a business. He had no idea that his skills would transform over the years and turn The Rescued Word into the rare and unusual business it had become. He'd been able to keep up with the changing times fairly well — in between the days spent on the slopes and along with his manual-typewriter repair skills, he'd taught himself how to restore old books to their former glory. He'd built his own printing press — one that was a "bona fide Gutenberg replica," or so he often said, after which he'd add some official-sounding lingo, as if an esteemed organization had given him the replica stamp of approval. Somewhere along the way, I figured out that no official experts had given the press any sort of notice at all, but it truly was an amazing machine.

Chester could even repair ink pens, the kind people spent real money for, the kind that were sought out when someone felt like they wanted to write something important or insightful. When I'd first started working with him at The Rescued Word, I'd been most surprised by how many people loved their pens. I preferred the throwaway variety myself, and I certainly noticed Chester's looks of perplexed dismay when I pulled out my BIC or Paper Mate, though he never said a word. When he added the sale of fine paper and modern-day writing instruments to his offerings, he created a business that was truly built to last.

"I can definitely fix that," I said to Mirabelle.

"Any chance I could get it back tomorrow?" Mirabelle said. "I have a letter for my grandson Miles. Oh, and I'll need more of that blue paper too. I can get that today though."

"You bet. I'll get this back to you by tomorrow," I said. I could, but it would mean working a little late, which was not a problem when it came to doing something for Mirabelle. I had to finish some work on a book that was due in the morning, but the printer was ready to go and the type blocks were in place.

"Oh, thank you, dear," she said as she placed a crooked, wrinkled finger gently on the back paper table of the typewriter. "This old thing is like a friend, a constant companion. I don't write stories anymore, but my grandbabies love receiving my typed letters. I would hate to disappoint Miles if my latest note wasn't sent in a timely manner."

"I understand. And fortunately, you're not the only one who loves these old machines."

"No? Gosh, most of the time I feel like I'm a dinosaur, a dying breed." She laughed.

"Not even close, Mirabelle. Some still like to write on old typewriters, and some just like to have them on display, but in working order. Nope, you're not the only one. This is, by the way, a very happy thing for The Rescued Word."

"Business is good, then?" she asked, her penciled-on eyebrows lifting above her thick glasses.

"Well, fortunately we do a little more than fix typewriters, but, yes, business is good."

"That's wonderful to hear. Chester and I talk about every manner of thing, but never

14

business. I worry about all of you over here. Bygone Alley is such a wonderful place. I'd hate to see anyone leave," Mirabelle said.

"I think we all stay pretty busy," I said.

The fairly level street that jutted off the steep slope of Main Street had long ago been affectionately named Bygone Alley for the old-time stores it held. Along with The Rescued Word, there was a yarn store with a couple looms, a beeswax candle store, a pocket-watch repair shop, a diner/cafe with a soda fountain, and the place where Professor Anorkory Levena taught Latin to people who actually paid him to learn the old, dead language. Though most of the services of those in Bygone Alley were from an earlier time and had been forgotten by many, all of us were still going strong, or strong enough.

I reached into the back of the Subaru and hefted out the almost ten pounds of Underwood. The No. 5s had at one time been the best of the best and used almost everywhere a typewriter was needed. They'd been known for many things, but they'd always been too big to lug around much, even if they had been called "portable."

I knew that Mirabelle's decades-old Subaru had logged about seventy thousand miles, because other than a few times a year to Salt Lake City, she only drove to a couple nearby places. She lived around the corner from Bygone Alley, on the street than ran along the non–Main Street side, and though the grocery store was at the bottom of a steep hill and around a tight S-turn, it was not far away. She'd also spent forty-five years working at the Star City Bank and Trust, but she'd walked to work every day. It had been an easy commute as she'd gone to and from the bank's Main Street location via Bygone Alley, waving to us every morning or joining Chester for coffee if she had the time.

I supported the typewriter with both arms as Mirabelle closed the rear hatchback of the car, stepped up to the sidewalk, and opened the front door of The Rescued Word, signaling me to go in first.

When my grandfather purchased the two-story brick building, it had been empty for a few years, but before that it had been home to the Star City Silver Mining Company, a company that had flourished in the late 1800s and early 1900s because of the vast amounts of silver that had been found in the mountains around the mining town now turned skiers' paradise. The first floor of the front part of the store was one big space that was filled with handmade wood shelving. The floors were also wood, original with plenty of long-ago-made scratches and marks to prove it. The walls were simple, now painted a soft blue where they weren't covered by shelves, either the shelves that Chester had built to hold the different types of paper we sold, or the now-antique shelving from the days of the mining company.

The mining company shelves extended down the middle of both of the sidewalls and were protected by ornately carved wooden doors depicting scenes of the beautiful and mountainous country and wildlife around Star City. The doors were works of art, and we'd had plenty of customers visit who just wanted to take pictures of the carved doors. We welcomed them in, and if Chester was in the mood, he'd come out and tell the visitors a story about the doors. He made up a different story every time. He figured he was just giving the visitors something fun to think about; I thought he'd probably get in trouble someday for his fibs, but he didn't seem to be concerned.

Filling the shelves were papers and note cards and envelopes of varying sizes, colors, and designs. Things were organized by color, and in some instances by complementary colors, like dark forest green and red. Or silver and gold. We had so many different animal note cards that we'd had to reorganize them by baby animals, adult animals, and then even further by which country they inhabited. Giraffes could be found on the Africa shelves, both under the baby animal and adult animal sub-categories.

There were windows along the top of the side walls that lit the entire space as the sun rose on one side and set on the other, finally slipping away every day behind one or another mountaintop, depending upon the time of the year. We had some light fixtures on the ceiling above but typically only turned them on in the late afternoon during the winter. Most of the time our cat, Baskerville, sat somewhere atop a set of shelves. He was there today, on the west side, enjoying the late-morning sun coming in the east windows. He'd move over to the other side soon.

The petite but surly calico meowed a suspicious greeting as he looked down upon us.

"Hello, kitty," Mirabelle said. "I don't think that cat likes me."

"Baskerville doesn't like many people," I said as I eyed the cat that I adored despite how he might feel about me or anyone else. He was the offspring of the very first calico who'd roamed the store. Arial had been my friend and companion whenever I'd visited The Rescued Word, my après ski buddy who'd sat with me while I drank hot chocolate and watched Chester either fix or print something.

Though I'd taken to skiing just like almost everyone else in Star City, I'd been the adolescent cursed with braces and glasses and wild, curly hair that went every direction except the right one. Chester, Arial, and the warm hot chocolate were my best friends for a long time. I still wore glasses, but the braces were long gone, and my curls had been tamed by some products that did what they promised.

Back then I had no idea that fixing typewriters, restoring books, printing things, and selling beautiful papers and pens would become my career. I just thought I was having fun. Arial had been a wonderful and loving cat. She had no idea that her son would turn out grouchy and misanthropic. I'd always love and care for Baskerville, though, if only because Arial would appreciate the effort.

Though Chester had built most of the non-mining-company wood shelves inside the store, my brother and I had built the two shorter shelves that took up the middle of the space. The shelves had taken us a long time to build, mostly because he'd been sixteen and I'd been six, and neither of us had the patience needed to finish such a project quickly, but Jimmy and I were still proud of our handiwork.

The paper products we sold were imported from all over the world. Paper was important. The way ink moved over the paper was important. Ink itself was probably the most important thing of all. Jimmy and I had a game we played — Chester's seven degrees of ink separation. Everyone and everything could be tied to ink in seven moves or less. Ink was somehow more important than blood; well, to Chester, at least.

The front portion of the store also displayed finer writing instruments and Chester's favorite pencil, the only one he'd ever use. Trusty No. 2 pencil–filled cups were placed all around the store. Many people bought a pencil or two, plucking them out of a cup on impulse, unable to resist the appeal of the memories the yellow No. 2s evoked.

I thought Mirabelle had come into the store to pick up more blue paper but we passed all the paper without stopping, and she was still behind me as we approached the back counter. I sent her an apologetic half smile when we both noticed my niece behind the counter, slunked down in one chair, her feet up on another as she moved with the beat of whatever song played in her earbuds. Her eyes were closed, and she had no idea that either I or a customer was in the building.

I supported the Underwood on my hip and knocked on the top of the counter, startling Marion to opened-eyed surprise. She pulled the buds out of her ears.

"Aunt Clare, Mirabelle, sorry. I didn't think anyone was in here," she said as she stood, because standing somehow must have seemed like the right thing to do.

"It's okay, dear," Mirabelle said. "Are you listening to one of those rapper singers?"

Marion smiled. "No, ma'am. I was listening to some country music." She looked at me. "I didn't know where you were. I walked this morning and saw Mirabelle's hatchback up but didn't know you two were behind it."

"Your Jeep okay?"

"Yeah. Just wanted to walk."

"We must have crossed paths. Do you know if Chester's in the workshop?"

"No. I just peeked back there and didn't see anyone."

"That's where I left him," I said, now curi-

21

ous but not concerned as to where my grandfather had gone. He never did like to stay in one place for very long.

"Maybe he went back upstairs," Marion said.

My grandfather lived upstairs, in the apartment he'd fashioned when my grandmother died twenty years earlier. When she died, their two children were already gone from the house, so he saw no reason to do much of anything but ski whenever he could and work. He sold the house and the lawnmower and moved to the second floor of his building, taking down walls and adding appliances to make it an open and comfortable space, particularly for a bachelor. Even though I do most of the work now, he claims he still loves living a mere twelve steps away from his store, and a quick walk to the nearest chairlift, of course.

"Maybe," I said. "Any e-mails?" She had become our stationery personalization pro, doing the work on the computer we kept behind the counter.

"I just got a couple of orders, but nothing urgent." She nodded toward the monitor.

I looked back toward the front, contemplating which task I wanted Marion to tackle first. As my eyes scanned, something flashed from somewhere, or had I just blinked at the wrong angle and thought I'd seen something? I couldn't be sure. I squinted and peered out the front windows, all the way to the diner across the street. Had the flash — what might have just been a brief reflection of the sunlight — come from outside, or perhaps the diner? I didn't see much of anything except indistinct summer-clothes-clad figures either walking down the street or moving around inside the diner. Whatever it had been, neither Marion nor Mirabelle seemed to notice it.

"The middle shelves could use some attention, dusting, arranging," I said. "And Mirabelle would like some more of her favorite blue paper. Would you gather that for her?"

"Sure," Marion said with a smile. She was mostly a good kid, but unfortunately she was not only a beautiful young woman with long blond curls and big blue eyes, she was also intelligent and seventeen, and better on a snowboard than almost anyone in town. Talks of her participating in the Olympics had gone from "maybe someday" to "probably the next winter games." Such a lethal combination created a number of sleepless nights for my brother, a single parent who tried not to be overprotective but failed miserably. I thought he was overcompensating for the fact that Marion's mother took off shortly after her daughter was born. She had left a note though, saying she was sorry she couldn't handle the responsibilities of being a mother at the tender age of twenty-one. We didn't talk about it much.

Everyone said Marion looked just like me, but my seventeen hadn't been a thing like Marion's. She'd been able to handle contacts, and her braces had been clear and barely noticeable. The hair products I'd found when I got older were at her disposal by age eleven, when she first started caring about her/our unruly hair. I still couldn't handle contacts, but I thought I wore my black plastic-framed glasses stylishly enough. Besides Marion's looks, though, her skills with a snowboard gave her a physical strength and confidence that would have been completely foreign to my teenage self. It was interesting to watch her from this side of those years and see just how much confidence could negate an undesirable trait or two.

"And let's turn the music off for a while and make this a no-earbud zone," I said.

Marion tried to stop her look of disappointment before it went too far. "Yes, Aunt Clare. Of course."

"Thank you." Mirabelle and I shared a

smile as Marion grabbed a duster from a shelf under the counter.

"You want to come back to the workshop with me?" I asked Mirabelle. It wasn't a question I asked most people, but Mirabelle had been in the workshop many times over the years. She and my grandfather sometimes shared their coffees back there as they shared stories about the days when snowboards hadn't existed and manual typewriters were all the rage and pretty much the only writing machines available.

"Sure. I'd actually like to talk to Chester if he's around," she said.

I thought I saw a pinch of worry in her eyes but it passed quickly so I didn't comment.

"Let's see if we can find him."

I repositioned the Underwood again and led the way down a short hallway and through a plain door. The back of the building had originally been used by the mining company as one of their small warehouses. Chester had found long-forgotten stuff like pick axes and lighted miner hard hats when he purchased the abandoned building. The apartment on the second floor didn't extend through this space, so the ceilings back here were the full two-story height, the back wall topped by the same kinds of windows that were in the front of the building, but these faced south, toward the rest of the town, the populated valley that stretched out from the bottom of Main Street. A concrete floor, metal shelves, a couple desks, some worktables, our type case filled with type blocks, other press supplies, and our printing press filled the space, but there was still plenty of elbow room. The shelves were currently topped with typewriters, typewriter parts, tools, press plates, and special paper that we didn't sell out front but used to restore some of the old books or for customers who hired us for small print runs.

The tall press always made me think of Frankenstein, something big and funny looking, put together well but with parts that didn't all seem to match, or at least were off sized. With a giant screw mechanism in its middle, its handle protruding outward, and the more sleek press plate extending out like a tongue, I'd long ago given it the name Frank. Chester had gone along and that was what he called it too.

The entire space smelled like books and ink and coffee, appealing and pleasant aromas, even when mixed together. At first glance it probably also looked like one big mess, but it was actually very organized. Most of the time I could find whatever I was looking for — even small tools or spare parts; Chester could find anything at any time.

"Oh! You're working on a book," Mirabelle said when she saw that I'd placed a readied plate on the press.

"I am. It's for a man whose father read to him from this book every night when he was sick for a few months as a child. The book has no financial value at all, but it means the world to the customer."

"What's the book?"

"*Tom Sawyer.* It's an old edition, but not a first; not even a second. There was just one page missing. I did some research to find the words that go on the page, but that was the easy part. I also had to come up with something that would re-create the design at the top of each page." I'd set the Underwood on a desk. Mirabelle and I both moved to a spot between Frank and another worktable. "See there?" I pointed to the curlicued pattern on a page of the book. "That was the hard part."

"Gracious, how did you do it? Did you have it — a stamp or something — made?"

"Nope, I got lucky. I could have had a steel type block made, but it costs quite a bit to have something like that tooled. The customer would have paid but I hoped to avoid that if possible. Chester has connections all over the world — people who collect stuff like these blocks. I found this exact one from a gentleman who lives in Romania. He's letting us borrow it."

Mirabelle shook her head slowly. "All for one silly little page in a book?"

I smiled. "Yep, one silly little page."

"That's amazing."

I didn't counter with how much fun it was. But it *was* fun to restore a book, whether one page or more, whether printing or rebinding or just cleaning it up a bit. It was also fun to bring an old typewriter back to life: make the keys work again, the bell ding properly, the carriage return smoothly. I'd found my career by accident, by hanging out with my grandfather and Arial when I was a kid. Chester had patiently taught me everything he knew about rescuing all sorts of words, bringing them back to life, perhaps even making them better than they were before.

Mirabelle was about to ask another question when a crash interrupted our conversation. The noise seemed to come from the space at the corner of the workshop, the area where my computer office was hidden behind another door. The staircase that led up to the apartment was on the other side

28

of my office and also hidden from where we stood. I was afraid Chester had fallen down the stairs.

I stepped around the press and the work-table just as a voice called.

"Clare! Get over here and help me, young lady!"

"Chester?" I said as I hurried.

I skidded to a halt once I turned the corner and faced both the stairs and the office. The good news was that Chester wasn't in a heap at the bottom of the steep steps.

But the news wasn't so good in my office. I wasn't sure exactly what had happened, but there was most definitely a heap of my stuff on the office floor, and my grandfather sat clumsily atop it.

2

"Chester, what happened?" I asked as I helped him stand.

"Oh, I got caught," he said.

Chester Henry was not delicate. Never had been, never would be if he had his way. He was seventy-seven years old but moved like someone much younger. He carried his six-foot frame confidently, his spine straight, with wide shoulders that were still not bony with age. He had a head full of thick white hair with a sizeable, perfectly groomed mustache to match. His skin was pleasantly wrinkled and probably permanently tanned with goggle outlines from years of exposure to the winter sun. From the age of about twelve, he'd also worn glasses. Since the moment he'd first donned them, he'd chosen round, gold wire frames. He'd met my grandmother not long after he'd first acquired the glasses, at the age of thirteen, and she told him that the round shape and the gold color made his blue eyes so "very lovely to look at." That sealed the deal and he'd never worn any other types of frames.

When not in ski clothing, his typical outfit of choice was a nice pair of pants, a button-up long-sleeved shirt with the sleeves always rolled up, and a sweater-vest, even in the summer. The only change that I ever remembered noticing was when he switched from wearing dress shoes to tennis shoes because they were so much more comfortable. That switch had come when I was probably six or seven.

Though neither physically nor mentally fragile, he did have an Achilles heel that kept him highly deficient in one particular area: technology. For some reason, he'd never quite understood cell phones, and computers had seemed hypocritical for someone "who fixed manual typewriters, for goodness' sake!" But I'd been pushing him to take the one-page, merely informational website that I'd created for The Rescued Word and expand it, hire someone to create a real online presence, something with a retail facet that would enable us to sell paper and pens to customers visiting us through the World Wide Web. He'd been fighting any such advancement, but we'd managed to get as far as letting customers know that we had a personalized stationery designer in house. One line had been added to our page: "Personalized Stationery Questions? E-mail Marion" and then her e-mail address. Her contribution to the business was growing steadily, but there was more we could do, more we could say to the world about our wonderful little shop nestled in our beautiful Utah mountain town. I'd tried and tried to show him other sites, how shopping carts worked, how easy it would ultimately be to oomph things up. And, though he hadn't bought on, I'd caught him a couple of times in my office, grimacing at the computer screen and moving the mouse. He'd never fess up to what he was really doing: trying to understand the universe inside that *dangburnit box,* but I knew.

"You got caught?"

"Yes. That wire was somehow wrapped around my elbow. When I went to stand up, I pulled it along the desk and it pulled everything down, me included. See, what I have told you about all this stuff?"

I inspected the "wire" and tried to visualize what had happened. It seemed that the cord from my mouse had somehow become wrapped around Chester, and when he went to stand, he pulled the keyboard and a stack of books that had been sitting on the corner of the desk onto the floor. And then he himself went to the top of the small pile. Just yesterday I'd been thinking about buying a wireless mouse. I guess I needed to get my own technology in gear.

"Are you hurt?" I asked.

"Of course not," he said as he straightened the bottom of his red sweater-vest and adjusted his glasses. "I was just afraid to stand up without you here in case I was still tied to that contraption. Who knows what I might have broken."

I nodded and smiled. "I understand. What were you doing?"

"Just fiddling around. Taking some time to figure out that crazy computer. See, the fates are against me, Clare, so very heavily armed against me. Every time I try to understand more, I end up understanding less, or creating a mess."

"It's not a big mess. Here, we can get it cleaned up quickly," I said as I made a move to reach toward the items on the floor.

"Hello there, Mirabelle," Chester said as he took a long-legged step over the pile of books and keyboard. "How wonderful to see you. Has Clare offered you coffee yet?"

The two of them left the vicinity of my office, evidently trusting me to handle the cleanup alone. I was sure they immediately ventured toward the coffee machine and the small table and chairs set at the other corner of the workshop.

Chester was typically pretty conscientious about cleaning up after himself. His hasty exodus was somewhat strange, but maybe he thought it would be rude to Mirabelle to pick up a few books before joining her. Maybe he was simply embarrassed and rattled. I didn't mind straightening things, but it was all just unusual enough that I became more curious about the entire scene, about what he'd been doing.

After I picked up the books — thankfully, none of them valuable or belonging to customers — and placed them and the undamaged keyboard and mouse back in their respective spots, I sat in the chair and pushed the button on the monitor. If he'd been on the Internet, he'd closed the browser. I clicked it open and immediately went up to the top bar to see the history of sites visited. Jimmy had taught me about checking the history back when Marion had been thirteen.

And suddenly, I didn't want to see what I was seeing. Chester had figured out how to maneuver, at least a little, through the Web. He'd gone to two sites — a search engine and then a site devoted to the treatment of pancreatic cancer. I clicked on the link to the cancer site.

I could barely read slowly enough to digest the words. Adrenaline sped up my heart rate and what I did read was so awful it was like looking at a horrible traffic accident. Words like "survival rate," "treatment," and "deadly disease."

Did Chester have pancreatic cancer?

No. No. I took a breath, let it out, and told myself not to jump to conclusions. None of this meant he had pancreatic cancer. Maybe he was having odd symptoms and was just researching. I'd done the same once for myself and become convinced that I had a deadly disease. It later proved to be nothing more than an allergic reaction to coconut. I was being ridiculous, thinking my grandfather had cancer based solely upon an Internet search. Besides, everyone knew that a deadly disease was attached to any Internet symptom search; one just had to click enough links.

I took a deep breath. I'd reacted way too quickly, and with disaster thinking leading the way. I tried to un-rattle myself.

"Get a grip, Clare," I muttered quietly.

But really though, why would he be looking for such a thing? Why would he use his limited computer ability to search for something cancer related instead of something about book restoration or typewriter repair? There must have been a solid reason for his curiosity. I'd have to ask. I hoped he'd have an answer that made me feel silly for my immediate panic and concern.

"Clare, I need you up front. We have a customer who seems unhappy and I don't want to bother Chester," Marion said from the doorway.

I cleared my throat. "I'll be right there."

I closed the browser and then pushed the button on the screen. I wished I'd never investigated, which was a phrase I'd heard Jimmy say a time or two when it came to his teenage daughter's online activities.

As I exited my office, I looked across the workshop. Neither Chester nor Mirabelle paid me a bit of attention. They were seated in facing folding chairs, each of them holding a mug of coffee and each of them with a serious, almost stern look on their face. Were they discussing something grave, something like pancreatic cancer?

Stop!

I'd have to find out later.

The unhappy customer was not dressed like our typical patrons. It was rare that someone who wore leather and chains visited our stationery store. During the summer, people frequently came in who'd been on a hike or were about to go on one, or perhaps just wanted to dress the part to blend in with the Star City population that was somewhat granola. Outdoor clothing and water bottles were common sights. But the tough-looking customer was holding neither a typewriter nor a book, so I quickly assumed he was there for paper or pens.

"Hi, I'm Clare, can I help you?" I asked.

"Yeah, I hope so. I want to buy a typewriter, one of those old kinds that don't get plugged in," the man said, his words and breathing oddly offbeat as if talking was painful, though he didn't look to be in pain.

He was probably in his midtwenties, however his drawn face and red-rimmed eyes belied the rest of his seemingly healthy, leather-clad frame, though the leather looked too warm and slightly too tight.

"I see. Well, sometimes we do sell typewriters on consignment, but at the moment we've got none to sell. I can take your name and call you if something comes in." I reached for a pen and a small notepad.

"No, I want to buy the one that you have in the back. I saw you carry it in."

"I'm sorry," I said as I pushed up my glasses. "I don't understand."

37

"The one that you carried in for that old lady. I watched you. I stood over in that diner across the street and watched you."

"It's not for sale," I said with a tone that hopefully told him the conversation needed to end.

Leather man didn't take the hint. Instead, he slammed his fist down on the counter and said, "No, you'll sell it to me now."

I really wasn't thinking about what I was saying or doing at that point; it was all mostly an intuitive reaction.

I grabbed Marion and half flung her behind me. "Get back to my office and call the police, Marion. Now."

I stepped into the space next to the counter where the man could have gone to follow my niece. That was definitely not going to happen, at least not without him shoving or tromping over me, dead body or not.

"You need to leave," I said to him.

He was momentarily startled, as though he hadn't realized the scene he was making. I heard the door to the workshop close and lock. *Good girl* ran through my mind, but I kept my focus on the man.

He shook his head and then he surprised me with, "I'm sorry. I'm under some stress and I shouldn't have acted so forcefully, but

38

I really need that typewriter. I'll pay a lot for it."

"I don't think it's for sale, but I'd be happy to find out and give you a call. What's your name and phone number?" I said.

The man squinted and pulled his mouth tight. He wasn't falling for my thinly disguised trick. I had no doubt that he wasn't sorry about his behavior. I also had no doubt that he was about to do something that might turn out to be bad for my health.

"Look, lady, I don't want to cause any problems, but I need that typewriter. Not one like it, not one similar to it, but that one. That specific one. Now."

"Why?" I said. And I was truly curious to know. Why in the world would anyone but Mirabelle Montgomery want Mirabelle Montgomery's old Underwood No. 5? It had some monetary value, but there had been so many of them made and used at one time that it wasn't worth more than a hundred bucks or so, and mostly it was just a personal treasure. What had Mirabelle said — an old friend?

"Because," he said as he pulled his chin down and glared at me.

I took a step backward. Was he going to charge at me? My system hadn't recovered from Chester's Internet search, and now it was infused with an even larger shot of adrenaline. I felt the pulsating fear in my throat and chest, but I tried to hide it with a firm glance up through my nerdy glasses.

He stepped forward but didn't charge. Somehow, even with knees that shook so hard I was bound to loosen a kneecap or two, I held my ground.

Fortunately, Star City was a small community, and my niece knew how to dial 911. The police station was down the Main Street hill off Bygone Alley, and the drive was fast and easy. The not-so-distant sound of sirens quickly became less distant. Just as I guessed that the police car with the loud sirens was turning onto Bygone, the man turned and retreated. As he darted away, something fell out of his pocket and slid under the front counter. He either didn't notice or didn't want to take the time to retrieve it. Whatever it was, I didn't immediately crouch to reach for it.

It took only a couple more seconds for the police car to park in front of The Rescued Word, but that was long enough for the man to have disappeared out of sight.

I grabbed the counter and took a deep steadying breath, or was it a bunch of breaths? I was too dizzy to know for sure. I'd need to keep it together for the police, not to mention for Chester. I wouldn't want to scare him more than he probably was already. I silently told myself I could fall apart later, much later.

Baskerville hopped up to the counter. He sat down and looked at me as a low growl rumbled in his throat.

"I appreciate the support, but you're a little late. You could have bitten his ankles or something."

The tip of his tail twitched before he stood, moved his body protectively in front of me, turned to face the front doors, and sat again as though he wanted to be the one to greet and talk to the police.

I ran my hand down his back as I took another steadying breath. He might not be the best cat, and he would never compare to his mother, but I was suddenly very glad he and I were both okay.

3

"He was wearing leather?" Jodie said.

"Yes, all leather from what I could see," I said.

"In this heat?" Jodie said.

"Yes," I said.

Jodie jotted another note in her notebook. To most everyone in Star City, Jodie was Police Officer Jodie Wentworth. She was also my best friend, had been since we were sixteen and I'd stopped hiding out in The Rescued Word as much. However, I'd still been too shy, but she'd been the opposite. Somehow, our opposites had attracted and the result had been a thirteen-year-long camaraderie. I'd seen her through a brief marriage and the resulting divorce, and she'd stayed by my side even after I'd broken up with her brother. Of course, I'd broken up with him because he'd been cheating on me, but still I'd appreciated where she'd placed her loyalties, ignoring the whole blood-being-thicker-than-water thing.

Jodie looked up from her notebook, her green eyes softening like they weren't supposed to do when she wore her uniform. "You okay, Clare?"

"I'm fine. Shaken up but fine. No harm done."

"Good," Jodie said. "Let me know if that changes at all. Can I get you a cup of water or something?"

"No, I'm fine." I smiled.

Jodie had always been such an odd mix. She was naturally pretty, not knock-out gorgeous, but pretty. Her green eyes were her best feature, but she mucked them up with way too much eye shadow. I'd told her this a number of times, but it hadn't stopped her from applying the powdery layers. She was petite and curvy in her uniform but walked with the heavy steps of either a medium-sized man on a mission or someone still in their ski boots. Her soft blond hair was always pulled back in a short, low ponytail — even when she wasn't working. I'd also told her a number of times that she had the type of hair and face shape that would be perfect for letting her hair down every now and then, but she hadn't taken that input either.

She was the youngest of five siblings, all boys except her. Her father had been a police officer and so was the brother that I'd broken up with. The other three brothers were firemen, and their mother had worked dispatch at the fire department for years. Though we lived in little Star City, we had our fair share of crime and villainy. Okay, probably just crime and fires, not so much villainy. Even though the Wentworth family members weren't required to be big-city cops and firemen, they had small-mountain-resort-town tough down to a science.

"Got it," Omar said as he appeared from the other side of the counter. In his gloved hands, he held the item the man in leather had dropped: a camera.

Omar Miller had been Jodie's partner for three years, and they worked well together. Omar and his wife had moved to Star City from California in search of easily accessible snow that could be skied upon as frequently as possible. Omar's wife, Jacky, had recently given birth to their first child, a daughter they'd named Star to honor the home they'd come to love. I'd mentioned to Jodie that I hoped a middle name had come into play because I didn't see Star from Star City wanting much to do with her first name once she hit junior high or so. Jodie still hadn't gotten back to me with an answer. Whenever Omar or Jacky was around, I could see dark circles from sleep deprivation under their somewhat swollen eyes. I wondered just how much skiing they'd get in this winter. Jodie assured me they'd already purchased Star's first set of skis.

Omar wasn't a big man, but he was — according to Jodie — the strongest person on the police force, his wiry but muscular arms able to lift heavier weights than all the other officers. I didn't understand weight-room jargon, but I'd been pleased to hear that Omar's talent had bothered Creighton, Jodie's cheating brother and a much bigger man who spent hours in the gym.

Omar's pale skin and white blond hair caused him to stand out in a crowd, almost glow a little, and when he was with his wife, who had darker hair and skin, they made a striking couple. It looked like Star had gotten her dad's complexion, but it might be too soon to tell.

"That must be what fell out of his pocket. I'm not sure if he noticed or not, but I really don't think so. I think he was too panicked to care," I said. "He wasn't really good at being . . . gosh, criminal-like. If that makes any sense. Maybe he didn't have much experience at it."

"I get that," Jodie said. "Let's dust for prints, Omar, but bag that first, please."

"Will do," he said as he followed her instructions. Omar had always been second fiddle to Jodie. He seemed to like it that way; so did she. It worked.

After Omar put the camera into a plastic bag he pulled out of his side pocket and then walked it over to a case he'd brought into the store with him, Jodie turned back to me.

"You say that Mirabelle's typewriter isn't valuable in any way?" she asked.

"No. Well, yes, there's a little monetary value attached to an old Underwood No. 5, but not much. Some people collect, some people still like to write with them, but not many. Mirabelle's is in great condition, other than the one small repair I have to make, but it's well used. I doubt even a serious collector would want it."

"Can we go take a look at it?" she asked.

"Sure," I said.

We left not only Omar in the front of the store, but Chester too. He'd come back in after seeing Mirabelle to her car and walking Marion home. Baskerville greeted him with an angry meow before jumping into

46

his arms. He petted the cat absently as he looked around the store. I caught his glance and signaled that Jodie and I were going to the back. He frowned and nodded and then cut a path toward Omar.

Chester had been stoically silent after all the ruckus. His face had pinched with worry and concern, but he hadn't become visibly upset or angry. I knew him well enough to know that he was in fact very upset and very angry. The idea that his daughter, granddaughter, and a beloved friend had been put in harm's way did not please him at all. I was sure he was holding his emotions in check so he appeared strong and in control. He was trying not to worry everyone else, but I also thought there was a chance he could blow at any second. Chester could huff and puff and flail his arms in a big way when he was upset. I hoped Omar wouldn't have to be on the receiving end of a Chester tirade, but I knew the police officer could handle it. It occurred to me that Chester shouldn't be taxing his emotions anyway. Even if he didn't have pancreatic cancer (oh, please no), he was in his seventies. No one got hurt, and there was no need to risk upsetting his health.

I turned and led Jodie to the back. Her heavy footfalls followed me to the desk with the typewriter. First, she lifted it.

"Both heavy and awkward. I love technology," she said as she placed it back on the desk. "Can't imagine life without my computer and a good word processing program."

"I agree. Mostly. Sometimes there's something quite wonderful about typing on these old things. The sounds." I pushed a key, creating the metallic click that almost everyone but the younger generations could identify with. I pressed the space bar enough to make the bell ring, which actually caused Jodie to smile. And then I returned the carriage. "See, you and I had computers, but there were also some typewriters around back in our high school days."

"I see what you mean, but I'm still choosing my computer. What's wrong with this one? Why did Mirabelle bring it in?"

"The 'L.'" I pushed the nonresistant and ineffective key. "The fix isn't a difficult one. I can have it done for her by tomorrow." I sent a quick glance toward the printing press. I still had the book to finish too, but I'd get everything done even if I had to work late.

"Why would someone want this typewriter?" Jodie said.

"I have no idea. There's nothing extra

special about it at all. If a person wanted one, they could probably find something online somewhere, and without much of a search."

Jodie tapped her finger on the boxy typewriter case. She picked it up again and with my help heaved it every direction, looking at the bottom, the sides, inside, at the keys.

"Is it made of anything that's valuable nowadays; you know, like copper or something? Copper's being swiped from everywhere."

"No, I don't think so."

Jodie put the typewriter back on the desk with a solid thunk. "You don't suppose that the man's desire to have the typewriter was more about Mirabelle than the typewriter itself?" she said thoughtfully.

A shot of concern rattled me. Did leather man just want to get at Mirabelle, and perhaps harm her in some way? The ideas didn't connect without more information, but still, the thought that someone might possibly want to do something bad to Mirabelle was worrisome.

"We've known Mirabelle all our lives, Jodie. I can't imagine that anyone would want to hurt her, but I suppose it's possible. You can never know everything about someone, I suppose."

"Right. Excuse me a minute," Jodie said as she reached for the radio on her belt and made her way back out to the front of the store. I heard something about sending officers to Mirabelle's house, but I didn't catch all the details.

Like everyone else, Jodie had been bewildered by the man's request for Mirabelle's typewriter, certain that there'd been some mistake, some sort of typewriter identity mishap. She hadn't recognized any part of my description of the man, and she'd been angry that I just hadn't handed the Underwood No. 5 over to him.

"Clare, it makes no sense that you wouldn't just give him the typewriter. It certainly isn't worth anyone getting hurt over."

It had been difficult to explain that my mind hadn't made it that far yet, that I'd only been able to think as far as not giving the man Mirabelle's prized possession. The wrongness of it bothered me. I supposed if he had hurt me or something more serious had happened, I would have given him the typewriter and whatever else he wanted with the hope he'd just leave.

I shivered.

I was glad nothing more serious had occurred.

I moved to the back door of the workshop

and confirmed that it was securely locked. A narrow old walkway ran behind our building, and the small Star City post office was directly across from our back door. The walkway had only one spot for entry and exit, directly off Main Street. It wasn't welcoming and no one really used it to get to back doors anymore. The backs of the old buildings had once been lit by charming gaslight replicas, but as those had broken over the years, most had never been replaced. The population and the tourist influx to Star City grew large enough at some point in the 1980s to forgo the charming hidden walkway adventures of the town for the streets that were out in the open, where lurking wasn't as easily accomplished.

The walkway was mostly a forgotten space, but still a manner by which someone could potentially get to the back doors of buildings. I hadn't heard of any problems lately, but making sure we were safely locked in was suddenly a priority.

Leather man didn't look familiar, but I didn't know everyone who lived in Star City. If he wasn't from here, he might not have known that the walkway existed, but I decided it wasn't a risk worth taking.

We had what I'd recently told Chester was a useless security system. There were cameras outside the front and back doors of The Rescued Word, and one inside the front part of the store as well as sensors on the doors. The cameras were, in theory, supposed to be wirelessly attached to a program on my computer. That program was supposed to record all activity, and the sensors were supposed to sound an alarm when someone used something other than a key to enter through the doors. The problem was that we'd gotten lazy. Again, the walkway was just an old unused space at this point, and nothing bad had happened inside the store before today. Neither the cameras nor the sensors had worked correctly in a long time, and we had made no effort to fix them.

I needed to turn on the computer and see if I could get them in working order before I went home. Home. Suddenly, I didn't want to leave Chester here alone, upstairs with someone like leather man roaming around. How could I get him to come stay with me for a few days?

My thoughts were interrupted by a forceful head butt to my ankle.

"Hey, Baskerville," I said as I crouched.

The cat was not in a good mood, though that was not unusual.

He meowed grumpily and then let me scratch behind his ears for a moment before he rammed his head against my lowered knee and then walked away. He looked over his shoulder as if to signal that I should come along, so I did.

He leapt up to the desk that held the Underwood. He sniffed at the machine and then sat and looked expectantly up at me.

"What?" I said. "That's Mirabelle's."

Despite Mirabelle's earlier evaluation that the cat didn't like her, he, in fact, liked her better than he liked most people. Or at least he acknowledged that he knew who she was. I'd seen him watch her from one of his high perches, his eyes following her as she shopped or just stopped by for a chat. For the most part, Baskerville ignored our customers, giving them quick, impatient glances and then resuming his solitary ruminations or whatever he did up there on the shelves. Not Mirabelle, though. No, he watched her, inspected her, seemed to consider her perhaps a bit closer to being worthy of his attention than the other customers.

"Clare," Jodie said as she came back through the door to the workshop. "You know we're taking the camera the guy dropped, right?"

"Of course."

"I'll let you know what we find on it."

"Sounds good."

"We have a little more information. There's a biker group in town. They're helping with a goat relocation project over in Purple Springs Valley."

"We have goats that need relocating?" I didn't go directly to the old inside joke between Jodie and me.

She and I (and probably others, but I couldn't be sure) had long called Purple Springs Valley Polygamy Springs Valley, because a family of polygamists had a small compound smack-dab in the middle of the valley bowl. Polygamy was neither legal nor an accepted practice in Utah, but it infrequently happened. There was no real predominant religion in our tourist town in the mountains, unless you called worshiping the snow a religion, and actually, lots of people did. And though the predominant religion in the rest of the state hadn't been keen on the idea of polygamy for decades, the miniscule percentage of those who still participated in the practice made it impossible for the state to escape the reputation that many Utah men folk liked to be married to more than one woman at a time.

The compound in Purple Springs Valley was the only one I knew of in the area and had at one time been the object of deep curiosity for Jodie and me. We'd peeked over the gray stone walls, we'd tried and fortunately failed to sneak into the compound once — this was long before Jodie became an officer of the law. We'd discussed the whole idea of polygamy many times over. We were thrown for a loop when one of our high school friends became wife number three in the family. How did Linea Christiansen, cute cheerleader, beer-drinking party girl, come to want to be someone's sister-wife? We'd talked about trying to find out, but we'd never spoken to Linea about her choice.

To perhaps further highlight our diverse population, a monastery also took some space on the far side of the valley. Hidden behind some tall evergreens was a quiet place with an ornate fountain in the center of a spread surrounded by sandy red stucco walls, where sworn-silent monks did two things: prayed and made wine. Their brand was called Purple, and though they weren't big producers, their wine was delicious.

A smattering of houses was also spread throughout the valley, and some others were hidden behind trees around its border. It was a great place to live. Despite the large number of people in both the polygamist compound and the monastery, there was lots of open space and beautiful views.

"Apparently, we do have some goats that need to be moved," Jodie said. "And this biker group, though they wear lots of leather and denim and make themselves look scary and tough, is a good group. They go around doing good deeds, helping out charities and such. However, maybe there's a spoiled apple or something in the bunch. We'll check them out."

"How are they relocating the goats?" I asked. "Are goats herdable or do they have to be sedated and transported?"

"I have no idea," Jodie said. "All I know is that the people doing the relocating are wearing leather in the heat of summer. Seems a little too coincidental if you know what I mean."

"I do."

Jodie turned to leave but I stopped her. "Hey, Jodie, before you go, can you help me get our security system back up?"

"Sure."

We set to work on the computer, the cameras, and the sensors. Though Jodie and I knew our way around the Internet far better than Chester did, we couldn't quite make everything perform together. However, Omar could, causing him to puff a little with masculine pride when he pushed

56

the buttons that finally got everything to sync correctly. Jodie let him have his moment, patting him on the shoulder with some manly thuds and telling him he did a good job.

Once the officers left, I found Chester standing by the front window and staring out at Bygone Alley. Baskerville sat beside him and looked at me as if to tell me now wasn't a good time to bother my grandfather. It didn't seem like Chester was looking for anything specific, just giving his eyes a place to rest as he thought. I swallowed hard and decided that, despite Baskerville's warning, it was time to face the fear that was still coursing through me even through all the other crazy and scary stuff that had happened today.

"Chester?" I began slowly. "You okay?" *You don't have cancer do you? Please tell me you are still healthy and strong.*

"I'm fine, Clare. I'm not happy about someone coming into our place of business and jeopardizing the lives of people I care for, but I'm fine. This world is crazy and only getting crazier all the time. The bold behavior of criminals does not bode well for any of our futures."

"No, but no one was hurt, so all's well that ends well, for today at least."

He nodded and smoothed his mustache with his knuckle.

"Can I ask you something?" I said.

"Yes. But later, Clare-bear. I have something I need to take care of. I'm closing the store for the rest of the day. I'm grateful that we've got the cameras working and I'd like for you to go home too. Take the day off."

"I might make it an early day, but I need to finish *Tom Sawyer* and I'd like to get Mirabelle's typewriter back to her."

"The police didn't take the typewriter?" Chester turned and looked at me.

"No, Jodie looked at it but there wasn't much to see."

"Hmm. Well, I suppose she knows best. Okay, that's fine, then, but I don't want the doors unlocked, I want the security system set to high if there is such a thing, and I want you to have your cell phone on you at all times."

I pulled my cell phone out of my pocket. "Got it right here."

"Good. I don't like this at all, Clare. Not even one little bit."

"Me either, Chester, but no one got hurt. All's well that ends well, right?" I repeated.

"So they say," he said doubtfully.

"I'll be okay. I have lots of work to do."

Reluctantly, Chester left me alone in the store. Well, Baskerville was there too. Chester didn't tell me where he was going and I didn't push too hard to find out. Baskerville climbed up to the east shelves to take advantage of the afternoon sun. He circled twice and then curled into a ball with his back toward me.

There had been no good moment to ask Chester the questions I truly wanted to ask him. Or I was just making excuses and was afraid of knowing the answers. We still had a serious conversation ahead of us.

I thought that I might be worried about being alone, but after I closed and locked the front door behind him, and then triple checked the lock, I realized I was grateful for the quiet time to get some work done.

I did leave the door — the one that Marion had been so smart to lock earlier — between the workshop and the front of the store open so I could better hear any noises from the front. I also triple checked the back door. I was as locked in and as secure as I could possibly be.

I decided to work on Mirabelle's Underwood first. The press was ready for *Tom Sawyer,* the press plate in place, but the task of printing the missing page would be messy and I'd need to clean up after I was done. I planned to save that for last.

I kept a thorough record of all of our book restorations, and placed a The Rescued Word watermark on each page that we altered or added. The mark was small and unobtrusive, but used so as not to deceive — or attempt to deceive — future owners of the books. The current owner of *Tom Sawyer* asked to have the page printed and simply placed in its proper space. He didn't want me to rebind the book with the page permanently bound inside. I didn't quite know why, but I was happy to do whatever the customer wanted. I gave the press one last inspection before I moved to my desk and Mirabelle's No. 5.

It really was a beast, but a beautiful one that was once well appreciated for its durability and ease of use. It changed the world of words, bringing a type speed with its numerous type bars that couldn't be matched by earlier 1900s versions of typewriters that had single type elements. Along with the speed, it brought a front stroke so that the typist could see what they were typing without lifting up the carriage. Though the No. 5 wasn't the first to do such a thing, that feature combined with the type bar, the QWERTY keyboard, and the ribbon inking (as opposed to rollers or ink pads) gave typed words quite the boost. Chester often said that the No. 5 revolutionized the entire world.

It was a square, squat, boxy machine, backside-heavy with a giant carriage, or that's how it seemed nowadays in our carriage-less world. Looking at the back through the open sides, it reminded me of a clock's inner workings, with a small hand crank that reversed the ribbon in front of the straight lines of key bars.

The keys were closer together than the keys of today's standard-sized keyboard, and they were smaller than what we've become used to. Round buttons made for petite hands and fingers back in the day.

I'd fixed unattached type bars before. No matter their durability, time and use could cause issues. Sometimes a typewriter fix was a matter of bending something or replacing a spring or a small screw. Though it wasn't a difficult fix, it required taking off the top carriage, unscrewing some of the casing, and then using some thin wire and a little precise soldering. Since I was already going inside, I thought I should inspect the other keys and type bars first to see if anything else needed attention.

I peered at the uniform fanned line of bars. Every one of them was still straight, though, expectedly, a little grimy and darkened from time and ink.

I moved the typewriter to the edge of the desk and crouched. This was the best angle to see the key bars' movement.

I pushed on the "L" key. Not surprisingly, it still didn't work. Then I started with the "Z" and continued back and forth over the keys. Every key other than the "L" seemed to work perfectly until I got to the "K." That one was a little sticky, which meant it might have become slightly bent. I stood, pushed on the key again, and observed its movement from above. Yep, it was slightly bent. I grabbed two sets of long-nosed pliers from a shelf, went back to the desk, and crouched again. I grabbed the arm and held onto it with one of the pliers. The bend was so slight that I decided I should just leave it alone. Just as I was about to release it, I noticed something on the side of it.

It was just a scratch, really, something that could happen accidentally over the years and something that I was only barely able to see through the grime. It looked like the number 6 had been scratched onto the bar. It suddenly seemed too precise to be random. Something in my gut told me to take a closer look. I reached for a small towel on the other end of the desk and gently wiped the arm as clean as I could. As I looked at it from the side, I could see that the mark was either a 6 or an upside down 9. However, it still could have been an accident, a fluke.

I started pushing keys again, moving slowly, looking now at each side of each bar, wiping ink and grime off most of them. I found the numbers 2 and 8. I decided I wasn't looking at an accident. These numbers had been placed on the key bars on purpose. Were they the reason leather man had wanted Mirabelle's No. 5? I became more anxious as I made each new discovery.

When I was done, this is what I had: five 1s, one 4, one 3, two 8s, one 0, one 2, one 9, and two 6s (if the 6s and 9 were to be read upright like I deduced), and an N and a W. So — 11111438802966NW.

Of course, I had absolutely no idea what it all meant. Maybe it meant nothing.

But at the moment my discovery seemed interesting if not important. I grabbed my phone from my pocket. I was going to call Jodie and get her to come back to the store, but I realized that she was done working for the day. I knew that it would not have mattered when it came to Jodie, but the numbers could probably wait until tomorrow. Maybe by then something would come to me regarding what they meant, and she'd have fresh eyes too.

I put the phone back in my pocket, stood up straight, and stretched backward, moving my neck and popping my shoulders. I needed a small break. Well, my eyes and shoulders needed a break before I continued.

I wondered where Chester had gone off to and why he hadn't come home yet. It wasn't like him to be out much after seven o'clock at night. The day had gotten away from me and it was already almost eight. I hadn't realized how much time I'd spent on the typewriter, and I still hadn't even soldered it yet.

As I thought about Chester, the pang of worry sprouted again. I hoped he was okay, both at the moment and in general. I tried to reach him on his cell phone but it went directly to voice mail, which wasn't unusual. He didn't much like his cell phone and often forgot to turn it on or even charge it.

I made my way to the darkened front of the store and peered out the window. Bygone Alley was quiet, as it usually was in the evening. The street was lit but only by a few old-fashioned streetlights that cast a warm if not bright glow. The diner across the street closed at eight on summer weeknights, but it looked like there were still a

64

couple of customers finishing up their dinners, or maybe desserts. Abraham, the diner's owner, made mouthwatering cream pies.

An old wooden ornate door was positioned to the left of the diner. It led to a small entryway and a skinny flight of stairs. At one time there had been a dance studio at the top of the stairs, a place where young children, mostly girls, had studied ballet with Nicolai Bartovsky, a Russian immigrant who'd come to Star City during our small and mostly unsuccessful gold rush in the mid-twentieth century. One small nugget of gold had been found in a stream at the bottom of a canyon, and it seemed the whole world heard about it — and this was long before the Internet-instant-news days. Chester told me that Nicolai hadn't found any gold, but he'd found a vital dance-student base, with mothers and fathers who thought the drive up from Salt Lake City was worth the effort even in the middle of brutal snowstorms so their children could learn ballet from a Russian dance master. Apparently taken by his attitude and accent, no one thought to check Nicolai's references. The town found out later, a few years after Nicolai's death, that he might have known a little ballet, but he was no master. Perhaps he had found gold after all.

For a long time after his death, the studio remained empty until Anorkory Levena — a regular old Utahn (southern red rock country) with a foreign-sounding name — came to town in the 1980s for the same reason Omar and his wife had: the snow. Having the greatest snow on Earth, or so one of our state campaigns advertised, drew many skiers and snowboarders to Star city. When Anorkory first came to town, he worked as a ski instructor at the resort, but those sorts of jobs weren't known for their comfortable salaries. Luckily he knew Latin and had become enamored with it during his six-year stint at the University of Utah. He didn't ever earn a degree, but he sure got good at Latin. Anorkory once told me that his mother often said to him, "If you had a passion for anything else like you have for that silly language, you would go far, my son."

It had taken him a while, but he'd built up a steady business full of people who actually *wanted* to learn Latin, or people who wanted their children to learn it. The road up from Salt Lake City had improved since Nicolai's time, but there were still snowy days to contend with. Anorkory's students didn't seem to mind. He might never be a millionaire, but he had a comfortable life that allowed for plenty of powder time in the winter, and a nice, big dance studio space to use as his classroom.

I'd never understood why anyone would want to learn Latin, but I was happy for Anorkory and his little gold mine too.

He was exiting through the ornate doorway as I spied out the window. Though it was summer in Star City, it only got uncomfortably hot a few days a year. And the mountain air cooled to sweater or light-jacket perfection almost every evening. No matter what the temperature was though, when he wasn't wearing his snow gear, Anorkory wore an old trench coat and a dramatic black scarf that made his hound-dog eyes look more artistic than sad.

He locked the door efficiently, his attention fully focused on each task he performed, which was something I'd come to expect from him, and took off down the sidewalk in front of the diner. I waved when I thought he looked my direction, but he didn't return the greeting. He must not have seen me.

The rest of the businesses were quiet, their windows lit with only a little backlight to deter potential thieves, but the owners and employees had all gone home for the day. I'd become used to being the last one to leave Bygone Alley because I often worked late, and even though Chester was usually upstairs, it was rare that I'd check in with him before I left.

A shiver snuck up on me as an image of leather man came to my mind. Truly, what might he have done if Marion hadn't managed to call the police in time?

"Stop," I said to myself. "All's well that ends well."

Baskerville meowed down at me from his perch.

"You should come down here and keep me company while I finish the typewriter and *Tom Sawyer,*" I said to him.

He looked at me a long moment, seemed to shrug, and then softly jumped his way down.

Together, we went to the back and got to work.

4

"Clare, wake up, honey."

I jerked my body upright, but my fuzzy brain lagged behind. Once I realized where I was, I noticed that both of my arms tingled painfully and hung uselessly from my shoulders. I'd been asleep at the worktable, my arms up and my head on them.

"Hi, Chester," I said and silently told my arms that the waves of pins-and-needles pain would pass soon enough.

"Late night?" he asked.

I blinked behind the glasses that I hadn't taken off and inspected him closely. Like me, he had on the same clothes he'd worn the day before.

"You too?" I asked.

He waved away my question and ran his fingers over the copy of *Tom Sawyer* on the side table.

"I looked at the page. You finished it beautifully, Clare. You are very gifted."

"I learned from the best," I said, trying to lift my arms, but they still hurt and were nonresponsive.

"Well, you surpassed my skills a long time ago, but I'm thrilled to be outshone." Chester smiled. "No one bothered you last night?"

"No one at all."

"Excellent. I took a gander in your office, to see what the cameras recorded. It looks like your computer is off. Turn it on later and let me know if there's anything to see."

"What? The computer shouldn't be off, Chester. The monitor should be on. It's supposed to be on all the time now. Maybe it's just in sleep mode or whatever. The security system is an old setup, and it won't work if it's powered off."

I scooted away from the table and stood. I hoped my arms didn't look too weird as I hurried to my office.

I gained back a little control and put my hand on the mouse, moving it, and then moving it more forcefully, but nothing came up on the screen.

"Shoot," I said.

With Chester watching over my shoulder, I pushed the power button. The buzz of the hard drive seemed to need to pick up steam before it could actually fire up.

Finally, after what seemed like a bazillion seconds, the monitor came on, showing my screen saver, which was a picture of Jimmy and Marion making silly faces.

I moved the mouse again and then clicked on the security system icon, bringing a four-squared picture into view. We only had three cameras, so only three pictures filled three squares. The fourth one remained black. The first picture came from right outside the front door. Though it was daylight, it was still early enough that there was no foot traffic yet to see. The second camera was placed on the wall behind the cash register, and I saw the empty but now lighted store in a fuzzy black-and-white picture.

I gave only a cursory glance at the third picture that displayed the back walkway before I clicked on the files-saved button. A few more frustrating clicks later, I was certain that the cameras hadn't recorded anything since only a few minutes after the police left the day before.

"Shoot," I said again. "I have no idea why the computer turned itself off, Chester. It's been so long since I've kept it on at night, I must have programmed in something to make it shut down if it doesn't get used for a certain amount of time, but I can't re-member doing that. I'll figure it out today

71

and change whatever settings need changing."

"That works. No harm done. You're fine. No one tried to break into the store. As you said yesterday, all's well that ends well." Chester smiled, but I could see a small bit of worry behind his glasses at the corner of his eyes.

"I'll fix it," I said as I clicked back to the live pictures.

Just as I was going to regroup and ask him again about his late night, my eyes landed on something unusual in the third picture, the one outside the back door.

The camera was aimed down the skinny walkway that was currently only barely lit from the rising sun. My eyes had somehow been drawn to the bottom right corner of the picture.

"Chester, does that look like shoes?" I pointed at two mostly shoe-shaped things in the corner.

"Maybe." He leaned in closer to the screen. "Maybe."

The black-and-white picture was less clear than the other two because of the lack of light and contrast. The walls, the windows, the ground, everything was crammed together with colors that were so similar that one item melted into the next.

"I think we'd better check it out," I said as I pushed the chair back.

Chester followed close at my heels and Baskerville darted in front of us. I hadn't noticed him yet this morning, but he moved as if he knew what we were doing and led us directly to the back door.

Neither Chester nor I were cautious as we opened the door. I unlocked the locks, turned the knob, and yanked it open, propelling myself out of the doorway without even one small glance in either direction.

The shoes I thought I'd seen on the screen would have been to our left, probably about ten feet away.

"Uh-oh," Chester said from directly behind me. He grabbed my arm and stepped around me, and with strength no seventy-seven-year-old man should have, pushed me back toward the door. But I didn't go back inside like he probably hoped I would. I followed directly behind him and Baskerville, who still trotted ahead, all the way to the shoes — well, boots actually — and sniffed curiously.

Chester crouched and put his fingers to the body's neck. "Nothing," he said.

"That's leather man," I gasped. Though he was on his stomach, his neck was turned

73

so that he faced sideways, and I recognized him, even with the piece of glass sticking out of his back He also still wore the leather he'd had on the day before. I crouched down and snapped my fingers, hoping Baskerville would come to me, but he didn't. Instead he moved to a spot right next to Chester.

"The man who came into the store yesterday?" Chester asked.

"Yes."

"Well, he's dead now." From his crouched position, Chester looked up and down the walkway.

There really wasn't much to see — a couple forgotten garbage cans, a broom. An old window frame leaned against the back of the post office. The glass had been broken out of it and made a puzzle-type pile on the ground around it. A piece of the window's glass had probably served as the murder weapon. There were lots of closed back doors and back windows, most of which had security grates over them. There was a general sense of old and grimy, abandoned but not filthy. At the far end, the walkway led to Main Street, and currently a slice of light shone from there. It seemed farther away than the five buildings between us, a long journey back to civilization even if it truly wasn't.

"Are you sure our cameras were out all night?" Chester said.

"One hundred percent positive," I said as my knees began to shake again.

"Let's get inside, call the police," Chester said as he stood, picking up Baskerville on the way.

Officer Creighton Wentworth operated differently than his sister, Jodie. They shared the same heavy walk, but for some reason Creighton's footfalls — even though he was six feet, five inches and two hundred thirty pounds of policeman buff — were less obnoxious than Jodie's. That was the only thing about him that was less obnoxious than his sister. He was big, overbearing, and awful, except that back when he and I had dated, I'd found him teddy bear adorable, both gentle and kind. When he cheated on me, those traits transformed. And when I wouldn't forgive him for cheating, he quit being so nice to me.

"Hang on a second, the officers didn't take the typewriter with them yesterday?" Creighton asked.

We'd already shown him the body and had had to listen to his exasperated questions as to why we'd run toward possible danger instead of immediately calling the police. Those questions had gone unanswered; even we didn't understand why we'd done what we'd done.

The body was now being attended to by Kelly, Creighton's partner and an even less-friendly person to be around. Kelly had become Creighton's partner about the same time of the breakup, so in all fairness I knew he'd only heard Creighton's version of events. It was understandable that he might think less of me, and I didn't much care.

Creighton and I were in the workshop. I was telling him what had happened the day before, the day I'd first met the live version of leather man.

"No," I said. "The police didn't take the typewriter, but it got a thorough inspection."

"Let me guess. My sister came out?"

"Your sister was thorough, Creighton. You know she's a good cop."

"She's also your best friend and not the person who should have come out and investigated a potential crime."

"So you should have been the one?" I said as I folded my arms in front of myself.

Creighton's brown eyes squinted briefly and the back of his cheek jumped as he gritted his teeth. "No, Clare, it should not have

76

been me either. It should have been some-one with no personal ties to you or your family, but apparently Jodie doesn't under-stand that rule. I'll be sure to tell her all about it."

"I know you will."

Creighton looked away as the line of his mouth went straight and hard. He looked back at me a moment later. "What else can you tell me? You said your security cameras didn't catch anything?"

"No, come to my office and I'll show you when they stopped working."

Creighton followed me to the office. Bask-erville was perched on the edge of the worktable, next to the No. 5. He didn't quite hiss as Creighton walked by, but he certainly sent him a dirty look.

"Stupid cat," he muttered quietly.

Baskerville was far from stupid. Snotty and standoffish, but not stupid. I didn't bother to point this out to Creighton though. I had done as much a time or two before. I'd save my sparring words for something else — I was sure he'd give me another reason to be irritated soon enough.

I sat in the chair and rolled it tightly up to the desk as Creighton moved behind me. He had to move in way too close to be able to see the screen properly. His chin was

77

directly above my right shoulder and I squelched an urge to lean to the left.

"I'm pretty sure this time notation is correct," I said as I pointed to the red neon-ish numbers and letters in the bottom right corner in the fourth square of the screen, "because that's right after Jodie and Omar left. And then, look, everything just goes black. I think I had it set to turn off, but I don't remember doing that. It's also an old computer. It could have done it on its own."

"I see. Well, it was good that you tried to have something working at least."

Now I did lean to the left and looked up at him over my right shoulder. I was able to inspect him from the farthest distance possible while still being seated. He was being complimentary and it sounded and looked sincere.

"Thanks," I said warily. "I did walk to the front and look out of the windows at around eight o'clock. I saw Anorkory leave his place, but he didn't see me watching him. I didn't see or hear anything suspicious all night."

"You were here all night?"

"I fell asleep at my table while I was working."

"I wonder if Chester heard or saw anything."

I shrugged. I wasn't going to be the one to tell Creighton that Chester had been gone all night, at least as far as I knew. The two of them could discuss that little tidbit.

I hadn't allowed myself to dwell on the fact that someone had been killed behind the building while I'd been in the workshop. Their life had been taken from them as I either worked or slept, with one mere wall in between me and the awful deed.

"Well, nevertheless," Creighton continued, "I'm pleased you have some sort of security system at all. Most businesses around here don't. Star City might be a quiet ski town, but we see crime, plenty of it. So good job to you and Chester."

I twisted my neck and looked up at him again. It was an awkward position and the space was too small and we were too close. I rolled the chair back a little and expunged myself from the crowded pocket. I slipped past him and stood on the other side of the desk, placing my hands on my hips in a pose that didn't hide how uncomfortable I was.

"Well, thanks," I said. "I'm glad we have something too, but we need something better."

Creighton shrugged. "Probably."

He took a few long-legged and authoritative steps out from behind the desk and led the way out of the office. I hesitated just long enough to keep the distance between us as far as might be considered acceptable. The back door to the building was open a crack since the crime scene people were still gathering evidence. He pulled it open wide and peered out.

"The body's gone," he said to me after he closed the door again.

"Did they take him out through the walkway, not through the building?"

"Must have."

I nodded.

"You can do whatever you need to do out there once everyone leaves. You won't disturb the crime scene. The techs won't go until they have everything."

"I haven't opened that back door in probably a year or so. I can't see why we'd need to go out there at all. At this point I'd like to seal it off, maybe cement it closed."

"Nope. Fire code won't allow that, but you can get some stronger locks and a security gate if you want."

"I'll look into it."

"Now, I'm taking this typewriter. I'll deal with Mirabelle if she doesn't like it," Creighton said.

"What will you do with it?" I asked.

"I don't know. Give it to our crime scene

people so they can look it over thoroughly. My sister's a knucklehead. She should have known better."

We'd been doing so well. For a good few minutes, Creighton and I hadn't said anything to each other that could be considered grounds for a fight. It might have been a record. But the insult to his sister irritated me just enough that I decided not to tell him about the scratched writing on the key bars. Even if they proved to be some code for finding a killer, I was just stubborn enough to want Jodie to figure it out before Creighton had the chance.

"Okay, but try not to tear it apart. Mirabelle has had that thing for a long time, and it's worth a lot to her, if not monetarily at least sentimentally," I said.

"No promises, but I'll pass that along."

Creighton lifted the typewriter like it was as light as an empty shoebox and placed it under one arm.

"Clare, call me if you need anything or if you hear anything or if you're concerned or scared. Or anything," Creighton said. "My cell number hasn't changed."

A flicker of regret over not telling him about the letters and numbers flashed in my chest, but then I remembered that not only had he just insulted my best friend,

81

but he'd cheated on me, so I managed to douse that flicker pretty quickly.

"Thank you," I said.

Without further good-byes, he marched out of the workshop. I followed behind slowly, only reaching the middle door as Creighton's feet hit the sidewalk outside The Rescued Word.

"Oh, hello, I'm sorry," I said to the man who was perusing our shelves of old-fashioned pens and ink bottles. "I didn't know we had a customer."

Technically, we shouldn't be open for another half hour, but with all the police activity in and out, the front doors had been unlocked.

"No problem. I was just looking around at all your stuff. What a great place," he said.

I'd never seen him before, and though he was dressed oddly, he wasn't wearing leather and didn't have a glowering look on his interesting face. And he wasn't Creighton. I decided that he was a welcome new sight.

He wore torn jeans that weren't torn in any fashionable way. They were also dirty. No, not dirty — dusty. His T-shirt had seen better days, and I did a double take when I read the words emblazoned across the front. "Geologists make the bed rock." I stifled a smile. He had to be at least in his midthirties, I thought, and was very tall, probably around six feet, five inches. He wasn't necessarily thin, but he was trim and in shape, the muscles in his arms well defined but not enormous. His skin was pale though I thought he might be sunburnt in a couple places; it was difficult to tell with all the dust. His dark, wavy hair was messy and needed some attention from a good pair of scissors. His blue eyes made a surprising contrast with his skin and hair. They were difficult not to stare at. He was handsome, but that wasn't the first adjective that came to mind as I looked at him. "Interesting" was the first word I thought of, followed by "handsome," then "tall," then, of all things, "cute."

"Thanks," I said as my eyes landed on the contraption that he held under his arm. I thought it was a mining helmet light, but I couldn't be sure.

"Oh," he said as he noticed where my eyes had gone. He lifted the thing from under his arm, looked at it, and then put it back where it had been. "It's a mining light. I was at the mine all night. Anyway." He shook his head. And then as if the transition made all the sense in the world, he continued, "I'm Seth Cassidy. You have my book, *Tom Sawyer.*"

"Oh! Yes, of course. I finished it last night. Let me go grab it."

"Thanks."

I'd never seen Seth before, but I'd met a geologist or two. Even an old mining town that didn't really do much mining anymore had need for them every now and then. We'd corresponded via e-mail and he'd sent the book via snail mail. He'd mentioned that he'd be in town to pick it up this week but hadn't given me any more details than that. I gathered the book, looked it over one more time, and then carried it out to him.

Seth had changed. He had somehow smoothed out his hair and the T-shirt slogan was no longer visible. Had he turned the shirt inside out, right there in the middle of the store?

"It's a beautiful book," I said as I handed it to him. "Very well taken care of."

"Thanks, yes, it's pretty special to me." He opened the book to the page I'd inserted. "Wow, this looks perfect. Really nice."

"I'm glad you like it."

"I do."

As he inspected the book some more, I inspected him. I thought he must definitely be close to my age. I couldn't stop myself from looking at his ring finger. No sign of a ring or a tan line on the finger that was part of a pair of strong, sure hands. But if he was, indeed, a geologist who worked out in the field, then jewelry might get in his way.

A moment later, he looked up and said, "Thank you. I can't believe I found you in Star City, of all places."

"My grandfather started this business a long time ago. He began by fixing typewriters."

"Wow, it was probably good to diversify considering what's happened to most of those."

"It was."

Seth looked at me a long moment, almost too long. I began to feel uncomfortable, so I decided to speak, of course choosing a cliché to move things along, because one can always count on clichés when trying to make a good impression.

"You new in town?" I cringed — only inwardly though.

"I am," he said happily. "I was sent here last year to evaluate an old mine. I left but then the job turned into a full-time reclamation gig this year and they offered it to me. I thought it sounded like a fun place to live." He paused. "Well, that made me sound like a kid right out of college. Truthfully, I was living and working in Alaska. I loved Alaska, but the winters were beginning to wear on me. When this job opened up, it seemed like a good opportunity." He smiled again. "And a fun place to live."

"It is a fun place to live," I said.

"I'm beginning to see that," he said.

I bet he cringed inwardly on that one, but he hid it well.

"I'm Clare Henry," I said extending my hand.

His hand was warm and calloused and strong, just like I thought. Probably dusty too, but I didn't mind.

"Nice to meet you, Clare."

We held on to each other's hands a little too long.

"Nice to meet you too, Seth."

We finally disengaged, and Seth retrieved his wallet out of his back pocket. "What do I owe you?"

We moved back to the cash register and completed the transaction. Seth was slow to put his wallet away and I didn't make any excuse to rush off to work.

After I'd placed the book in a bag, he said, "Clare, is there any chance you'd be available for dinner sometime in the near future?"

"I think I might be," I said.

"Good, I'll stop by again soon to ask you

more formally. I'd like to prove to you that I do know how to clean myself up and I do have clothing without suggestive sayings written across the front."

I laughed, probably a bit too loudly. "I'll see you later."

I liked the way he looked at me through the front window and waved as he turned right, toward Main Street.

"Well, that hasn't happened in a while," I said aloud as I put my hands on my hips.

In fact, a spark like that had been such a rare thing over the last several years that I began to wonder if Seth had been real, if any of that had actually happened. I'd given him back his book though. The book was real. I'd worked hard on that book, so our conversation must have really happened, right?

"What hasn't happened?" Chester said from behind me.

He and the cat in his arms must have come in too late to see the town's newest geologist.

"Nothing, Chester. But I need to talk to you. Do you have a minute?" It was time.

"Of course, my dear."

With Baskerville on his lap and as we sat in facing chairs in the workshop, Chester assured me that he did not have cancer. He promised me that he was healthier than the proverbial horse, that he was going to live to be at least one hundred and twenty years old, and that I had nothing to worry about.

"Then what's going on? The search for pancreatic cancer? You've been a little less like yourself lately."

"I have? I haven't meant to be. I think you're imagining things, Clare. Now, if I haven't been around the store as much lately, it's just because I've been busy with a few projects."

"See, that's what I mean. You never have projects, unless they have something to do with The Rescued Word. You're not a multi-tasker, you've said so yourself."

"Well, I have some now. They have nothing to do with cancer, of the pancreas or any other body part, and they have nothing to do with my imminent death because it isn't imminent. Maybe I'm working on a surprise."

"What kind of a surprise?"

"Clare, if I told you, then it wouldn't be a surprise, now would it?"

"Why were you looking up pancreatic cancer?"

"I wasn't. Maybe that arrow mouse thingy hit something that was about pancreatic cancer but I wasn't looking at it."

What he said was possible, but I also thought he was lying about something I couldn't pinpoint. However, I was relieved because I didn't think he was ill. I believed he would live to be one hundred and twenty, or at least close. If he was sick, I would have seen more signs, like a decrease in his energy level or appetite. There was something else going on though, and I'd figure it out eventually.

Baskerville looked at me and yawned. He blinked and seemed to want to tell me to get over whatever was bothering me.

"Okay. For now," I said. "Also, you should probably know that Creighton took Mirabelle's Underwood. He said his sister should have taken it yesterday."

Chester cringed. "I was afraid that might happen. I had thought about calling Jodie and telling her to take it, but I didn't want to interfere."

"You think she should have taken the typewriter?"

"Sure, it was the item the man was after. If I were a police officer, I'd want to become totally acquainted with that machine. Know it from carriage return to space bar."

I thought about the numbers but decided not to tell Chester about them quite yet. I wasn't sure why I wanted to keep the find to myself. Maybe I thought that if he had a secret, then I should too.

"That makes sense," I said. It did, but I felt disloyal to Jodie for even thinking it let alone saying it aloud.

"Mirabelle's not going to be happy that her Underwood will be detained," Chester said.

"You don't think they'll tear it apart, do you?"

"Oh, holy moly, I hope not. If so, we'll have to search the universe for a replacement. Mirabelle will be devastated."

"I'll go talk to her. I'm caught up on everything here."

"Good, she'll be happy to see you even if your news isn't the best. And I plan on remaining closed again for the rest of the day. I already called Marion. I'll put a note on the door to ring the bell if someone needs something."

We were a small staff, but it was rare that someone wasn't around to help the customers. In even rarer moments when no one else was in the shop and the front doors were locked but Chester was home, he left a note out front that asked the customers to push a button on the outside of the building to the side of the entryway. The button was attached to a buzzer that extended up

90

to Chester's apartment as well as a hollow tubelike space that carried voices back and forth. It was an old system put in by the mining company, but one Chester still used. If someone needed something, they could communicate with him via the tube, and then he could come downstairs and help them.

"I don't know, Chester. Should we just close all the way? No note? I don't want you answering the door with no one else here."

He looked at me through his glasses with a stern squint.

"I will not live my life afraid, Clare. This is not only my place of business, but it is my home. I will conduct myself as I always do."

"I understand," I said, but the corner of my mouth twitched. I liked it when Chester became adamant about something. And at the moment it proved to me even more that he was still the same old Chester. If he did, indeed, have health problems, he wasn't letting it change him in any way.

"Good, now, go see Mirabelle and give her the less-than-happy news. She'll take it better from you than she would anyone else."

"Will do," I said.

91

Chester put the note on the door and locked it after me. He waved and I watched as he and Baskerville made their way through the store and to the back.

He seemed perfectly fine.

I hoped he truly was.

5

"I have some sugar cookies," Mirabelle said. She was standing in front of her pantry, holding an old, wrinkled bag of cookies. From my vantage point in the kitchen doorway, it looked like it might just be an empty bag.

"None for me. Just some coffee would be great," I said.

Mirabelle had never gotten into cooking or baking or anything overly domestic. Her house was neat, but always a little dusty. She was fond of frozen pizzas and ice cream sandwiches. She was still thin and in good shape, so no doctors had thought it necessary to chastise her for her eating habits.

She was also very fond of coffee; hot, hot coffee that burned weaker humans' mouths. Whenever she offered a cup, I took it but didn't drink from it right away. I didn't know how she got her coffee hotter than anyone else could get theirs, but it was a talent I respected with my few-minutes-to-cool rule.

"Just as well. These are so old they might break teeth." Mirabelle folded the bag and threw it in the garbage can under the sink. "Sit. The coffee will be ready in only a few minutes." She eyed me sideways as I sat. "You didn't bring the No. 5. Is there a problem?"

"The police took it. Well, Creighton took it on behalf of the police. Have you heard the news about what Chester and I found behind our building?" Getting the story out quickly was the best way, like ripping a Band-Aid off instead of pulling it slowly.

"No."

I told her about leather man's tragic demise.

"He deserved it," she said without any remorse whatsoever. "How dare he come in and threaten you and Marion, or anyone else for that matter? How dare he!"

"Anyway, Creighton thought that your No. 5 should be looked over thoroughly by the crime scene techs. Just in case there's any sort of evidence or a clue that will lead to the killer."

"I guess I understand that reasoning, but I hope they don't hurt it. I'll call Creighton and let him know I'd like to get it back in one piece. Did you have a chance to fix it?"

"I did," I said as Mirabelle set a steaming cup on the table in front of me. She sat in another chair.

Mirabelle lived in a small square house with a spindled front porch and white shutters. The siding was pale pink, pale enough that it was difficult to identify the color unless you looked very closely. The inside was made up of simple old and comfy furniture. Her living room fireplace was framed in decorative tile that had been painted with all different sorts of kittens. The house was very different than my small chalet-type house that sat at the top of Main Street, but I thought Mirabelle's home fit her perfectly. Even though Mirabelle had never had a cat — she was a dog person — the cute kittens worked.

Her side of the street held six houses that had been built during a Star City silver-mining boom. They'd originally been houses for miners and their families. They were all small and square-ish like Mirabelle's, but I'd heard that some had held large families, kids packed side to side like sausages on cots or mattresses. All six houses had been refurbished over time, and though they were still small, they were pretty adorable and were featured in a Star City postcard collection that many of the gift shops sold.

"I saw something," I continued after Mirabelle had taken her first hot sip.

"What do you mean?"

"I saw something interesting on the typewriter," I said. "Well, on the key bars."

"What did you see?" She placed her mug on the table and leaned forward a little.

"There were numbers and letters scratched onto the sides of the bars."

"Really? I don't understand. Scratched onto the metal?"

"Yes. Someone used a sharp tool and scratched them onto the bars. You never saw them?"

"No. I've never looked at the sides of the key bars." Mirabelle's eyebrows came together. "You know, the older we get, the more we forget. I realize that's not a big epiphany, but there it is. However, I am certain I never scratched anything onto the side — or any part — of the key bars. I'm pretty sure no one I know did either. I don't have any memory of anyone doing such a thing."

"Have other people typed on it?"

Mirabelle laughed. "Of course. My children and grandchildren have all played on it. I wouldn't be surprised if one of them came up with the idea, for whatever reason, but I don't think so."

"Where did you buy it?"

Mirabelle closed her eyes and leaned her head back a little. "Gosh, Clare, I'm pretty sure I got it in Star City, but I can't remember where exactly. There couldn't have been many choices back then. Wait, there was an appliance store on Main. It's long gone, but I think I might have gotten it there. It was a place that at one time, when I was a little girl, sold iceboxes and those washing machines with rollers. Do you know what I'm talking about?"

"I think I've heard of the store."

Mirabelle bit her bottom lip. "That's what I remember at this point, but I'm just not sure."

Main Street had seen every form of retail outlet over the years. Currently, to best cater to the resort tourist community it was mostly populated by a number of restaurants, a few bars, and lots of art stores. The buildings that housed the stores were all old, many of them with brick walls and iron-paned windows, charmingly left over from the mining town days.

I ventured a small sip of coffee. It was hot but almost manageable. "Did I tell you what the guy who came into the store looked like? I mean, really looked like?"

"You said he had dark hair and wore leather."

I tried to give her a better description. I told her about his round face, that his dark hair was thick and straight, that the leather he wore seemed too tight for him. I also mentioned that his eyes were brown and unfriendly.

"Sound familiar at all?" I said.

"I'm afraid not," Mirabelle said. "But I'll keep thinking about it. It was so strange that he wanted my typewriter and only my typewriter. Those carved numbers might have something to do with it. Do you remember what they were?"

"Sure." I'd written them on a piece of paper. I pulled it out of my pocket and showed it to her.

"I have no idea what they mean," she said after a quick glance. "No idea at all."

"Me either. I didn't tell Creighton about the numbers. I know that's bad, but I thought I'd tell Jodie first. He was insulting her police skills."

Mirabelle smiled. "I'd do the same thing, particularly if I had your history with Creighton."

"Well, it's a little childish, but I figure he'll find the numbers or Jodie will tell him after I tell her."

My phone buzzed and jitterbugged across the table.

"Oh, speak of the devil. Excuse me, Mirabelle." I picked up the phone. "Jodie?"

"Hey, you're closed."

"What?"

"The Rescued Word is closed. You at home?"

"No, Mirabelle's."

"I just heard from Creighton. He picked up the typewriter. He's right, I should have taken it in. I'm not happy with myself, so I need to do something proactive. I'm heading out to the goat relocation group to have a look around. You want to go with me?"

I'd never seen a goat relocation before. "Sure. Are you outside the Word?"

"I am. I'll wait for you. *Hasta.*" She hung up.

"That was Jodie," I said. "She heard from Creighton and she'd like some company. This is terribly rude, but do you mind if I go with her?"

"No, go, tell her about the numbers. Tell her to take the credit for seeing them before. He'll be mad she didn't tell him earlier, but still . . ."

"I will."

Mirabelle walked me to the door and we hugged, but she was clearly distracted.

"What's up?" I said, thinking maybe I should stay with her instead.

"I'm trying to remember more about my No. 5. Why can't I remember?"

"Mirabelle, I can't remember what I did last week."

"Right, but, well, I can't help but think I'm forgetting something important. Go, go with Jodie so I can have some time with my thoughts. I'll call you if I remember."

"Okay." I turned to leave but turned around again. "You sure?"

"Go, Clare," Mirabelle said as she scooted me out of the house and then shut the door behind me.

Mirabelle's street was just around the corner from Bygone Alley. I walked down the sidewalk in front of Mirabelle's and turned onto Bygone, meeting up with Jodie only a few minutes after saying good-bye to Mirabelle.

Jodie stood in front of the store and was in civilian clothing, which was a surprise. In fact, she wore jeans and a T-shirt that was destined to soon hit the rag pile. The thin white cotton wasn't really all that white anymore.

"We're not official?" I said as I gave her a once-over. I was far from a fashionista and my clothes were frequently spotted with ink, but even I knew it was better not to wear grungy T-shirts after the age of seventeen. Jodie struggled with these sorts of things, but her choices today were an even bigger surprise than normal.

"You're never official," was all she said.

"Good point."

"I'm off duty until later. I have my badge and gun, but I think that a pack of goat-moving motorcycle riders might be more apt to talk to me if I'm not in uniform."

"Another good point. Who's driving?"

"I am. Come on." She turned and walked to her old Bronco. She was not in a good mood and I knew why, but I also knew she would prefer to be grumpy than talk about it.

I hopped into the passenger side and buckled up.

"So, tell me about this goat relocation project," I said.

Her grimace perked up to a look of tolerance. "It's all about the ecosystem. Goats, wolves, hunter, prey. The project's causing an uproar in some circles; other circles are pretty pleased. They are mountain goats and about fifty of them are being moved to the La Sal range down south a ways. Apparently, there used to be goats there, but there aren't any longer and we have way too many roaming around Polygamy Springs Valley. They're bringing other more vicious animals to the area. Specifically mountain lions."

"The people living out there are upset?"

"The wildlife people are concerned that if the mountain lions go there, they'll just keep moving closer to Star City. The canyon is a gateway canyon." Jodie laughed at her own joke. She was coming out of her funk.

"Guess what?" I said.

"What?"

"I know something about the typewriter key bars that Creighton might not have discovered yet."

"Oh?"

After I told her what I'd found, she pulled out her cell phone and called her brother.

"Take credit. Say you saw them when you were there yesterday and you just hadn't put it in your notes yet," I said.

Jodie smiled my direction and said, "Thanks, Clare, but I can't do that. Creighton was right to be mad at me, but just letting him know about this will help even if I wasn't the one to discover it."

She didn't take credit for the find but she also did what she could not to throw me under the bus. She told Creighton that I'd forgotten to mention the numbers to him because I'd been working late and my brain didn't function well with so little sleep, especially after finding a dead body. I didn't care much whether Creighton was mad at me or not, but I appreciated Jodie's BFF loyalty.

"The numbers are interesting," Jodie said after she ended the call. "Any idea at all what they mean?"

"Nope," I said. "I've never seen such a thing before. Once, on an old Remington, I saw that someone had scratched their name on one of the key bars, but there was nothing cryptic about that."

"No." Jodie stared out the front window. "We'll work on it. Creighton appreciated the call. He wanted me to tell you thank you."

"He's welcome," I said flatly.

Jodie laughed again. "Still not ready to cut him a break, are you?"

"Oh, look, a motorcycle gang," I said as we rounded a ridge that opened below to Purple Springs Valley.

There were probably a couple hundred people in the valley below us, and most of them wore denim, leather, and/or bandanas. Many of them had their names patched onto the back of their denim or leather, like they were members of a sports team. I thought that was an odd feature, but it probably helped with the simple task of remembering who was who. Their motorcycles were parked along the side of the road at the bottom of the curvy switchback we traversed. The line of bikes was even, all of them leaning to their right just like obedient but slightly off-kilter soldiers.

"Considering the attire — minus the name patch, which would have been helpful — you would think that our mystery murder victim/potential typewriter thief came from this group, wouldn't you?" Jodie said.

"Or he wanted everyone to think that he came from this group," I said.

"That's right. Looks are often deceiving," Jodie said. "Let's go mingle."

Jodie expertly steered the Bronco down and around the curves in the switchback. She parked at the end of the line of bikes and we got out of the truck. It was obvious we weren't part of the group. I now understood why Jodie had worn what she'd worn, but her effort at dressing appropriately for the crowd seemed forced. I just stood out like a sore thumb in my khakis and girly pink short-sleeved shirt.

The valley was spectacular though. You could see part of the monastery's walls and a few discrete houses around the perimeter, as well as the polygamy compound that sat in the middle and stood out even more than I did with its high gray stone walls and promises of the secret stuff going on behind them. I had come to the conclusion that there probably wasn't much secret stuff going on, but it was impossible not to speculate. The motorcycle group was spread out just this side of the walled compound in the middle, leaving the other side open with a multicolored sea of wildflowers and tall green grasses moving every direction with the light breeze. It was storybook charming, even with the motorcycles, the riders, and a big truck with "Utah Division of Wildlife" emblazoned on the side of its cab.

Almost all of the goat relocaters looked our direction at once, their patched-on names disappearing as they faced us. Their faces were decidedly not friendly and welcoming, but suspicious and maybe a little mean.

"Hang close by me, Clare. We'll be okay, but I'm not afraid to shoot if I have to."

"You got it."

6

Our initial hesitation — well, *my* initial hesitation; Jodie was secure with her solid, confident footsteps and loaded gun in her back waistband — proved to be a hasty and poor first evaluation.

The group was called Angels for Animals. They were all motorcycle riders in the strictest stereotypical sense of the word. Most of them were at least a little rough around the edges, many had tattoos, and some had cigarettes hanging from their lips. None of the cigarettes were lit, and though I wasn't sure why, I didn't think I needed to ask. As we moved toward them, Jodie briefly told me that many of them had arrest records, although the policy to join the group noted that no violent criminals were allowed to be a part of AFA.

The first person to approach us was a big guy with an eagle tattoo covering his entire right forearm. His long gray hair and beard must have prematurely taken on that color, because the rest of him looked to be in the buff thirtysomething range.

"Help you?" he said. He wasn't unfriendly, but he didn't smile right away.

"Yeah, we're looking for someone who might know someone else," Jodie said.

"I see," the man said with raised gray eyebrows and a knowing half smile. He twisted his top half a little and pointed to the name on the back of his denim vest and then faced forward as he held out his hand. "I'm Mutt."

"I'm Jodie, and this is Clare."

He shook our hands and looked us both in the eyes so hard I thought I should feel a burn.

"Walk with me. We'll see what we can figure out before we get others involved. I'll be watching the fringe area though. You two reek of cop. Well, you do." He nodded at Jodie. "If anyone here has done something wrong that they haven't paid the price for yet, they might try to run. Keep your eyes open and check your six every now and then."

"I thought this wasn't a violent group," Jodie said.

"That's what's in our mission statement, but we have enough members who've had

107

enough run-ins with the law that we think it's prudent to be careful," Mutt said.

Jodie nodded but didn't seem concerned. She did have her gun after all. I'd definitely stick close by her just in case.

We stepped away from the bulk of the group, most of which went back to their duties. From our lower valley bowl vantage point I could see that some goats were in what looked like a temporary pen of sorts. The dozen or so animals seemed content, not panicked because of the walls around them. Next to the pen were some large containers, and I watched as a goat was loaded into one container and then slowly lifted up and onto the flatbed truck. My animal-loving side wondered and worried about the whole operation, but Jodie had assured me that the goats weren't being harmed and that they would end up happier with fewer predators where they were going. I wondered if she was just appeasing me.

"What's up?" Mutt asked.

"There's been a murder in town, over in Star City," Jodie said.

"That's never a good thing," Mutt said, though he didn't sound defensive.

"No, never. Some strange circumstances have brought me out here to ask your group about the victim. He was dressed all in leather. Frankly, he looked like lots of people here look. I'm wondering if anyone might know him." Jodie pulled a picture out of her back pocket and showed it to Mutt. The picture was of leather man in my back walkway.

Mutt took the picture and inspected it closely. A moment later he shook his head. "I don't think I know him. He's dressed like we dress. And though most people here have their name on their back, not all of them do. He could have blended in, but . . . well, I hate to stereotype my own group, but he actually looks a little more clean-cut than the rest of us. Look at that haircut. It looks styled and coifed." Mutt smiled then, right at Jodie.

She smiled back. Oddly, and probably inappropriately, the whole thing made me smile too.

"We're all a bit scruffy. We like it that way," Mutt added. He stopped smiling so brightly, but I'd witnessed his and Jodie's momentary eye lock. Mutt was a big guy, tall with muscled shoulders that had tattooed arms attached to them. He was not Jodie's type, but Jodie's return smile made me wonder if that could possibly change. That's the thing with a long friendship;

lifetimes can be read in one simple smile.

"What do you do for a living, Mutt?" I asked unabashedly.

"Oh, I'm a computer programmer down in Salt Lake City. I do contract work, always moving from one company to the next."

"Computer programming? That's a pretty good living, huh?" I said.

Both Mutt and Jodie looked at me.

"Yes, ma'am," Mutt said. "And I make enough money to be able to take some time off and do good works." He winked at me.

Jodie rolled her eyes my direction. "Anyway," she said. "I think I'd like to walk around and talk to some others too, if you don't mind."

Jodie didn't care if he minded or not, but I understood she was easing her way into the group and she knew Mutt could grease the wheels.

"Don't mind a bit. If anyone is uncooperative, just give me the high sign. I'll straighten them out right away."

"Thanks."

"One more question before you leave, Mutt," I said. "I'm just curious. Are you married? In a serious relationship?"

"Clare, you are an embarrassment to our gender," Jodie said.

"I am not married, nor am I in a serious

relationship. I have a four-year-old daughter and I get along with her mother very well, but we just couldn't stay married to each other. Just in case you need to know." Mutt smiled again and then walked back toward the group.

"Clare. Really?" Jodie said.

"There was a spark between you two. We're way beyond being coy if there's a spark," I said, thinking about Seth and how I wished I'd asked him more questions about himself or at least had Jodie there to embarrass me like I'd embarrassed her.

"A spark does not always a flame make."

I laughed. "That's poetic of you, but still, there was a spark. I think you should ask him out."

"Come on. Let's go *ask* some questions to other people. Stick by me. We're in because Mutt approves of us, but we still need to be on our toes. If there is a murderer in our midst, they will try to avoid us or run. We don't want to put anyone, ourselves included, in a position to be harmed."

We met Ingrid first. She wasn't as friendly as Mutt, but then she didn't seem to be attracted to either Jodic or myself, so she probably saw no need for an extra dose of polite. She had long brown hair and green eyes. She didn't recognize the victim.

After many more conversations with many more bikers, no one said that the murder victim looked familiar in any way.

"That doesn't mean they're telling the truth, or that they aren't in denial," Jodie said in a side conversation to me. "People don't want to recognize murder victims because they fear that someone may suspect they had something to do with the crime, even if they're completely innocent. What I've been looking for is a quick reaction. If someone was close to the victim, it would be difficult to hide their emotions. I haven't seen any of that, so I think that if anyone we've talked to did know him, they only knew him as one of the group, not as someone they were close to."

We spent a lot of time talking to bikers and watching the goats being loaded up for transport. Everyone was very gentle and patient with the animals. I ended up taking a couple of cards from different members of the group. I had no idea why I'd need an Angels for Animals group in the future, but one never knew.

I found a pen in my pocket and started writing down names from the patches I saw on the backs of the cards. Jodie hadn't ordered anyone to talk to us and she had done nothing to make sure we spoke to every single person there, but I wasn't good at remembering names. It was almost a reflex for me to want to write them down.

As we were leaving three hours later, Mutt hurried to catch up to us. I stepped away from his and Jodie's conversation and slid into the Bronco. They weren't discussing the murder; the smiles on their faces made that clear.

"He asked you out, didn't he?" I said when she got into the truck.

"None of your business."

"He did. He's sweet."

"I'll let you know." She smiled at me.

"Yay," I said. I could tell she didn't want to talk about it any further, and though that might not always stop me, I changed the subject. "Mirabelle bought her typewriter back in the day. Where might she have purchased it from?"

Jodie thought a long moment as she steered the Bronco toward the switchback road and then said, "O'Malley's."

"No, they own the bar on Main Street."

"The family has been in Star City for a long time. They've owned lots of businesses. They used to own a popular appliance store in town. This was before both our times, but I've heard a little of the history. The bar's only been around since the nineteen seventies."

"O'Malley's, huh? I don't remember knowing about their previous business ventures. Haven't a couple of the O'Malley boys been in prison?"

"Auto theft and check fraud." Jodie knew her arrest records.

There was no way to connect the modern day O'Malley criminals to their ancestors who might have sold Mirabelle her typewriter, but I was still curious about the history.

"You want to go to dinner with me at O'Malley's tonight?" I said.

"I would love to, but I'm on duty in a couple hours. Night shift tonight. Real duty. None of this plainclothes undercover stuff," she said.

"Yeah, we're kind of badass, aren't we?" I said.

"I am. You, not so much."

"Hey."

"Okay, okay, you can be badass too if you want."

"Oh, I want. I definitely want."

7

The trip back to town took about fifteen minutes. We made some more small talk and got caught up on each other's family member's heath statuses on the way. When we pulled up in front of The Rescued Word, Seth, the geologist, was peering in the front windows. He'd changed clothes and brushed his still-too-unruly hair. He wore a nice but casual collared short-sleeved shirt, jeans, and funky green tennis shoes.

"Who's that?" Jodie said.

"A customer. I refurbished *Tom Sawyer* for him."

"He's adorable," Jodie said with eyebrows raised my direction. "Shall I come with you and ask if he's married and if he has a good job?"

"He's a new geologist in town and I don't think he's married."

"Ah, I see. Do you suppose he's looking for you or Chester?" Jodie honked the horn, causing Seth to jump and turn toward us.

Jodie smiled and waved. Seth waved hesitantly, until Jodie pointed at me in the passenger seat. Then Seth smiled and waved back confidently.

"It's a wonder anyone has ever wanted to date either of us," I said without moving my lips from a smile.

"That's true. You might want to go see if he has another book hidden in his pocket or something. I'll talk to you later."

"Thanks for letting me play cop today."

"Don't tell Creighton about any of this," she said seriously as she sent another glance to Seth.

I hopped out of the truck and Jodie pulled away from the curb, revving the engine much more than I thought was necessary.

"Hi," I said as I walked toward Seth. "Everything okay with the book?"

"Great. It looks really fabulous," Seth said. He looked around uncomfortably. I had the sense that he felt exposed out in the open.

"Oh, good. Glad to hear it. You want to come in? We closed for the day, but my grandfather owns the place. He trusts me with my own set of keys."

Seth smiled. "Well, I was just coming by to see if you wanted to go to dinner. Tonight would be great, but if that's short notice, maybe some other night." He looked relieved to get the words out.

"Thanks for the invitation," I said. The day had gotten away from me and I wasn't exactly sure what time it was. I didn't want to look at my phone but a quick glance at the shadows along Bygone made me think it must be almost six. What had I said to Jodie — there was no longer any need to be coy? I knew that the best thing was to play at least a little hard to get, but I just didn't want to. "Sounds great. I accept."

"Oh, good. Any chance you'd like to recommend a place? I haven't been in town long enough to know what's good and what isn't. Pick something expensive. I'd like to impress you."

I laughed. "You like garlic burgers?"

"I do, especially if both my date and I eat them."

"There's a place just around the corner. It's a bar/restaurant called O'Malley's. They have the best garlic burgers."

"Perfect, although it doesn't sound expensive, which means we will probably have to go on two dates. This one and an expensive one very soon."

I liked his smile and his style. It was obvious that he was a little nervous, but he was trying to combat that with humor. He certainly wasn't shy.

"Okay," I said. It had been a long time since someone of the opposite sex had been nervous around me. He was much more put together than he had been earlier, though I didn't think he'd been wearing glasses when he came in to pick up the book. He wore them now. They were black framed like mine, but the frames were even thicker and maybe a little nerdier. They looked great on him though and made him look both smart and extra interested in what I was saying.

"I'm ready any time you are, but I understand if you need a minute or two. I'll wait out here."

"Let me run inside for just a second. My grandfather lives upstairs; I can use his sink to wash my hands. I've been hanging out with a bunch of goats."

Seth blinked and his eyebrows rose.

"And, I mean that literally. I'll tell you all about it. If you want to head on over to O'Malley's and get us a table, I can just meet you there."

"Oh, my mother would not approve. I'm afraid I'll have to wait close by and escort you. Since we're walking, I'm sure I'll get a call this evening about not opening car doors for you — she can sense that kind of stuff."

"Even when we don't need a car to get there?"

"She's good."

"Come on in. You can wait inside."

I unlocked the front door and pushed it open. Normally, Baskerville would be up in the apartment with Chester if he were home. At the moment, the cat was high on the east shelves again taking in the rays coming from the sun setting through the western windows. I assumed that meant Chester wasn't home. Once again, I wondered where he was.

The cat looked down and acted as if he was just going to grace us with a nod of acknowledgment before going back to the blissful sun soak. But he noticed Seth and must have realized that this was a human he hadn't had the chance to judge yet. Perhaps Baskerville was savvy enough to understand that I was going on a date with the man in the bright shoes and glasses, and the cat wanted to inspect him and offer him a chance at approval.

Baskerville jumped down, from the top shelf to a middle shelf. He sauntered down the top of that shelf, keeping his eyes on Seth, and then stopped when he came to the end. He sat and looked at Seth disapprovingly before sniffing once quickly in my direction.

"That's our cat, Baskerville."

"He's a beauty," Seth said. "I get the sense that he'd rather I didn't pet him. What do you think?"

I shrugged. "Give it a try."

Seth laughed. "I'm game."

He stepped toward the shelves. Baskerville watched him and leaned away only a small bit as Seth's hand came forward and landed on the back of the cat's head. For a minute, I thought Baskerville might screech and run away or bite Seth — he's more prone to harmless, playful bites than real ones, but he was unpredictable enough for a moment of worry. Surprisingly, he sat still and then leaned into the sure hand.

"That's impressive," I said.

Seth smiled at me and then looked at the cat. "Good work. I'll pay you later."

Baskerville might have liked the head massage, but evidently he wasn't in the mood for conversation. He sniffed again, turned, and jumped back up to the top shelf.

"I'll be out in a sec," I said to Seth as I took off toward the back of the building.

The workshop was quiet and dimly lit, with only the light coming in from the high windows. Everything seemed to be in place. The back door was securely closed and locked — I checked it yet again. I climbed the old staircase that at one time led to the mining company's managers' offices. Chester had told me that all the people who did the hard work had desks on the first floor, but the managers had offices upstairs where they mostly hid from anxious prospectors who thought they'd make a fortune in Star City. Some had, but most hadn't, and those who hadn't were sometimes so unhappy with the outcome of their mining adventures that they came into the offices angry and with a good shot or two of booze boosting their courage. Lots of people resented the success that was had by the Star City Silver Mining Company, and lots of mining failures thought the Star City company owed something to those who hadn't succeeded. After all, the prospectors had worked hard; maybe the mining company should share the wealth. The managers let the office workers, most of them women, deal with the issues. Men were less likely to pick fights with women, though it had happened a time or two.

The stairs were made of old, worn oak, and the railing and banister were wrought iron. No one ever cleaned the thin crevices in the designs, so the banister was always a little dusty. I noticed it today more than normal and thought I might have come up with a job for Marion.

Once I reached the top of the stairs, I knocked and announced myself. "Chester!"

His apartment was one big room, except for the walled-in bathroom. The inside walls had been torn down when Chester moved in. A support beam had been added along the ceiling to keep it from collapsing, but Chester had insisted on keeping the old gold-specked (not real gold) linoleum floor and the roll-out windows that had been part of the original building. He'd also kept the tiled walls, which were different from anything I'd ever seen. The tiles were mostly white marble, except for a row of diamond shaped ones that ran around the middle of the entire space and were flecked with the various types of precious metals and minerals found in the mines around Utah. There was some silver, of course, and, among other things, gold (real gold flecks) and zinc.

A kitchen of sorts lined one wall — a small oven, small fridge, small microwave, and a round table with only two chairs. A living room area was in the middle — a comfortable couch and a reading chair with a lamp over the back and stacks of books about to tumble over on each side. Chester always had lots of stacks of books about to tumble. A bedroom took up the other end. The bed had been made hastily and without much concern whether someone would see that the old quilt wasn't straight. The furniture wasn't worn so much as just kind of old. It was definitely from a different time, but comfortable-looking and suited to someone who didn't much care whether or not his bed was well made.

"Chester!" I said as I approached the bathroom.

He wasn't in there either.

I hurried in and washed my hands and scared myself when I looked in the mirror. My hair needed a brush, and my face needed a full shower and makeover. There wasn't time for much more than using Chester's brush to do a little something with my unruly curls.

There was one good thing about accepting a last-minute invitation for a date: There wasn't time to worry about what you were going to wear or look like. You just had to go with whatever was already in place.

I made my way back downstairs, slowing my rushed pace at the middle door. Seth was still trying to work his magic on Baskerville.

He stood next to the shelves with his hands in his pockets as he looked up at the cat on the top shelf. He was saying something that I couldn't hear. Baskerville had the tips of his paws over the edge of the shelf and his chin rested on the paws. The cat looked amused or bored or perhaps curious; it was hard to tell.

"Hi," Seth said when he saw me approach. "I'm trying."

I looked up. "He hasn't turned his back to you or hissed yet, has he?"

"No."

"Then there's a chance."

We stood there a minute, just smiling at each other. Finally, Baskerville had enough and he meowed disapprovingly.

"Shall we?" Seth said.

"Sounds good."

I locked the door and we set out for the short trip to O'Malley's. On our way, we passed something that was rare to Bygone Alley — a new business was moving in. The spot next to The Rescued Word had for years been home to a beekeeper and his honey company. He'd sold all kinds of beekeeping equipment and freshly harvested honey. The owner of the store, Earnest Battleboro, had passed away a few months earlier, and new businesses had been vying to stake a claim on the place since the moment the landlord announced it was available.

Ultimately, a chocolate store would be taking the space, but not just any chocolate store, one that did things the old-fashioned way, apparently. I didn't know what that meant yet, but I looked forward to trying out their products as soon as they were open. So did Chester.

We also passed a fiber store, full of everything that had anything to do with knitting or crocheting or whatever one did with yarn or the fibers it came from. I'd never been interested in such things, but I sure liked the owner, Kristina Leamens.

"You've been here all your life, then?" Seth said as I gave him a brief rundown on the stores and history of Bygone Alley.

"I have, and I've worked with Chester almost forever too. I enjoy what I do. I feel like I've never really had to work, ever."

"I get that. I've never worked for family or for myself, but I love what I do. It makes all the difference, I'm sure," Seth said.

"I know a geologist is all about rocks, but what does that mean exactly?" I said.

"Lots of things, but you're right, we're all about that stuff. We're a strange group, more prone to caves than the outside world." He stopped and looked up at the small hand-painted sign above the door that said "O'Malley's." "Looks like we're here. I'll tell you more during dinner." Seth pulled the door open.

We were greeted by the noise of a boisterous crowd. I'd had an O'Malley's garlic burger a time or two, but it had been a while. I'd forgotten what a rowdy place the bar was. The three well-placed televisions were always on sports channels, and cheering and booing were encouraged.

As the joviality wafted through the door with the scents of beer and garlic, I wondered if we should go someplace else, but Seth was sending an interested glance inside. And I really wanted to talk to Oren O'Malley. I led us forward.

8

Oren was behind the bar, playing the stereo-typical part of an old Irish pub owner very well. He was a big man with short dark hair, big blue eyes, and rosy cheeks — though I knew the rosy cheeks weren't from alcohol, but from the hard work of running a bar. He didn't drink, never had according to Chester.

He wasn't an overly friendly man, always a little suspicious and cranky, but he was mostly well liked throughout town. His sons, Brian and Timothy, had been a chal-lenge, both of them choosing paths that had landed them in prison a time or two. I wasn't sure, but I thought one was still residing there.

"I see a table close to the bar. Will that be okay?" I said above the noise.

"Sure, fine," Seth said as he smiled and was bumped by a waitress balancing a pitcher on her tray.

We threaded our way through the crowd, and as we approached the table, another man was on his way to it from the other direction. He noticed there were two of us, most likely on a date, and bowed out of the race. Seth and I thanked him as he smiled and moved on.

"That was helpful," Seth said. "I'll buy him a drink."

At least that's what I thought he said; I couldn't hear him very well.

We were at one of the five tables that were close to the bar. These tables were set up a little higher than the rest and were separated from the others by a thick brass railing. The other tables were all regular sized and just as packed with patrons as our higher-up ones were.

"What can I get for you?" the waitress said. She was petite and had perfected her "bar voice" so that we could hear her easily.

Seth nodded at me.

"Garlic burger, loaded, fries, and a diet Coke," I said.

"I'll have the same, but make mine a real Coke. She's driving," he joked.

The waitress wasn't amused, but I thought the bad joke was kind of cute. I chuckled.

"I'm not much of a drinker," I said when she'd left.

"Me either, though if I knew you better, I might get a beer. Maybe next time," Seth said.

I glanced over at Oren O'Malley, but he wasn't doing much of anything interesting as he simply tended bar.

The waitress was back only a moment later with our drinks.

"Here you go. Coke and Diet Coke. I'll have my eyes on you two. If you get out of hand, I'll take those car keys," she said without a smile.

"Thanks, we appreciate that." Seth grinned.

"I have a question for you." I leaned over the table toward her. "What have Oren's sons been up to?"

She blinked at me and said, "Who wants to know?'

"My grandfather owns a store on Bygone. He knows Oren, and I was just inquiring for him."

"I expect they're fine."

"Is either of them still in prison?"

"Oren doesn't pass out their addresses to the staff," she said.

"I see."

"I'll be back with your burgers," she said.

"Thanks."

Seth looked at the man behind the bar

and said, "Is that Oren?"

"Yes."

"If you don't mind me asking, why are you curious about his sons? Don't get me wrong, I'm not the jealous type, and since you mentioned prison, I'm not sensing any competition."

"No, no competition. It's a long story and one that seems silly to share here and now. It's all about a typewriter though."

"Oh, how mysterious," Seth said.

"Sorry. Tell me what you're doing as our new town geologist."

Before the burgers arrived, Seth managed to tell me about his contribution to some mine reclamations. The mines had long ago been emptied of their resources, and the plan was to make them more like they used to be before their local ecosystems had been destroyed and the land had been dug through. It was clear he loved what he did, and I was impressed, asking if he might show me a site or two one day. He said he would — and soon, if I was up for it.

When the burgers arrived, I couldn't help myself and asked the waitress one more question.

"Didn't the O'Malleys used to own an appliance store? I think it was even located here, where the bar is," I said.

"I've never known this place to be anything but what it is," she said before she walked away again. I watched her go directly to Oren. It was obvious that she told him I'd been asking odd questions.

But they weren't all that odd really, were they? If we'd sat at the bar, I would have asked the same things directly to Oren.

"Let me guess," Seth said. "You're looking for a typewriter that was sold in the appliance store."

"Sort of, but not really," I said, but I was distracted by watching Oren and the waitress watching us — well, me. They didn't seem to have any interest in Seth.

I waved it away and tried to ignore Oren for the rest of the evening. It wasn't easy. Every time I looked his direction, he was looking at me.

"I'm sorry. I'm not being the best date, am I?" I finally said.

"It's fine. I'm intrigued. I'd like to help, but I'm not sure how."

From there, the date went from distracted to almost impossible. We were bumped into, sloshed upon, and elbowed more than a few times. The volume of the crowd became unbearable, and once we were done eating, I was sure we both had heartburn and ring-ing ears, and Seth was as ready to leave as I was.

"I'm sorry about that," I said when we finally escaped the bar. "I should have picked a better place."

"Don't worry about it. I'll research and find a quiet place for the next one."

"The next one? I doubt I would want to go out with me again after that."

"You'd be wrong," Seth said. "Hey, I'm parked in front of your store, but I'd love to give you a ride home."

"Actually, I live right at the top of this street. Bygone Alley is halfway between where we are right now and my house. If you're up for it, we can walk up and then you can go halfway back down to get your car. It would give me a little more time to prove I'm not a completely horrible date."

"I like that idea." He seemed momentarily perplexed before he smiled again, but I didn't ask about the confusion.

We walked slowly up the hill, passing restaurants; gift shops; a drug store; another smaller, even more unappealing bar; a coffee shop; and a stained-glass-window store (I always thought it belonged on Bygone Alley, but it had been on Main Street for years). We also passed one of the main theaters used during the Star City Film

Festival, which had turned into a huge international yearly festival for independent filmmakers. Star City residents mostly loved and looked forward to the festival. It certainly brought a lot of business and Hollywood stardom to the area, but it also brought lots more people, and though Hollywood types were interesting, like any other large group, there were always some less desirable visitors.

If I were to have rated my date behavior, I probably would have given myself a four, at tops a five out of ten. I hadn't been as attentive as I should have been, and the location I'd picked had been a total fail. As we sauntered up the street and I gave a mini Star City tour, I couldn't quite figure out how to bring my rating up. It was probably beyond salvage, so I was surprised that when we reached the top of the hill and my small blue chalet, Seth actually confirmed that he'd like to see me again soon.

"Really?"

"Yeah. You know, it was so difficult to hear each other that we didn't have to deal with trying to fill awkward silences."

I laughed. "That's true."

Of course there was no avoiding the awkward moment of good-bye, but Seth did something unexpected that made my heart speed up a beat or two.

He held out his hand to shake. I laughed a little and reciprocated. But when he had my hand in his, he gently tugged me forward and kissed me on the cheek. At the moment — in fact, throughout the entire miserable date — he'd been really adorable, albeit in kind of a nerdy endearing way. The kiss moved him up from adorable to super-almost-irresistible adorable.

I had to fight the girly urge to put my fingers over the spot on my cheek that he'd kissed.

When he turned to walk back down the hill, I forgot all about the misery at O'Malley's, and only looked forward to seeing Seth again, hopefully very soon.

9

My house had been in my family since Chester first moved to Star City. Though he and my grandmother had never lived in the little blue chalet at the top of the hill, they'd been the first ones to purchase it. They thought it would make a great rental property — what visiting skier in their right mind wouldn't want to stay in the small blue house that was high enough on the hill to have a view of the Star City valley below and the mountains beyond? And not only were the views and the access to all the town's amenities great selling points, but so was the access to the slopes. There was a ski-in-ski-out point up two houses and around a small curve.

Once my father had been old enough to have a place of his own, he'd become the chalet's renter. He and my mom had lived there through Jimmy's birth but needed more space when I came along, so we moved into a house in the valley, close to all the schools. A few years ago and long after both Jimmy and I had grown up and left home, they purchased a condo in Arizona and a condo in Salt Lake City. I didn't think their snowbird lifestyle would last, and I missed having them close by. Jimmy and I had frequently discussed when we thought they might be back to Star City full time.

After we moved to the bigger house, the chalet had reverted back to being used for tourists — all of them giving it rave reviews regarding its charm and location. When I was old enough, I moved in. Chester didn't want to worry about what would happen to it after he was gone, so he told me I could only live there if I bought it from him. That was an easy decision, and I didn't pay nearly enough for it.

I loved Little Blue.

The main level was mostly just one big open space except for a couple pillars and a breakfast bar that separated the front living space from the back kitchen area. A window-walled dining room also extended out from the side of the kitchen and couldn't be seen from the living room because it was tucked behind another wall. The dining room offered a perfect view of the biggest, most challenging slope at the resort. You could have dinner with friends and watch experts elegantly ski down the hill or brave novices roll down it. I'd yet to witness a serious injury, but I'd cringed and held my breath waiting for someone to stand up again a time or two.

I had the original dark wood floors polished and the inside walls painted a light cream color. The furniture was contemporary, not woodsy like the furniture in most of the log-cabin-type chalets in the area. There were windows everywhere, one on each side of the front door, and along the sides and back of the house. There were also two skylights on the peaked ceiling over the bedroom loft. Though the ceilings were low on the sides of the loft, the full-floor setup made for a fairly spacious bedroom where I had the most comfortable queen-size bed ever invented, a half bathroom, a walk-in (though not deep) closet, and a seating area. On clear nights, I spent a lot of time either in bed or on a chair looking up at the stars through the skylight windows. There was a reason we'd been given the name Star City, and on clear nights that reason was bright and breathtaking.

I'd barely had time to kick my shoes off by the front door when a knock startled me. I figured it must have been Seth, and I thought it was kind of cute that he'd wanted to see me again only a few moments after we'd said good-bye.

But it wasn't Seth.

"Clare?" Oren O'Malley said as I opened the door.

"Mr. O'Malley?" I said. I looked around behind him, but there was no sign of anyone else, including Seth.

"Yes. Can I come in?"

I wanted to say no, but there probably wasn't any harm in letting him. My family knew his family, even if we weren't close enough to visit either of Oren's boys during their incarcerations.

"Sure," I said as I stepped back.

Oren's steps were short but not terribly slow. His big body somehow looked more like it was scooting rather than walking as he made his way to my couch. He sat down with a gigantic plop and sigh.

"Did you walk up here from the bar?"

"Yes, I followed you and your date. Who is he? I've never seen him before."

"A friend," was all I said as I took a seat in the chair next to the couch. Our families definitely weren't close enough that I thought my date's identity was any of Oren's business.

"He likes you. You like him?"

"Mr. O'Malley, what can I do for you?"

"You can tell me why you were asking so many questions about me and my family and my past business."

"I didn't think I was asking anything that should warrant being followed home."

"Any questions rouse my suspicion," he said as he sat back on the couch and rubbed his finger under his nose.

"I just wondered about your family's past businesses and if you all sold typewriters, particularly if you sold one to Mirabelle Montgomery back in the day."

Oren looked at me a long moment and then laughed. It was a big belly laugh that brought tears to his eyes.

"Clare, either you're making that up, or you certainly like to add drama to something that would warrant no drama whatsoever. Why didn't you just come up to the bar and ask me these questions?"

"Because you were busy and you kind of scare me."

After another moment of study, he laughed again. It wasn't as big as the first laugh, though.

"Why in the world would I ever scare a Henry? Your grandfather and I have known each other forever. He knew my father."

"He might know you and our families

know each other, but I don't know you all that well," I said.

Oren nodded and I realized that he did everything big. Even his nod was bigger than a regular person's nod.

"True. Mostly. You know my boys though."

"I do," I said, hoping I didn't give away my feelings for those boys in my tone.

"Why were you asking about them?"

"That was just my curiosity. I'm sorry. None of my business really." I hadn't in any way tied one of the O'Malley boys to the body behind The Rescued Word, but their past behavior made me wonder. I didn't want to be that honest with Oren.

"I know they've not been the best of boys, but they will get better," he said.

"I'm sure."

"No, really, Brian's been pretty good for two years now, and Timothy will be released from prison very soon, maybe in the next couple of days. He's a new man, Clare. In fact, and you're going to think I've gone off my senses, but you might want to consider getting to know Brian a little better. A date or two wouldn't hurt. A couple dates never hurt anyone. If you're not serious about the guy from earlier, that is."

Or unless Brian has become some sort of

serial killer.

My imagination got the best of me for a moment, and Oren's sudden matchmaking ideas were unexpected.

"We'll see, Oren. I went to high school with Timothy and I think I knew Brian a little. He went to school with my brother. I don't think either Brian or I thought of each other in dating terms."

Brian had been a miniature version of Oren but goth: all Irish eyes and ruddy skin, but with black clothes and black-lined eyes. He and I had never even had a conversation I could remember, let alone a flirtatious glance. Even though he was in my brother's class, they never hung out either. Jimmy was the clean-cut football player; goth hadn't been part of his high school world. I'd seen Brian around town (when he wasn't in prison, of course) a time or two since high school but probably not in a few years. He'd lost the goth look but gained a dangerous edginess that gave his eyes a mean slant. I hadn't struck up any conversations with him after high school either. I felt a little sorry for Oren and what I interpreted as his hopes for his boys to settle down and into something more normal. I wondered how many bar patrons he'd considered as possible dates for his sons.

But even if it was a character flaw on my part, I couldn't find it in myself to leave the past behind. There was no way I could date someone who'd spent time in prison for auto theft and check fraud. Twice, if I remembered correctly. I was pretty open-minded, but not quite that open-minded.

Also, there was that geologist and our potential future friendship to consider. No, I wasn't going to date Brian.

"Ah, fooey," Oren said. "You're both grown up and look at life differently than when you were young 'uns. I'm telling you, Clare, there might be something there. Keep him in mind."

I nodded as ambiguously as possible.

"All right, well, let's get back to the typewriter business that started all of this in the first place. You want to know what, now?"

"I guess . . . First, did O'Malley's Appliances sell typewriters? Maybe used ones?"

"Sure, probably, I think I remember that."

Why in the world hadn't I just gone up to the bar to ask Oren these questions? They were harmless, if handled directly. In fact, an even better idea would have been to call Oren during the bar's quiet time and ask him over the phone. I'd turned this all into something it hadn't needed to be.

"Any chance you sold one to Mirabelle Montgomery?" I said.

Oren didn't laugh this time, just smiled and shook his head a little. "Clare, I suppose that if Mirabelle Montgomery bought a typewriter during the time that O'Malley's sold typewriters, there's a good chance we sold her one. Do I know about that particular moment? Do I still have any sort of sales records from back then? No, my dear, I'm afraid I do not."

I grimaced. "I know. It was stupid of me to think that it was possible."

"Why is this something you need to know?"

"Mirabelle has had a typewriter for years. It's an old Underwood, and I'd like to see if we can track down more of them. I know collectors." It was a believable lie. And I really did know collectors.

Oren shook his head. "Check out the Internet."

"We have, and we will some more. Look, Oren, I'm sorry I was so weird. I really didn't mean to be. You're right, I should have just come up to the bar and asked you about the appliance store. There was no need for all the cloak-and-dagger stuff, and if I wanted to know about your sons, I should have asked you that directly too."

Oren rubbed his chin, and like all his other movements, this one was supersized and kind of rough. I wondered if he hurt himself, but he didn't act as though he did.

"There's something you're not telling me, Clare Henry. Any chance I can get it out of you?" He smiled a too-toothy smile, trying to make me think he could handle being jovial just fine.

This time I laughed.

"No, I'm not hiding anything. Except, maybe I should tell you that I did kind of like that guy I was with. I should probably exhaust that romantic avenue before Brian and I get engaged or anything."

"I see how you are," Oren said jokingly. "Well, we'll give this new fella a little time, but I'm going to plant the seed in Brian's mind."

"Sure."

Oren's departure was friendlier and less suspicious than his arrival. I watched his funny short-stepped shuffle as he made his way down my porch steps and then the sidewalk back toward the bar. He reminded me of a Weeble, and I was glad he didn't fall down. I didn't think I could get him upright on my own.

It had been a full day, and I was tired enough to crawl into bed without giving

Seth, Oren, Chester, Jodie, or the twinkling stars above another thought.

10

Though The Rescued Word could get pretty busy, I'd never seen the crowd inside comprised solely of people I knew.

As I strolled toward the door, I stopped short. Instead of going right in, I peered inside and took a moment to evaluate the crowd, quickly deciding there might be too much company in there, and I might just want to go home and come back again later.

Chester was there, seemingly both irritated and amused by all the different conversations that were taking place, his attention flitting from one person to another.

Creighton was also there, holding Mirabelle's typewriter as he talked to Mirabelle — I assumed they were discussing the typewriter. Actually, Mirabelle was probably telling Creighton to give her back her property and he was trying to explain the police procedure for doing that. How they'd come to be at the store together was a mystery.

Marion and her father — my brother, Jimmy, were also there. Those two were off to one side, probably discussing something that caused all parents and teenagers to look annoyed, not just them.

Jodie and Seth were there, standing next to each other and chatting in a front corner of the store. They looked friendly enough, but Jodie was surely grilling poor Seth about his income and health and relationship history. I felt sorry for him, but I deserved it, I guess.

I decided it was best to go in and get it over with, whatever *it* was. As I opened the door and went through, the first person to greet me wasn't a person at all, but Baskerville. He wasn't on a high shelf yet, but jumped up from the floor to one of the middle shelves as I entered. He had a throaty meow/growl he often used to show his displeasure. He sent one of those my direction, though I knew it wasn't about me. He was relaying his displeasure at so many humans in his space.

"I know, but I suspect they'll all be gone in a few minutes. I'll kick them out if I have to," I said to him as I scratched behind one of his ears. His look told me that he certainly hoped so.

"Clare, hi!" Jodie said with a too-friendly smile and wave.

I nodded her direction.

"Hi, honey," Chester said as he leaned on a middle shelf, taking on a long-legged Fred Astaire pose. "We have company."

"I see that. I'll be with you in a second, Jodie and Seth," I said. I didn't acknowledge Jimmy and Marion. They might not be there for me, and they were family; they could wait.

"Creighton, I see you brought Mirabelle's typewriter back. You done with it?" I said.

"We are," Creighton said. "We got the numbers and letters, but we have no idea what they mean. I asked Chester if he had any idea."

"I don't," Chester said.

"Right," Creighton said to him. "Anything special about typewriters that would cause them to have that stuff scratched on the bar things?" Creighton said to me.

"Key bars. No, nothing that I'm aware of," I said.

"I see," Creighton said. I caught his quick but questioning glance toward Seth. I also caught Jodie's smile and Seth's confused and uneasy demeanor. Poor guy; between my friends, my family, and my own behavior on our first date, surely he'd given up hope that things were going to improve.

"Can Mirabelle have it back?" I asked.

"Yeah, Creighton, can I have it back?" she said to him but smiled at me.

"I just wanted to make sure Clare was done fixing it," Creighton said. "And . . ."

"I am done fixing it. And what?"

"I'll be happy to carry it back to your house, Mirabelle," Creighton said, doing one of the things that Creighton did best: throw in something gentlemanly every now and then to keep everyone on their toes.

"No, that's okay. I brought the car over today. Grocery store day," Mirabelle said.

"I'll be happy to take it out to the car," Creighton said.

"No, it's okay. Just set it down. I want to . . . Just set it down, please, Creighton," Mirabelle said. For an instant I felt a little sorry for Creighton and his genuine attempt to be kind to Mirabelle.

Creighton set the typewriter down next to Baskerville, who sniffed at the short return bar. The slots below in the low shelf held pastel-colored papers on one side and dark greens and reds on the other. I called it our holiday shelf; one side reminded customers of Easter and the other side, Christmas.

Creighton steeled himself and then turned to Chester. "Thank you. We'll let you know

149

if we need to look at anything in the store more closely." Then he turned to me. "Clare, I need to talk to you further. Can you come with me back to the station?"

Chester stopped leaning and stepped toward me, and Jodie moved around Seth and joined us too. Jimmy and Marion stayed back from the crowd. I could see the look of indecision pass over Jimmy's features. He wasn't sure whether his daughter needed to witness whatever would happen next.

"Why do you need to talk to Clare?" Chester said.

"Police business," Creighton said.

"It's official business, Clare. I'm sure Creighton hadn't planned on announcing to the world that he wanted to talk to you, but the store was pretty busy this morning and he probably couldn't figure out a better way to do it," Jodie said with just enough bite that everyone in Star City probably either heard or felt the shockwave from her stern tone.

I didn't envy her position of being both Creighton's sister and my friend. I also didn't feel sorry anymore for Mirabelle's snootiness toward Creighton.

"Is this about the murder?" Chester said.

"It's police business," Creighton repeated.

"I see," Chester said.

"Look, I'm going to go back to the station, and you and Jodie can come in together when you're done here," Creighton said, attempting to be gentlemanly again, but it didn't work this time.

No matter what, Creighton was a police officer first. It was unlike him to behave any way but authoritatively. I wasn't sure whether to be interested, bothered, or slightly honored that he was giving that persona a brief rest so I wouldn't feel weird about being taken in by the police in front of family members, a long-time customer, and a cute guy who, by now, was probably wishing he'd never let me rescue his copy of *Tom Sawyer.*

However, I was mostly nervous. No matter who the police personnel were, no matter if they were friends or old boyfriends or just people you knew, being asked to talk to them regarding official business was nerve-racking.

Jodie looked at me and nodded, her eyes both pained and stern. She was not happy, but she was also a police officer first. I suddenly wondered where her and Creighton's partners were.

"Of course," I said to Creighton and then to Jodie. "Can I have a few minutes?"

"Yes. Just go with Jodie when you're

ready," Creighton said.

"Does Clare need an attorney?" Chester asked.

Creighton shrugged. Jodie said nothing.

"Excuse me, I need to make a phone call," Chester said before he turned and took long, fast strides toward the back, his dress-pant-clad legs still reminding me of an elegant dancer.

"Wait a minute, Creighton. You don't think Clare had something to do with the murder?" Mirabelle said. "That's preposterous!"

Creighton sent Mirabelle a sad smile but he didn't say anything. He looked at me again and said, "Just go with Jodie. I'll talk to you when you get there."

"Okay," I said reflexively as I watched him make a quick exit out the front door.

After we dated, my relationship with Creighton had been full of strife and sarcasm on my part, attempts at apologies and then anger on his part. The cheating had occurred almost two years ago now, and recently I'd sensed that maybe I was finally getting to a place where I didn't want to be sarcastic or punch him in the face every time I saw him. I wasn't sure whether that was forgiveness finally creeping in or not, but it had been nice not to have such a fiery ball of anger in my gut. Even with his official invitation to the police station, that gut fire didn't ignite fully, but I doubted I'd be forgiving him today.

Jodie nodded at me again and then moved to the front of the store and pretended to look at our display of African animal note cards. Jodie barely did e-mail; I doubted she'd ever sent a handwritten letter to anyone, but the African animal cards being of interest to her was more believable than if she'd gone to the baby animal note cards.

Mirabelle sidled up next to me. "It'll be okay, Clare. Don't worry."

"I'm not worried," I lied. "Can I take the typewriter outside for you?"

"You want me to drive you out of here? I'd do it."

Thank goodness for Mirabelle. "No, but thanks though. I just wondered if you'd like a hand out to the car."

"No, I'm going to go bother Chester a bit," she said. She put her hand on my arm and pulled me farther away from everyone else, closer to the sidewall where the baby animal note cards did, in fact, reside. She lowered her voice and said, "I stopped by to talk to you. I remembered where I got the typewriter."

"Where?" I said, glad for something to

distract me from Jodie's sour observations of the cards up front.

"From the newspaper. The editor, Homer Mayfair, sold it to me." Mirabelle said.

Homer Mayfair was a legend, at least in Star City, maybe in the whole state of Utah, but I couldn't confirm it. At one time though, people from all over the world might have heard of him. It was during his time as editor at the local small newspaper, the *Star City Brilliant* (meant to refer to a star's brilliance, not anyone in particular's intelligence level, and we had to explain that far too often), that our town became famous for our mining successes as well as Homer's run for mayor in the early 1970s. His campaign tactics had been noisy and obnoxious and garnered the attention of national media, particularly when he used his peg leg (a real one, just like pirates used to wear in the olden days) to get the sympathy vote. He hadn't won the race, but lots of people who'd never given us much thought ended up hearing about Star City and its perfect snow. Our ski resort saw its first big bump of winter visitors. Things had been crazy busy ever since, and among locals the credit was often given to Homer's peg leg. Or "To Homer's Peg!" as it was toasted in local bars on the eve of resort opening day.

I thought Homer was still alive and I was pretty sure his leg was still wooden, but he didn't get out all that much, so the story of his legend hadn't been extended much past the 1980s. I knew he'd at one time been friends with Chester — pretty good friends, I thought.

"Thanks, Mirabelle," I said. "I appreciate the information and your support. I'll be fine. Go on back with Chester. I'll talk to you later."

"Will do. Yes, you'll be fine, Clare. Don't let Creighton or Jodie bully you into anything."

I smiled. "They won't."

After Mirabelle walked away, I chose to tackle whatever Jimmy and Marion needed next.

"You okay, sis?" Jimmy asked.

"I'm fine, but what's up?"

"Now doesn't seem like the right time, but I have to get to work and I wanted to have this discussion before I went," Jimmy said. He sent a sideways look toward Seth, then glanced at Jodie and took a few steps so that he was directly next to me, with his back to both of them.

"Is the murder the reason you need to talk to the police? I'm worried," Jimmy said. He was a nice-looking man with blond hair, a baby face, and naturally dark eyelashes that clashed with his blond hair but highlighted his blue eyes.

"I'm sorry, Aunt Clare. I didn't think he'd get so freaked," Marion said.

"What's on your mind, Jimmy?" I said.

"Do you think we ought to install more security, perhaps hire an armed guard?"

"He's out of control, Aunt Clare," Marion said.

"I'm not. This is not just about you, Marion, this is about Clare and Chester too," Jimmy said. "If the police want to talk to Aunt Clare . . ."

"I'll be fine, Jimmy. I haven't done anything wrong."

"Of course you haven't, Clare. I know my timing is bad, but maybe that's because I'm simply too late. We should have taken care of this years ago."

"It's okay, Jimmy. You're a parent; you should be worried about Marion's safety and well-being. Marion, that's what parents do. We've made sure the cameras are working better, but we're not going to hire any guards, armed or not. Though I can't guarantee that nothing bad will ever happen here again, I think we're over the scariest part. You know things are typically pretty quiet."

"I do, but, Clare, someone was killed."

"I'm aware of that."

"Dad, come on, leave it alone. Aunt Clare and Chester will make sure I'm safe."

"Oh! Do you think Marion should quit working here?" I said.

Jimmy just looked at me, his mouth in a straight line.

"You know," I continued, "I don't think Marion should quit, but it might not be a bad idea to take some time off until we figure out what's going on."

"Really?" Marion said, clearly hurt that I'd sided with Jimmy

"It hadn't occurred to me, Marion, but your dad might be right. We have no idea what happened. Take a few days off and we'll see if we find out more. Jimmy, I get it. I get your concerns. I'm sorry Chester and I didn't think about it first. Chester walked her home, but maybe Marion shouldn't be here right now. I'm sorry, sweetie, but I've got to side with your dad on this one."

Normally I found Jimmy's overprotective ways aggravating, and though he might be overreacting a little, I agreed that better safe than sorry was the correct choice this time.

Marion's pretty face fell along with her wide but trim athletic shoulders.

"Everything would've been fine," she said.

"Go lift weights or run or whatever it is that you do to look like you look," I said. "Better yet, ask a boy out or something."

"Clare," Jimmy said with a sigh.

"Sorry, but you know what I mean."

"I do," Marion said. "I don't like it, but call me when I can come back."

"Of course," I said, the image of the dusty banister coming to my mind, but only briefly. Jimmy was right: Marion should take a few days off. The dust would still be there.

Trying to keep a balance between teenage dejection and grown-up acceptance, Marion marched out the front door, following the same path that Creighton had taken, however, she and Jodie had a quick friendly word before she left.

"The police want to talk to you?" Jimmy said again.

"It looks that way."

"Do you know something that will help them solve the murder?"

"I don't think so, but I'll find out when they ask me the questions."

"Fair enough. I know Chester is probably getting you an attorney right this second, but I can help find one if you need me to."

"I'll let you know. Thanks, Jimmy"

"And thanks about Marion. I know you think I'm out of control, but I really ap-

158

preciate your support on that one," Jimmy said.

Though he was older and his forehead permanently creased, his baby face made him look younger than me. Even in my late-teen years I'd often been mistaken for the older sibling, but the mistake had never bothered me. Before he'd become a dad, he'd been a great brother — caring, kind, and only a little overprotective of his baby sister. He was still a great big brother, but all his energy was geared toward his dad role, which was the way it was supposed to work.

"My pleasure, and though your reactions are typically over the top, I'm with you on this one. I have no idea what might happen next around here."

Jimmy hugged mc tightly. He smelled like a floral-scented body wash. Marion must have done the shopping recently. After the hug, he filed out of the store too. He and Jodie smiled at each other but they didn't chat.

"Hi," Seth said as I stepped toward him. He'd been holding some No. 2 pencils and rearranging thcm in the cup. He put them on the shelf against the wall, in a square space above one of the carved doors. "I'm sorry about contributing to the crowd this morning, but I thought it would be rude if I left. Or you might think I'd let a silly police officer or two scare me away." He scratched the side of his head and looked at me with amused eyes. His hair was brushed but still messy. He didn't have his glasses on, but his T-shirt and jeans were both clean, wrinkle-free, and void of any clever slogans or declarations.

"Actually, if everyone hadn't been here with their own agenda, it would have been a good time to introduce you to some of them. Maybe next time," I said.

"Sounds good. In fact, I'm so certain that you will be set free after your time with the police that I was wondering if I could get your number since I failed to ask for it last night. And when I have your number, I'm going to call you and see if you want to go out to dinner again sometime soon."

I laughed. "I'd be happy to give you my number."

"That's good news." Seth looked back at Jodie, who smiled and waved at him. "I have a confession."

"Uh-oh. Okay."

"I'm staying in an apartment just across from your place. For some reason I thought it might be weird to tell you that last night, but now it feels weird that I didn't."

I remembered his perplexed smile when I told him where I lived. It made more sense now. "Oh. Well, as confessions go, that one's not bad."

"There's more. I spied on you and saw the bartender stop by your house."

"That's a little weirder, but not bad."

"I wonder about your relationship with him, but it's none of my business. Should I just step back? He could probably beat me up with one hand tied behind his back."

I laughed again, and it felt good to release a little nervousness. "No, he's a family friend, I suppose, but he probably wants me to have his grandchildren, a task I won't be taking on. Yeah, he wondered who you were and why I had so many questions about his family, and ultimately why I didn't just go up and talk to him in person. Actually, I wonder the same thing too. I made a big deal about nothing."

"I see. Well, I'd love to have the answers to all those questions myself, but I feel like it's too soon to be that nosey. Anyway, I have a cool thing at my place I'd like to show you."

"Really?" I said.

"Yeah, it's a geode. It's very pretty."

I was surprised by how I was suddenly very interested in seeing Seth's geode.

"How about I call you later?" I said.

We exchanged numbers, and Seth was the next one to leave the store, he and Jodie sharing wary smiles. They'd probably like each other when they got to know each other, but I couldn't be sure.

Once he was gone, Jodie sauntered toward me. Her steps were unusually light, which was how I knew she was nervous too and not pleased about what was about to happen.

"What the hell is going on, Jodie?" I said.

"Clare, you were here all night when that man was killed."

"So?"

"We have to ask you some questions, and it should be done in a police setting. I'm sorry. You have to know how sorry I am."

I kept the look on my face as disagreeable as possible. She somehow took that as an agreement.

"Good," she said. "Come on and let's just get it over with."

I walked to the back and told Chester and Mirabelle I was leaving. Chester was on the phone, the landline attached to the wall with the stretched and kinked cord now dirty from spending its life in the same space as so much ink. He put his hand over the mouthpiece and told me that his attorney would meet me at the station. He also told me I shouldn't say one word until the attorney arrived. He offered to come with me, but I told him to stay at the store. He wouldn't rant and rave like he probably wanted to with Mirabelle sitting in a chair with her cup of coffee, which was good for everyone. Mirabelle told me again that I would be fine. I hoped so.

As I turned to leave the workshop, something started to claw its way up from my subconscious. There was something about Mirabelle . . . I turned around again and saw her sitting with her legs crossed, her coffee mug perched on her knee. She wasn't looking my direction now, her gaze focused on the steaming cup.

What was it, what did my subconscious want me to pay attention to? It was something to do with Mirabelle, but I couldn't pinpoint exactly what. It wouldn't come clear. I stood still and looked at her for so long that Jodie finally said something.

"You coming, Clare?"

"Yeah," I said absently. "Yeah."

As much as I didn't want to, I went with her.

11

The Star City police station broke tradition with the town's older architecture. The station, located at the bottom of the long Main Street hill and then over two curvy streets, wasn't far, because nothing was far in Star City, but walking back up the hill when I was done would be more a hike than a leisurely stroll back to work. I hoped Jodie would give me a ride. The station had been built in the early '90s, its angular, sloping but not peaked roof topped with dark green tiles. The rest of the small structure was also angular and had been a source of contention when it was built. People had thought it was too modern. Now it was just too '90s.

Jodie wouldn't say more except that neither she nor Creighton would be questioning me because we were all friends, or at least had once been. We just knew one another too well. I didn't listen closely to her official explanation.

"Will I be put under arrest?" I asked as she pulled into the long but skinny parking lot.

"No," she said. I wished I'd heard a little more confidence in her voice.

"I probably will be advised by my attorney not to answer anything, don't you think?"

"Possibly."

When she parked in her self-awarded space by the front door, we got out of the Bronco. Jodie pulled open the station door and let me go in first, but once inside she walked past me, her heavy footsteps having returned as we made our way down the hallway.

"In here," she said as she pulled open another door.

The light was bright and the walls were a drab gray, making the room immediately unpleasant. However, I'd been in it a time or two when I wasn't under suspicion of murder and I'd stopped by to pick up Jodie on our way to lunch or dinner or something else more fun than police business, and it hadn't been so bad then.

It wasn't a big room, but it was one of the bigger ones in the building and the spot where six cops, Jodie, Creighton, their partners, and two other officers had their desks.

Creighton stood up from his chair and met us halfway across the room. "You won't be questioned by one of us," he said.

"I know. Jodie told me."

"You don't need to worry about this," Creighton said, his tone friendlier than it had been in some time.

"Got it," I said.

Even though Creighton was a lot bigger than Jodie, they had matching angled shoulders. I'd never noticed the genetic trait before, but as I followed them, I saw how their right sides were both slightly lower than their left ones.

"Officer Streed, this is Clare Henry," Creighton said after he opened a door and signaled me into a smaller room, obviously built to question suspects without distractions that might interrupt the interrogation. It even had the mirrored glass I knew was one-way only.

"Have a seat," Officer Streed said without standing. He barely looked up from the papers on the table in front of him.

Creighton nodded at me and then closed the door, leaving me to fend for myself. I didn't spot Jodie anywhere behind him.

I sat and remained silent.

Finally, after what seemed like a long, rude passing of time, Officer Streed looked up. He was probably in his forties, with a deeply receding hairline and heavy dark circles under his brown eyes. I couldn't remember ever seeing him anywhere around Star City, and I definitely didn't know him.

He pushed a button on a small digital recorder in between us on the table. "Clare Henry, this is to advise you that this conversation is being recorded." He stated the date and then jumped into the questions. "Where were you the night of —"

But I cut him off. "I'm waiting for my attorney before I talk to you."

"Whatever you want to do." He clicked off the recorder and leaned the chair back a little. "I just have a few quick questions though. You could be out of here in a jiffy."

"I'll wait."

The door opened before Officer Streed could fit in more motivational commentary.

"I'm Ms. Henry's attorney," said the man who came through the doorway.

Both Officer Streed and I were at an immediate loss for words. The man who came through the door wasn't a man exactly. It was probably only last week that he was considered a boy. It looked like everything he wore — his suit, shirt, and tie — was too big for him, as if he'd had to dig through his father's closet for the clothes. His short brown hair had been combed sideways, and it looked like he'd used some gel to keep it in place, but the effect was definitely more like spit from Mom's finger. His pale skin and thin face made him seem even more youthful, if that were possible. I was sure that Officer Streed regretted sharing with me a look of disbelief, but he hid it quickly.

"All righty," the police officer said before he clicked on the recorder again. "Come on in."

"I'm Danny, I mean Dan Nelson," he said as he shoved his briefcase under his left arm and extended his right hand to Officer Streed.

Officer Streed shook, but not without a suspicious squint at Danny, I mean Dan. Dan and I shook too. As we did, he smiled as if to reassure me he could handle this.

"You know my grandfather?" I said as he pulled back the chair next to me, noisily scraping the feet over the '90s linoleum.

"Well, not really. My father knows your grandfather. I just recently joined my father's firm. Dad's fishing today."

"Have you been to law school?" I said.

"Of course." The smile disappeared as he sat in the chair and scooted it forward.

"Passed the bar?"

"Yes. Just last month."

"I see," I said.

Officer Streed had the gall to smile big. I was surprised he didn't lick his lips.

"Excellent," Officer Streed said. "Let's get started."

"Uh, no," Dan said.

"Why not?" Officer Streed asked.

"Because my client isn't under arrest. She doesn't have to answer any of your questions. She can leave if she wants to. Do you want to?"

"Wait. I didn't *have* to come in?" I asked.

"No, you weren't arrested," Dan said. "Want to leave?"

I did want to leave. I also wanted to have some serious conversations with Jodie and Creighton regarding how I would never trust them again. But I was kind of curious too. What evidence did they have that made them want to question me? How could they possibly have anything?

"What are the questions?" I finally said to Officer Streed, but I turned to Dan then and added, "I'll answer only what I want to answer. You tell me if I should skip something."

They both nodded, Dan with a scared enthusiasm, and Officer Streed with impatient irritation.

Officer Streed began. "You first saw the

169

murder victim when?"

"The day before he was killed — or is that the day of, if he was killed that night?"

"I understand what you mean," Officer Streed said. And then he recited the dates attached to the events so they would be recorded. "Please give me the sequence of events as you remember them from that day."

I saw no problem in relaying the sequence of events, and Dan didn't stop me as I went through them step-by-step. Actually, I tried very hard to give as many details as possible, like the fact that leather man's eyes seemed to be rimmed in red. Officer Streed didn't interrupt and he didn't take notes. He kept his sad-dog eyes on mine. He might not have even blinked.

When I finished, he said, "Before that day in The Rescued Word, you'd never seen the victim before?"

"No, never," I said.

"Anywhere else?"

"No, nowhere else. Never."

Officer Streed nodded and opened a file. "I'm going to show you some pictures." He pulled out a small stack and fanned them in front of me. They were all of Mirabelle, Marion, and me in The Rescued Word.

"I've never seen these pictures before, but

I know the people in them," I said. "These were on the camera? I thought I saw a flash or something."

"When did you see a flash?" Officer Streed asked.

"When Mirabelle and I were talking to Marion before we went to the back."

"Why didn't you mention that in the sequence of events?"

I swallowed hard. "I guess I forgot. These were on the camera?"

Officer Streed didn't confirm or deny that these were pictures found on the camera that had fallen out of leather man's grasp or pocket or wherever it had come from as he'd turned to escape from the store.

"How about these? Have you ever seen these pictures?" Officer Streed said as he pulled three more pictures from the folder and turned them over. One picture was me on my front porch, holding a cup of coffee. One was of me leaving Little Blue, stepping off the stairs and onto the sidewalk. I was holding a bag that I sometimes used to carry books back and forth if I didn't want to leave them in the safe. There were just some books I felt shouldn't be left at the shop. Chester understood this and never argued when I told him I was taking a book with me. The last picture Officer Streed turned over was the most bothersome one. It was of me at my kitchen sink. Whoever had taken this picture must have been up on the side of the mountain with a strong telephoto lens.

"This was the same day he came into the store. I had that bag and I know I wore that shirt." I pointed at the middle picture. Then I pointed at the kitchen picture. "This is from that day too. I don't remember that moment, but it must have been before I went into work. To answer your question though, no, I've never seen these pictures before. They bother me."

Officer Streed nodded, but now his eyes weren't glued to mine; he was looking down at the pictures.

"Where were you the night the murder occurred?"

I looked at Dan, who clearly wasn't sure whether I should answer or not. I thought he might shrug, but he managed to look completely unsure of himself without needing the shoulder move.

"I was at The Rescued Word all night. I was working on a project, and then I fell asleep at my desk," I said. Truth was truth, I decided.

"Did you see or hear anything unusual?" Streed said.

"No."

"Did anyone knock on either the front or the back door?"

"No. Well, not that I heard."

"What about your grandfather? He lives in the building, right? Was he there?"

"I . . ."

"Hang on, Clare," Dan said. "Let's let Chester answer that for himself."

"All right," Streed said. "When was the last time you saw your grandfather before you spent the night working?"

I looked at Dan, who did shrug this time.

"Earlier that afternoon. He left the store around six o'clock," I said.

"And then when did you see him next?" Streed said.

"He woke me up the following morning."

"You were sleeping — where?"

"At the worktable. That's where he woke me up."

"But you have no knowledge of where he was overnight?"

I thought for a moment. I didn't have to answer. I could lie, but that wasn't a good idea either. Finally, following Dan's earlier lead, I said, "I think you should ask Chester where he was."

"I will," Streed said. "I wasn't asking you where he was, though. I was asking you if

173

you saw him."

"I didn't see him overnight," I said. "He might have been in his apartment above the store though. He's over twenty-one. I didn't ask him. He doesn't have to check in with me." This was kind of a lie. We did check in with each other out of common courtesy, but not all the time.

Was that a good or bad answer? It seemed bad, but I didn't want to make it worse by showing uncertainty or concern. I didn't need to push up my glasses, but I did just to give myself a minute to regain my composure.

"And do you have any knowledge at all about what might have happened to the murder victim, the circumstances behind his murder?"

"Not at all."

"You and your grandfather found the body."

"Yes."

"I'd like that sequence of events too."

I did as he asked, taking him through seeing leather man's shoes on the computer screen and then finding the body outside in the alley.

"Your cameras just go out that night?"

"No, in fact that was the first time they'd been *on* in a long time. We'd become

174

spooked when the man came in earlier demanding the No. 5. We decided to make sure the cameras and sensors were on and the program was working. We didn't do that very well, unfortunately."

"Number 5?"

"The typewriter. An Underwood No. 5."

"I recommend you get your system fixed."

I nodded, but only a little. I didn't want to agree with Officer Streed on much of anything at the moment.

"Any chance your grandfather turned off the cameras in the middle of the night?"

A thread of panic zipped through me, but again I tried to remain neutral. "No chance at all. My grandfather stays away from all that stuff. He doesn't understand any of it."

Officer Streed nodded coolly now. "Perhaps you or your grandfather were so scared by the man's intrusion into your store that one of you thought you should take the law into your own hands?"

I knew this was the part where the person being questioned should see that the officer was just trying to shake things up, and the person being questioned should remain obstinately quiet.

However, I pulled in a breath as if to protest.

Fortunately, my attorney was better than

his first impression had indicated. He put his hand over one of mine and said, "That is not really a question, Officer Streed, and my client will not be answering it or any more that you might have. We're done here."

I shut my mouth and let the air travel out through my nose. Of course, my nose whistled. Everyone in the room acted as if they hadn't heard it.

"All righty, then," Officer Streed said. "Until next time."

He reached forward, clicked off the recorder, picked it up, stood, and left the room without any further comment.

"Thank you," I said to Dan. I wasn't sure what else to say. It occurred to me that he might want to know without a doubt that I was innocent and I was pretty sure that Chester was too, but strangely it didn't seem like the right time or place to make such a declaration.

"You're welcome. Sorry my dad couldn't be here. He's somewhere where there's no cell phone coverage."

"You did great. I'm glad you were available."

"Well, I really did go to law school and I really did pass the bar, but only recently."

"At least you passed," I said.

I kind of expected him to say "barely," but

he didn't. He just smiled.

"If they had any evidence, they'd keep you or arrest you. They clearly have nothing and are just looking for something, anything. The pictures of you at your home are probably the big reason they're looking for a connection."

"Those pictures bother me."

"I can understand that, but though I think you should be careful, it appears the man who took the pictures is gone, and perhaps he was only taking them because of your connection to typewriters, the one he came in for specifically. Again, always be careful, but they probably aren't any cause for alarm."

"Okay," I said, but uncertainty filled my voice.

"Can't blame the police, really. They are trying to solve a murder; they gotta start somewhere. I'm here to make sure they don't get out of hand. Here's my card with my cell and my office numbers. Call me if they want to talk to you again, or to your grandfather."

Dan stood, so I did too as I took the card. He shoved his skinny briefcase back under his arm and opened the door for me.

He followed me out into the big room, now populated with six officers attempting to look like they were doing something po-licelike. But I knew they were all watching me expectantly, wondering what this turn of events might do to my friendship and ex-relationship with two of their fellow officers. And I was sure they were also watching Jodie and Creighton with critical eyes. Would they do their jobs or would they cave because of our histories together?

I didn't much care what the other offi-cers, including Creighton, thought or did. I was only interested in letting Jodie know that I felt hurt and betrayed. I thought she should suffer at least a little.

When I stopped at her desk and she looked up at me with as even a glance as I'd held for Officer Streed, Dan stopped next to me. He looked at me with raised eyebrows.

"Oh, Jodie's a friend. I'm not going to answer any of her questions either." I sent her a much harder and more impatient look. She withered slightly, which wasn't her style.

"Very good. Call me," Dan said before he turned and left, nodding confidently at a couple of the other officers and seeming not to care that they didn't return his friendly greetings.

"I will." I turned toward Jodie when he was gone. "That was awful."

"Coffee?" Jodie said as she stood. "Next door?"

She led the way out of the station. I followed behind, but not obediently. I tried to act as if she just happened to be going the same direction I was going. I glared at Creighton. He ignored me. I glared at Omar and Kelly. They didn't ignore me, but they didn't smile either. I glared at the two officers I didn't know; they just blinked at me.

In only a few moments, we were next door to the police station, in a small coffee shop that was built more for drive-thru or walk-up business than for inside customers. But there were two small tables available for those who wanted to come in and sit.

Jodie ordered our coffees as I took a seat at one of the tables. Shortly, she brought over two very large cups and set one in front of me. Before she sat, she placed an envelope on the table next to her coffee.

"I had no choice, Clare. You had to be officially questioned," she said as she scooted in her chair.

"No, I didn't, apparently. I wasn't under arrest. You couldn't have forced me. I could have said no. I feel tricked."

"Fair enough, but you have to understand it was a necessary move *on our parts,* and if you'd said no, you would have looked guilty

179

in the eyes of our chief. There are procedures we are required to follow, and we are searching for a killer. Omar, Creighton, Kelly, and I discussed the best way to handle it. It had to be done."

"Why didn't you or one of them question me?"

"Come on, you're smarter than that. Think about it a second." She took a careful sip from her cup.

I took a sip too. The coffee helped.

"All right," I said a few moments later. "Conflict of interest."

"Right. There was no way I or Creighton or anyone else you know for that matter could have talked to you. We all love you. There's no way we'd be objective. We had to get someone to come up from Salt Lake City, and we asked specifically for someone who wasn't a hard-ass to do the job. You weren't even in there very long."

The resentment that had balled in my gut was loosening a little, but that might have only been the coffee.

"Here, I've got something for you." Jodie slid the envelope toward me.

"What is it?" I asked before touching it.

"Just open it."

I lifted the flap and pulled out the few pieces of paper that had been folded inside the envelope. At first glance the papers looked official, but I didn't zone in on any of the specific words.

"It's a background check on your new boyfriend," Jodie said.

My mouth fell open and I refolded the papers. "You're kidding, right?"

"No, not at all. While I was at it, I did one on that Mutt character too. He did ask me out."

I couldn't help myself. "And?"

"I'll only tell you if you look at what I found on Seth James Cassidy."

"It's just awful that you did this," I said. "Where's the mystery? Where's getting to know each other?"

"It's still there. These reports don't talk about all the *legal* bad habits people have, just the illegal ones. I'm sure learning about how they pick their noses or chew with their mouths open will still be delightful discoveries. All the report will tell you is if he's ever been married, where he's lived, and if he's ever been arrested for anything." Jodie sounded like both a police officer and someone who'd gone through a bitter divorce, so bitter that I wasn't allowed to say (or even think, she'd said) her ex-husband's name. I bit back the name now along with the desire to call her a cynic. If that's what

181

she was, she had good reason to be. Old what's-his-name was a jerk to the highest degree.

"It seems like such an invasion of privacy," I said.

"It is, but a worthwhile one."

I looked at the envelope. "I don't want to look at it."

"Fine, but keep it. You might want to at some point. You can thank me now though. For the report, for the coffee, and for finding a police officer who would question you gently."

"I'd like to be mad a little longer."

"Sure, but when can I expect you to get over it?"

I sighed. "Maybe by tonight."

"That'll work. I'm going out with a man named Mutt tonight. There are just some things you can't even imagine happening, let alone predict. So I'll be okay with you being mad a tiny bit longer. Are you going out with your new boyfriend?"

"I might be going out with Seth, but I'm not sure. I think we should stick with *potential* new boyfriend."

"It's about time you get back out in the world."

"You say that like it's something I've been able to control. I haven't been asked out all that much since . . . since your brother." I was surprised by the lack of venom in the word "brother."

Jodie laughed. "That's because the vibes you put out are that you don't want men looking at you or calling you or texting you, and you definitely don't want them asking you out."

"I do not."

"Come on, Clare. You're gorgeous and for the most part smart." She smirked at my rolling eyes. "There's not a single man who's met you or seen you across a crowded room that didn't want to ask you out."

"That is so not true."

"Okay, whatever you say, but nevertheless, Seth is cute. If only it weren't for . . ." She bit her bottom lip and eyed the envelope.

"I'm not taking that bait. I'll ask him about his criminal record."

"You should."

The radio on Jodie's belt beeped and a voice said. "Jodie, you there?"

"I'm here," she said as she pushed its side button.

"We've got a problem. We need you and Omar at a scene right away."

"Gotta go. Can you get back to The Rescued Word on your own?" Jodie said as she stood and sped out the door without waiting for my answer. I watched her hurry away and tried to still be mad at her, but mostly I admired her dedication to her job.

I sighed as I thought about the trek up the hill, but I didn't mind getting back to work on my own. Police stuff was more important than my stuff anyway.

12

I threw Jodie's partially drunk coffee away but took mine and the envelope with me as I left the coffee shop. I thought about throwing the envelope away, but I didn't want whatever was inside it to be floating around out in the world for anyone to read. I debated shredding it when I got back to the store, but I wasn't exactly sure what I'd do. For now I folded it into threes and put it in my pocket. I didn't want to think about it or the pictures or if the answers I'd given to the police were acceptable.

It was a perfect sunny day with a clear blue sky. Because of the high elevation, Star City never got too hot in the summer and humidity was close to non-existent, so it wasn't unusual to enjoy three straight months of weather perfection; more, of course, if you also enjoyed the snow. There were many Star City residents who thought the pleasant summers were a pretty big inconvenience when it came to their worship of the white stuff.

As I set out up the hill, I noticed that there was a tantalizing smell coming from somewhere not far away. I let my nose lead me about halfway up the block and down a small side street similar to Bygone Alley, but not as charming. A roasted-almond cart had been set up. The owners were testing their product, considering whether they would open for the winter season. I was happy to be a taste-tester and gave the cart cook a thumbs-up regarding the almonds. I told him that the winter months would be an even better time to sell the warm snack.

I should have been in more of a hurry to get back to work, but I meandered out to Main Street, glanced in a couple of store windows, and found some bright orange cowboy boots that Jodie would love and some earrings Marion might get for her next birthday.

I wasted just the right amount of time apparently so that when I started up the hill again, I happened to see someone who seemed familiar standing at the opening of the walkway behind Bygone. The opening was mostly hidden by overgrown vines from bordering buildings and a bus stop sign that, though small, somehow drew eyes to it instead of the entrance. Some instinct buzzed in me and I stopped walking and watched him. He looked so familiar. How did I know him?

He glanced around furtively. If he'd really been looking closely, he would have noticed me standing partway down the hill, watching him as I pulled another almond out of the paper cone and put it in my mouth.

But he didn't see me. He didn't think anyone was watching him. Suddenly, he darted into the walkway.

"Wait, was that an O'Malley?" I said aloud to myself. "Brian, I think."

He was too far away for me to be sure, but there was something about his dark hair and ruddy complexion and the untrusting slant of his eyes. I hadn't seen him for some time, but I thought I'd just watched Brian O'Malley disappear into the walkway. Where a man had recently been killed.

I rolled the top of the cone down, clutched it in my fist, and took off in an awkward uphill run.

I was used to the elevation, and though I'm not in bad shape, I'm in better shape in the winter. By the time I made it to the walkway, I was pulling in noisy, deep breaths.

I pushed away the vines and peered in.

The view from this direction was much different than the view from outside the back door of The Rescued Word. From here, it wasn't really a walkway as much as an unpleasant space wherein one might choose to walk if they had absolutely no other path to take.

I didn't see Brian O'Malley. I didn't see anyone.

Why would he have gone in there? Where did he go? Why did I care? I didn't have answers to any of the questions, except that I knew I did care, or was, at least, very curious.

I looked around, much as alleged-Brian just had, but I didn't see anyone paying me any attention. Star City had its fair share of summer tourists, but the streets weren't busy at the moment. The few people who were here were more interested in looking into store windows or pushing themselves to make it up the hill than in what I was up to.

As I stepped into the walkway, I knew two things for certain. One, the back door to The Rescued Word was locked tight — or at least I hoped so. I'd checked it recently enough. And two, there was no exit on the other side. One way, the same way, in and out.

I decided I wouldn't venture far.

The path curved a little to the right about five feet in, and once around the curve, I could see the entire length of the space, the buildings' backsides, the uneven path, and the thin rectangle of blue sky above. The broken window that had been leaning against the wall was no longer there, nor were the pieces of broken glass that had been on the ground around it.

There were no people. The walkway ended with a brick wall that was the entire height of the buildings. It wasn't as foreboding as I thought it would be. The light from above helped give the area a warm glow, and there were no bad smells. Given a little TLC, I thought it could be cleaned up enough to be cozy.

I wasn't going any farther though. I'd seen someone who looked like Brian O'Malley enter. Where had he gone? As I took a step to turn around, a back door not far from The Rescued Word's back door bounced open with a sharp noise. I saw it as it propelled out and then shut again.

Had Brian gone in through that door?

I hurried out of the walkway and ran around the corner to Bygone, continuing to move quickly as I looked in windows. I saw familiar store owners and employees —

some of them waved — but I didn't see Brian.

I stopped in front of the empty store and put my face to the window to better inspect the inside of the shadowed space. I didn't see anyone, but I saw evidence that someone had been there, or some*thing.* Among construction equipment, a white bucket on its side rolled slowly toward a wall. Either someone had just knocked it over or the building had become home to critters or ghosts.

In a flash, I saw the light change toward the back of the space. There was a counter with a saw on it blocking the back door, but the light flickered just like it would if the back door had opened and then closed.

I took off in a sprint to get back around the corner, but I wasn't quick enough. As I came out to Main Street, I saw a figure I thought was the person in the alley running down the hill, darting around a now slightly larger group of tourists and light poles. If he was running, he must have known someone was watching him, or trying to watch him.

I debated following him down the hill, but I didn't have it in me. I probably couldn't catch up to him, and he'd already been enough of a disturbance. I'd tell Jodie about him though, right away if possible.

It was as I stood there, telling myself it was okay to give up the chase, that something else occurred to me, something completely unrelated to the man running down the hill. That thing that had been trying to rise from my subconscious when I'd watched Mirabelle sip her coffee suddenly became crystal clear. It was as if the adrenaline shooting through my system knocked stuff back into place, stuff that my time in the police station had temporarily scared away.

Mirabelle had told me that she'd gotten the typewriter from the old newspaper editor, Homer Mayfair.

Mayfair. When Jodie and I had visited the bikers and the goats, I'd seen the name "Mayfair" on the back of a jacket — denim or leather, I was pretty sure. I thought I'd written the name on one of the cards I'd taken. Where had I put those cards? Hopefully I'd find them somewhere in Little Blue.

Oh, I had lots to tell Jodie.

I hurried back to The Rescued Word, glancing inside the future chocolate shop on the way but seeing nothing new. I was going to call Jodie from the privacy of my office. Even though I knew she was currently busy, I'd leave a message for her to call me as soon as possible.

However, I was diverted again, but this time it was a good diversion.

13

A new customer with an old book was always a welcome sight.

She sat on a chair next to the counter. Like Mirabelle had, she held a cup of coffee on her knees as Chester sat in another chair facing her. I hadn't noticed that I was still breathing heavily, but when I saw her, I tried to calm down, and I used my hands to smooth my hair that was undoubtedly a wild multi-directional mess after the chase I'd just participated in. The envelope was in one pocket, so I put the wrapped-up almonds in the other pocket before I opened the door.

"Clare! You were released. I was just telling Olive here about our recent adventures. I thought you might return soon, and she didn't want to have to make another trip up from Salt Lake just to talk to you if she didn't have to. I told her about the murder and the man after the typewriter. I believe she's found it all quite delightful," Chester explained.

"I have," she said sincerely.

"Hi, Olive," I said as I approached them both, briefly wondering how Chester had managed to go from concerned about me handling a police interrogation to making me a main character in one of his stories. Maybe he'd talked to Dan.

It seemed as though it hurt her to bend her neck enough to look up at me. She was older than Chester, or at least she looked it. Her back was hunched even as she sat, and her rheumy eyes registered what I interpreted as pain. I glanced at the fingers around the book she held on her lap. They were bent almost all the way sideways. Our new customer was crippled by arthritis. No wonder Chester had brought some chairs up front. And no wonder she didn't want to make another trip from Salt Lake. I wondered how she'd made this trip up on her own.

"You the Clare Henry I've been hearing about?" she asked with a twinkle in her watery eyes and a small nod toward Chester.

"I am."

"My granddaughter is so very talented, and I have no doubt I'm leaving you in good hands." Chester smiled and then stood to leave me the chair. I took a seat and saw relief wash over Olive's face. She didn't need to look up to see me any longer. Chester patted my shoulder. "Wait until you see what Olive's brought you to rescue. Once in a lifetime. I've tried to tell her, but I'll let you give her the details."

Chester excused himself and went to the back.

"I've brought a book for you to fix. What do you think?" She lifted it from her lap. I reached forward to take it from her before she had to go too far.

"Let's see," I said as I set the book on my lap. "Oh my, Olive. Oh my."

It was a first edition of *Tarzan of the Apes* by Edgar Rice Burroughs, a book published in 1914. With its dust jacket — its almost perfect dust jacket.

"Olive, this is a very valuable book," I said, my mouth suddenly dry. "Are you aware of its worth?"

"What would you say?"

"I'm a restorer, not a dealer or appraiser, but give me a second and I'll give you my best guess."

The dust jacket was simple. A black figure, like a silhouette, of Tarzan sitting on a tree limb, a white background, and some green leaves. The edges of the jacket were bent slightly in, but only slightly. I about cried as I gently removed it and placed it on the counter. I lifted the simple maroon cover emblazoned with the title in black lettering and looked through the pages, using my knuckles more than my fingertips. I found nothing wrong with the book. It was as close to perfect as I'd ever seen.

"What needs to be restored?" I asked.

"Go to page seventy-six. There, you'll see some pencil writing. I did that when I was a child. The book was my father's."

I turned to the page and saw the writing. It said: "Jonny is a booger." I laughed.

"Jonny a relative?" I said.

"My brother. He *was* being a booger, but I should have never written that in the book. I wish I wouldn't have. Now I need to sell it, but it has to be in the best condition possible. What can you do?"

"I see. Well, I can clean the page with the pencil markings. You're smart that you didn't just try to erase it yourself. That might have damaged the page. The binding is beautiful and doesn't need any attention. But I have to be honest with you, I think you can sell it for quite a bit of money even if you leave Jonny's behavior issue on the page."

"Would fixing it lessen the value?"

"No."

"What would you do?"

I looked at the penciled words again. They would not be difficult to erase.

"I can erase the pencil right now if you'd like. I just need a few minutes."

"That would be lovely, Clare. What is the book worth?"

I took a deep breath and let it out slowly. I had never held or worked on a book worth so much before. "Olive, you can probably get a lot for this book. A lot. But I'd like to do a little research if you wouldn't mind. Give me a couple days to look up some things. I'll get back to you quickly." I wasn't an appraiser and I didn't want to set her expectations too high. "But it's about the dust jacket, Olive. Dust jackets are rare, well-preserved dust jackets even more so. And a dust jacket along with a first edition book being in such great condition is as rare as a unicorn. Rare is what gets the big bucks. This is a big-bucks book."

Olive's eyes got big and her hunched back straightened as much as I thought it could.

"Holy . . ." she said.

"Yeah." I laughed. "You want me to run back and take care of the pencil?"

Olive nodded slowly. "Yes, please." She

looked at her coffee cup. "You don't by chance have anything stronger?"

We didn't, but I did top off her coffee before I carried the book to the back — as if it were a crown on a pillow.

I cleared off my desk and wiped it down before I set a protective film over it and the book on top of the film. I washed my hands and donned gloves and a surgical mask. I didn't use gloves all the time, but today I wanted total protection. First I used my phone to take some pictures of different parts of the book: the copyright page, the title page, the spine.

"How about that book?" Chester said as he came around the wall that hid the stairs.

"Chester, it's *Tarzan,*" I said.

"I know, my dear. Good memories. It's also pretty valuable, huh?"

"I've never . . ." I said.

"I know. I once printed a title page for a first edition *Gone with the Wind* with an only slightly mauled dust jacket. I thought I was going to have to seek therapy afterward, but I didn't. What are you doing to it?"

"Just removing the pencil marks. It's an easy fix, really."

"Fabulous. The torment will be over quickly. Good luck. I'll keep Olive company while you work."

I got to the task at hand.

I unwrapped a new art gum eraser. Slowly and gently, I ran it over the pencil marks, removing "booger" first. I dragged the eraser from the inside to the outside of the page. Then I used a fine brush to move the eraser pieces off the page.

When Olive had written the words, she hadn't pressed very hard. It only took about two minutes to remove the pencil marks. When I was done, I hadn't changed the color of the paper, and there were no telltale indentations on the page. It looked as good as new. Easiest job I'd ever had, except for the stress involved.

I took it out to the front to show to Olive and then put the dust jacket back over it. I wrapped the whole thing up in a paper bag, breathing a sigh of relief when it was covered and safe.

Olive laughed. "You're glad that's over?"

"I am. And, Olive, it was an honor to work on your book. Thank you," I said.

When Olive asked how much she owed us, both Chester and I insisted we couldn't take a dime, that the chance to see, touch, and work on her book was greater than any fee we could charge. She tried to argue, but she knew she couldn't win.

I offered to walk her and her book out to her car.

"You know," she said as we made our way outside, "everyone knew about your grandfather and his store in the old days."

"That's always fun to hear," I said.

"Do you know that when he built his printing press, he made national news?"

"No," I said. "I knew it was kind of a big deal around Star City, but I never knew it was something that was of interest nationally."

"It was. Chester Henry was — and still is — quite the character. The big newspapers back east ran a story that had first run in our very own *Salt Lake Tribune.* I remember it all. Chester beamed in the picture that was in the paper. The reporter who wrote the story made Chester out to be a big deal, but your grandfather was humble about his skills. It wasn't just anyone who could build a working replica of a Gutenberg press, but he made it sound like he put together a simple puzzle. I think the article was in the 1960s maybe."

"I've never seen the newspaper story."

"I'm sure it's been archived at the paper, but you should see if Chester has a copy. He might, I guess. I remember both Chester and the reporter being a pretty big deal for a short time." Olive smiled back into the past.

"Did you know Chester before today?" I asked.

"Oh, I suppose we've met over the years, but he doesn't remember me. I'm not the famous one, and age changes the way we look."

"Did you know him well?"

Olive shrugged and smiled again. "I probably had a crush on him, but lots of women did, particularly after that article. He was so dashing. No straying eyes for Chester Henry though. He loved his wife."

"Yes, he did," I said.

Olive drove an old Mercedes sedan. Powder blue with a diesel engine that belched loudly and spit out a puff of smoke when she turned the key. The book was safe on the passenger seat, and her feet reached the pedals just fine, but the arthritis made me worry about her safety.

"You all right, Olive? I'd be happy to drive you back to Salt Lake."

"Oh, don't be silly. This car and I can read each other's minds. Thank you, Clare. Tell Chester thank you too."

With that she pulled away from the curb, and I waved as the car moved slowly down Bygone Alley. I hoped she'd be okay, and I was really glad we hadn't had anything stronger than coffee.

As I reentered the store, I was met by two less-than-cheerful characters. Chester stood beside the counter and Baskerville sat on it. I wondered where the cat had been when Olive was there. Normally, he liked to inspect new people.

"Clare, now that we've taken care of business, come and tell me what the police wanted with you. I hope the attorney arrived in time. I'm sorry it was the boy. I'm thinking of suing the force over the mere idea of bringing you in for questioning," Chester said.

Evidently, Baskerville agreed with Chester. He looked at me and shook his head in disapproval of the police but nodded in agreement with Chester's idea to sue.

Chester must not have talked to Dan.

"Let's go in the back. I'll tell you everything," I said.

14

I didn't tell Chester *everything.* He didn't have blood pressure problems, and I had no desire to bring them on. And Baskerville paid such close attention to what I said that I was concerned he'd run away and wreak havoc on the police or one of the officer's animals. It was a ridiculous notion, of course — that Baskerville the cat understood what I was saying and that he'd be capable of seeking revenge, but sometimes I wondered.

"So, they didn't really want much of anything?" Chester said after I told him about Officer Streed's questions.

"That's correct. They just wanted to get the timing down, perhaps some of the logistics behind finding the body. Nothing serious."

Chester somehow made a noise that sounded exactly like "harrumph." I was impressed.

"Well, that's good. I'm still going to have a talk with Jodie and Creighton anyway."

"They'll probably want to talk to you too. Find out where you were that night," I said. I didn't need to add anything else, and I didn't need to look at him with raised eyebrows. He knew I wanted to know what he'd been up to too.

He opened his mouth as if he was going to say something, but then he shut it again and frowned. After he shifted in the chair, he decided to speak. "Well, I'll be happy to tell them."

"You will?" I said.

Baskerville meowed the same question.

"Of course. They're the police."

"They're also Jodie and Creighton. Well, *they* probably wouldn't question you, but you've managed to put them in their place a time or two over the years." I smiled.

The corner of Chester's mouth twitched. I'd wanted to say something that would make him less concerned, less wound up, and I'd found the right thing. Though Chester had always respected the police and the job they did, he'd fearlessly given both Jodie and Creighton a piece or two of his mind whenever the need arose.

"Well, I have no place telling them their business, I suppose, but they made you go in there, Clare. That will bother me until I get a chance to let them know how I feel," he said less adamantly.

"I understand." I did — he was only being Chester.

Baskerville understood too. He blinked slowly and arrogantly. He was sitting on my desk, soaking up our conversation, his head moving back and forth like he was watching a tennis match. I scratched behind his ears, which even misanthropic cats liked.

"All right. If you're okay, do you mind if I step out a bit?" he said abruptly.

"Uhm. Sure. What're your plans?"

"Nothing, I just want to run some errands. I won't be long."

"Okay, what errands?"

"Just errands. Do you, by chance, have some plans with that tall young man who was here earlier?"

I blinked. I supposed it was okay for him to be cagey with whatever was going on in his life even as he expected me to answer honestly about mine. "I imagine there will be another date in the very near future."

"Another one? Well, this is good news. Tell me about him."

"Not much to tell. I don't know him all that well yet. He's a new geologist in town."

"Ah! Well, the geologists I've met take

their rocks very seriously, and I can't think of any way to say that other than the way it sounds like a double entendre, but none intended. I hope he's a nice man and I hope you enjoy his company."

"Thank you, Chester. I hope so too."

"All right, now I do have to go. I need to run upstairs first and grab something and then be on my way."

I nodded at him suspiciously, but he didn't seem to notice as he hurried away, a marked pep in his step.

I didn't mind being alone. I wasn't worried for my safety. It was daylight and the back door was as locked as it could get. Besides, I had plenty to do. Other than making that call to Jodie, the press and the type blocks needed some attention, and I needed to clean up from the *Tom Sawyer* project. Also, the giant screw part of the press felt like it had a catch. I wanted to try to fix it by myself before I asked Chester to work on it. I got a huge kick out of fixing things on my own. And I'd received an e-mail a few days earlier inquiring as to whether or not we were set up well enough to do a short print run of some books for a long-published *New York Times* bestselling author who had a house in Star City. He was interested in using our equipment to do all the work himself, including binding the books. I thought it was a book of his poetry, but he'd been just as cagey about the book as Chester was about his personal life. I hadn't crunched the numbers or evaluated if it was truly feasible (or if I wanted someone — *New York Times* bestselling author or not — hanging out in my workshop, getting in my way for however long it took him), but I really needed to get back to him.

I'd get to it all but not quite yet.

I sat at my desk. So did Baskerville — he sat on a corner, his tail wrapped tightly around his feet. He did this when he wanted to stay out of the way. I pretended to be busy as I looked intently at a piece of junk mail. I thought that Chester would be in too much of a hurry to notice it wasn't important. I was right.

He bounded down the stairs, carrying something under his arm. I thought it might be a book, but it was wrapped in a white paper bag. It wouldn't be a customer's book, but one from his own private tumbling stacks upstairs.

"See you later, dearest," he said to me as he continued his quick pace around the wall and out of the workshop.

"Later," I said.

The second I couldn't hear his footsteps, I jumped up and hurried to the middle doorway, with Baskerville at my heels. We peered out and watched as Chester grabbed a piece of pastel lavender paper from the Easter side of the holiday shelves and held it gingerly by its corner as he went through the front doors. Then he turned left.

I hurried through the store, pulling my keys out of my pocket as I went.

"Sorry, boy. I need to do this on my own," I said as Baskerville jumped up to the holiday shelf. He seemed just fine with me leaving him in the store and twitched a whisker before climbing up to the sun.

I turned the window sign to "Closed," left the store, and then locked the door behind me. I leaned out from the small entryway just in time to see Chester turn right at the end of Bygone. If he'd turned left, I would have wondered if he was going to visit Mirabelle. But turning to the right didn't tell me much of anything. I knew *of* some people who lived on that part of the mountainside, but I didn't know any of them personally.

I continued to move quickly, darting around a few people, smiling and saying "excuse me." Just as I reached his ornate door, Anorkory stepped out and onto the sidewalk. I dodged him expertly.

"Clare!" he said as though he wanted to talk a second.

"Hi, Anorkory. Gotta get somewhere. I'll stop by later."

"*Tempus fugit;* so does Clare," he said with a chuckle.

Latin humor. I couldn't help but smile as I waved backward.

I made it to the corner just in time to see Chester's destination.

Just like on Mirabelle's side of the street, the houses on this side were fairly small and built close together, though not cute and boxy enough to be on a postcard. Chester practically danced up the front stairs of the third house in from the corner.

The only way I could see what was happening now was to either cross the narrow street or walk to the middle of it. The house wasn't far away; there was a very good chance that Chester would turn around and see me.

But curiosity guided me now. I crossed all the way because someone in the middle would have been a more curious sight than someone on the other side.

I gained a great view of the white house with the wide front porch just as the door opened. A woman swung the door wide and then smiled big at Chester. I only saw her briefly, but it was clear she wasn't young or even middle-aged. She was probably at least seventy but, as Chester would put it, a really good seventy. Her long hair was still mostly black but streaked with gray, and it fell softly to her shoulders. She was dressed in nice brown slacks and a satiny beige blouse. After she smiled, they kissed. It was a quick kiss but by no means chaste.

"You have a girlfriend?" I said to no one. "Why wouldn't you tell me?" Though I'd never known Chester to date anyone on a serious basis, I and the rest of the family would never have criticized him for doing so. My grandmother had died a long time ago. We'd often talked about how nice it would be for Chester to have a little romance in his life. A gruesome thought suddenly occurred to me, and I spoke aloud again. "Oh, I hope your girlfriend doesn't have pancreatic cancer. She looks very nice."

I put my hands on my hips and stared at the house. It was a chalet like Little Blue, but it was more squat, making me think it didn't have a loft bedroom. As I'd seen Chester on the porch and then kissing the woman, it seemed like he fit well with the space. I had to admit, though, I was kind of hurt that he didn't want to share the news, even if it was no one else's business.

I turned to make my way back to the store, feeling way too conspicuous until I reached Bygone. I'd think about how to handle letting Chester know I'd followed him, but for now I had to get back to my original plan.

I pulled out my cell phone and called Jodie.

15

"Clare, you okay?" Jodie said as she answered.

"I am, but are you? Are you still at that crime scene?"

"Nope, on my way back to the station."

"Come by The Rescued Word? I've got more information."

"On my way."

Before I reached the store, I heard a siren come to life. I didn't think I'd made my information sound like an emergency, but sometimes Jodie liked to turn on the siren just because she could.

She pulled to a stop in front of the store just as I got the front door unlocked.

"What's up?" she said as she joined me.

"Come in," I said as I pushed through with her at my heels, almost closer than Baskerville could manage.

"Hey, all is well," I said up to him.

He sent an impatient blink to Jodie and

then put his head back down on his paws, closing his eyes on the way.

"Have a nice day to you too," Jodie said to him.

"I have some weird puzzle pieces that might be relevant to the murder," I said as I continued to lead her to the back. This time I closed the middle door. I didn't want to risk anyone overhearing anything I had to say.

"Great. Tell me."

We sat, but I didn't offer coffee. Jodie leaned forward in her chair with her elbows on her knees and her attention fully on me.

"Remember our time out with the biker gang and the goat relocation?" I said.

"Of course."

"Do you remember seeing the name Mayfair on the back of one of the backs?"

"I'm not sure. Not really. Not right at the moment at least. Why?"

"Well, Mirabelle remembered where she got the typewriter. She bought it from the old newspaper offices. At the time, the editor was Homer *Mayfair.* I am ninety-nine percent sure I saw that name on a vest or jacket or something. I think I wrote it on one of those cards, but they're at home — I think — and I haven't run up there to check."

Jodie looked off into the distance and bit her bottom lip. She understood what I'd said and how I considered the information relevant, but she was just running it through the Jodie-meter.

"Well, that's interesting, I suppose. There could be a connection. It's not a common name, but it's not totally uncommon either. The purchase was a long time ago. I don't know. I'll take a closer gander at the Mayfairs just in case."

"There's more," I said.

"Wow, didn't we just talk to you at the station a little bit ago? Couldn't you have shared all this then?"

I gave her a sour look. "No. All this has happened since I left the station and had to walk up the hill to get back to work. By the way, I wouldn't have told Officer Streed anything. You know that, don't you? You know that I would only tell one police officer anything. You. You're the only one." I took a deep breath and let it out.

Jodie sighed too, but hers was less a release and more an attempt to keep her patience level intact. "I know, Clare, but please understand that the police have to at least give the appearance that we're doing things the right way. I'm truly sorry. Creighton's sorry too, but he'll never tell you."

"I appreciate your apology again, and I don't want one from Creighton."

"I understand. We good, then?" Jodie looked up at me from under tight eyebrows.

"Yeah, we're good."

I told her about the man I had followed who I thought might have been Brian O'Malley. The breaking and entering was much more interesting to her than the flimsy Mayfair connection I'd tried to make. She radioed the station, asking Omar to meet her in front of The Rescued Word as soon as possible. She also asked him to track down the empty building's landlord if he could.

Omar arrived only a few moments later. Now there were two police cars parked on Bygone. One never got much attention since everyone knew Jodie and I were friends, but two garnered curious looks out of store windows.

"You going to look at that background check I did on your new boyfriend?" Jodie asked as we stepped outside again, this time to greet Omar.

"Probably not."

"Suit yourself, but you should. Excuse me, Clare." She lifted one finger as if to tell me to keep back, but I didn't want to so I stayed close.

"May I come with you?" I said before the partners could even tell each other hello.

"No," they both said instantly.

"I'll stay out of the way. I can show you what I saw."

"No, Clare," Jodie said. "Go back inside. This is police business. Official police business. You told me what you saw. I can figure it out."

"I'll hold my breath so I don't disturb any dust or anything."

"Clare," Jodie said.

Omar put his hand on Jodie's arm. "She can't come into the building, but once we make sure all is clear, she can come into the walkway, right?"

Jodie blinked and frowned at her partner. "If we make sure it's clear, then maybe."

"Thanks," I said, and I started walking toward Main Street before Jodie changed her mind.

At the bus stop sign and the overgrown vines, Jodie instructed me to wait until she and Omar could investigate. They tore the vines away and went through carefully, in cop mode, with their guns drawn but held low. I thought they were far more terrifying than Brian O'Malley had been. It seemed to take a long time, but I didn't even peek into the space as I waited. They'd intimidated me well. No passersby seemed to have any idea what was going on, and only one bus stopped. The driver opened the door and looked at me expectantly. I told him thanks and waved him on.

"All right, Clare, we've cleared the walkway and the building. I'm not sure what you're so curious about, but go on back. Jodie's there. I'm going to stay out here while you take a look," Omar said as he came through the opening, his gun safely holstered now.

"Thanks," I said as I walked past him.

The slight jog to the right kept Jodie hidden from me for a couple of steps, but a second later I saw the full expanse of the walkway and where she was in it.

She'd crouched and was looking at something on the ground, next to the building.

"Clare, step back. Get Omar back here again," she said without fully turning in my direction.

I did as she asked and then stayed close by Omar as he hurried to join her.

"What's up?" he said.

"Look there. I think the techs missed something." She pointed.

We were on The Rescued Word side, in between our back door and the empty store's, which was currently wide open.

217

Briefly, I wondered if it had been opened by Jodie and Omar or if they'd found it that way, but now wasn't the time to ask. There was something much more interesting to see.

"Is that a license plate?" Omar said as he got a little closer to where Jodie was pointing.

"Looks like it. A motorcycle plate," she said.

Omar took a couple pictures on his phone of the plate in its location before Jodie, with gloved hands, lifted it from the short tangle of weeds it had been mostly hidden in.

"Wyoming," she said.

The plate had only four numbers, and the word "Wyoming" was set along the bottom. The background picture was of one of the state's better-known natural features, Devils Tower, a circular butte in the land that had been a landmark throughout history but was famous for being the spot where Richard Dreyfuss met the aliens in *Close Encounters of the Third Kind.* Jimmy and his friends had climbed it back when they were in high school.

"And a relatively new one at that." Omar pointed at the year that was imprinted on one side. "They kept their registration up. The tags are current."

"Well, this should help us find someone to talk to," Jodie said. She looked back over her shoulder up at me. "At least someone who isn't you."

"Good news for me," I said.

"Very," Omar agreed.

16

A date for the evening with a geologist and his geode became solidified with one quick phone call. The day was pretty well shot when it came to getting any real work done, so I locked the front door one final time and decided to call on an old friend before I got ready for the date. Well, one of Chester's old friends, technically.

I knew exactly where Homer Mayfair lived, if he was still alive, and I was pretty sure he was. I had a distinct memory of Chester taking me to his place when I was a teenager. Homer had three big scrapbook-like volumes of old newspapers, and he wondered if Chester would come out and see if there was any way to bring the paper and ink back to its former glory. Chester had told him over the phone that restoring newspaper wasn't like restoring old books, that microfiche had been made to save the newspaper stories, but Homer still asked

Chester to come out and look at the items himself. I went along so I could learn how to gently tell a potential customer that there wasn't anything we could do for them.

I also remembered that there had been a moment of animosity between the two of them, though I couldn't remember the exact details. Homer became suddenly upset with Chester about something, but they both ended up almost joking about it. Though the memories weren't clear, I didn't want to bother Chester or let him know what I was doing. If the moment was right, I'd ask Homer.

I made the short hike back up to my house and hurried in for the keys to my car. I did a quick search for the cards I'd written the goat relocation names on but couldn't immediately find them. I'd have to search later.

Homer lived in Purple Springs Valley — well, along the perimeter of the valley, up the side a bit, opposite the monastery, and neatly hidden by a curtain of aspens. If he'd wanted, he could have observed the goat relocation activity from his front porch, and no one would have noticed him watching through the trees.

He'd been one of the first people to build a home in Purple Springs Valley. One of the attractive features of Star City is that even though it's small, it has almost everything anyone would need. You could travel over a short mountain pass or around a mountain slope and build your house out in the woods, get away from it all but be back in the middle of it all in only a few minutes. If Star City didn't have what you needed, you could drive thirty more minutes and be in Salt Lake City. If you couldn't find what you were looking for in Salt Lake, then you truly didn't need it.

When Homer built his home on the edge of the valley, he probably thought he would be out there on his own forever. Even though it was Utah, no one could have predicted that a polygamist family would have dared be so bold as to settle so close to the town that was "in Utah but not of Utah." Over the years, a few other houses sprung up along the treeless valley floor as well as amidst the white-trunked aspens along the upward-sloping perimeter. There were even a few houses higher up, mostly hidden by the tall evergreen pines. It was always cold inside the tree line. Even though Homer's abnormally wide log house wasn't up far from the valley, I rubbed my arms from the chill before I knocked on the front door.

I'd come the same way Jodie and I had,

but there were no motorcycles, no riders, no trucks, and, I assumed, no more goats in the valley. If the project had caused any damage to the land, it had sprung back quickly with wildflowers and tall grasses upright and filling the open spaces.

To the side of the house and back a little was an empty old barn and corral. I hadn't remembered the barn and corral from my last visit, and I hadn't noticed it until I got out of my car on this trip. The barn might have been painted at one time, but it was now just old splintered wood that looked to be one heavy snowfall away from collapsing. The only animal in sight was an old black Lab that had laboriously lifted himself up from his resting position next to the porch to greet me.

It seemed like there were no people anywhere. There were no cars. The dog looked old but well taken care of.

"Hey, boy," I said as I held my fingers down so he could sniff me. "Not of the guard dog variety, huh?"

His tail wagged.

The front door of the house opened before I expected it to, a small slit at first, but then wide.

"Help you?" Homer said from the doorway. He was old, but that wasn't a surprise.

He'd been old when I was a teenager. He was older than Chester but I wasn't sure by how much, small with deeply sunken wrinkled cheeks and only a few wisps of hair on his head. He wore a white sweatshirt and faded jeans. Winter attire on a summer mountain day. I resisted looking down to see if he still had the peg leg sticking out from the bottom of his jeans.

"Hi, I'm Clare Henry. I work with my grandfather, Chester, at The Rescued Word in Star City. May I come in?" I said.

"I know who you are. I know who your grandfather is too. You figure out a way to fix my newspapers?"

I was impressed that he remembered. "I'm afraid not. I have a few questions about your newspaper days though."

"Really? Well, come on in, then."

Homer stepped back and then disappeared somewhere inside. I heard the knock of the tip of his leg on the wooden floor, but I'd lost sight of him by the time the dog and I entered the house.

"Homer?" I'd said as the dog and I moved past a dark front room, blinds over all the windows shut tight, and then down what seemed like the main hallway.

"Back here. Come on. Be careful. I have some junk I need to get rid of," Homer called from somewhere down the hallway. I hoped a wardrobe wouldn't be waiting for me at the other end, beckoning me to come inside, but the house most definitely felt secretive and shut off from the rest of the world. A scent of old long-ago-read ink and dust filled the air. It wasn't altogether unpleasant, but it made me want to clean, and very few things had that effect on me.

When we came to a fork the dog took over, veering right. He looked over his shoulder so I obediently followed.

I wondered what the floor plan of the house had been titled. "Maze" came to mind. I passed two shut doors, one on my right and one on my left, before I came to an open door. Light blazed out into the hallway from inside, and I took two quick steps to reach the hopefully safe oasis.

"Come on over and have a seat." Homer signaled.

I'd seen messy. I'd seen piles and stacks of stuff. Chester's precarious book piles had always been a part of my life. I'd seen cramped rooms. But I had never seen anything like the room that Homer Mayfair's dog and I walked into. It was a big room, probably almost the size of The Rescued Word's retail space. I was reminded of a cave my parents had taken my brother and me to when we were little. The cave was full of stalactites and stalagmites. Earth formations protruding out from both the floor and the ceiling. There were so many varying-sized stacks of things in Homer's room that I wished I'd remembered which ones — stalactites or stalagmites — had been the formations jutting up from the cave's floor. Whichever it was, Homer's office was so plentiful with them that between the mess and the closed-tight windows, an immediate sense of claustrophobia came over me.

The stacks weren't made of earthy things though; they were made of newspapers, books, boxes, and pieces of paper. Homer's desk was at the far end of the room, and the top of it was no less messy than the rest of the space, though the stacks were shorter. As he sat, I noticed an old fireplace behind him that looked like it hadn't been used in some time. I decided that was a good thing. There was so much paper in the room that one tiny stray spark would quickly set the whole house ablaze, maybe the whole valley.

The dog at my heel, I wove my way carefully to a seat across from Homer. I didn't trust myself to roam freely without toppling something, so I was glad to be seated. The dog had handled the journey like a pro, not tipping even one stack. Granted, he'd probably done the walk a thousand times, but I was still impressed. I patted his side as he sat at my feet.

After I sat down, a low bench behind Homer and to the right of the fireplace came into view. Lined up along the top of the bench was a row of old typewriters. None of them looked familiar, but there was an old No. 5 in the group, though it was in terrible shape.

"How's your grandfather, Clare? He doing okay?" Homer asked, interrupting my typewriter perusal.

"He's doing very well, thanks. He stays busy."

"He knows the store will be in good hands when he kicks the bucket."

I smiled. It was a reality, I supposed, but not one I liked to discuss.

"So, what can I do for you?" he asked.

Homer's forearms were on his desk, his fingers entwined. He wasn't tall and his pose made him seem extra short, as if he was a kid peering over a candy counter, but a kid with an old face.

His brown eyes were bright with curiosity and intelligence, but though he'd welcomed me inside, I didn't see much kindness in his expression. I saw impatience.

"I was wondering about your typewriters." I nodded toward the bench.

"You were?" He looked over his shoulder at them. "You need something to fix?"

"No, actually we're pretty busy."

"So, what, then?"

"Back in your newspaper days, do you remember selling some typewriters?"

"Of course. We sold them all the time. We'd get new ones and have to do something with the old ones."

"Do you remember selling one to Mirabelle Montgomery?"

Homer's eyes actually lit brighter as he sat up straighter. "I'm sure I remember selling one or maybe even two to her. She used to write those dirty stories." He laughed. "Oh, I so loved to read her stories. My colleagues did as well, but none of us could ever admit it because we were serious journalists, after all, no time for frivolous fiction. Wasn't that silly? Mirabelle's stories would be tame compared to some television commercials today let alone some books that are being written. Let me think. Oh, yes, she wrote a story about a sheik and his harem. She had a talent for describing what was going on behind their tent bedroom walls without ever giving the specifics. Gracious, she was a pro at it. She might still be." He laughed again, the impatience gone. "Yes, I'm certain I sold her at least one typewriter."

I smiled. "I just fixed one and she's kept it in great condition. She still writes letters to her grandchildren on it. I wouldn't be surprised if she still writes fiction too, but she says she doesn't."

"That's a shame. She had a real talent, but perhaps not a good fit for this time period." He shrugged.

"Well, I liked her typewriter so much that I was wondering if you had any more like it. Chester and I have talked about putting up a display in the store with some antique typewriters, and I thought I'd see if you had more and if they were for sale."

As much sense as that might have made, it was a complete lie. In fact, Chester and I had once had a typewriter display, but every time we put a new typewriter out someone came in and wanted to buy it. Chester could never tell them no, so our display was always unfinished.

"Oh, well, let me think." Homer sat back in the old squeaky chair. "Best guess is that I sold her an Underwood No. 5, but I can't be totally sure. We sure went through a lot of them."

"Oh, yes, that's the one," I said.

"I have one over there," he said. "But it's in terrible condition. You wouldn't want it. What was wrong with Mirabelle's?"

"The 'L.' It was an easy fix."

"Excellent, so she's got it back, then? It's working?"

There was nothing strange in his tone, nothing to make me think he was fishing as to the whereabouts of the typewriter. But I didn't want him to know it was at her house. I might be paranoid, but I didn't want *anyone* to know it was there.

"No, actually, the police took it."

"The police? I don't understand. Why?" he asked.

"Did you hear about the murder downtown?"

"No," he said, and it sounded genuine. "You might find this hard to believe coming from an old newspaperman, but I don't pay much attention to the news anymore. It's either too awful to digest or in the case of the paper too loaded with error. It drives me batty wondering what happened to all the editing practices I put into place. Anyway" — he waved away his complaints — "no, what murder? Who was killed?"

"I don't know, but the man who was killed had come into The Rescued Word asking specifically about Mirabelle's typewriter.

The next day his body was found in the walkway behind Bygone."

"That's terrible. And strange. What would he have wanted with Mirabelle's type-writer?"

"That's also why I'm here. I wondered if you might know."

"No idea." He shook his head slowly, but I saw something else there. Or I thought I did.

Was I imagining that Homer was trying very hard not to show me that he did know why Mirabelle's typewriter was wanted by a man who had ultimately been murdered? I thought I saw forced control in the push of his fingertips that were now on the top of his desk and the small catch in his breath-ing, as if his throat had tightened up but he was trying to will it loose without me notic-ing.

"Is it worth a lot of money?" he asked casually but with some of that tightness in his voice.

"Maybe a couple hundred dollars, at most," I said.

"Then I have no idea," he said, his eyes locked onto mine.

Were we playing chicken?

I nodded but didn't break eye contact. "Homer, how're your kids? Don't you have a couple? And your grandkids?"

The transition was awkward at best, but he didn't seem to notice. In fact, he seemed relieved to change the subject.

"Sure, two boys and a girl in Salt Lake City. Their kids are your age or older. Out of school, trying to make a life."

"Are their kids in Salt Lake too?"

"Some are. A couple are south in St. George, and one granddaughter moved to Alabama. Why?"

"Just curious. I hope everyone is well." When the silence continued two long beats, I asked, "Do you mind if I look at those typewriters?"

"Of course not. Make yourself at home."

I inspected him to see if there was any hesitation, but there was only sincerity in his offer.

There was no polite way to ask him to leave his own office, but I wished there were. Or that he'd leave on his own, maybe offer to go get us some coffee or cold drinks. But he didn't leave or offer anything. He remained in his chair, turning it so he could observe me as he rested his chin on his tented fingers.

I stepped carefully around the dog, the desk, and a few stacks of books. Any other day, I'd also be curious about the books.

But not today.

The old Underwood was first on the bench and truly was in terrible shape, with missing button tabs over the keys and no ribbon inside. The black case was scratched and dented on one side. There was no fixing it, but I was sorry for its condition and I hoped it had seen a long stretch of good years.

A yellow (even the keys were yellow) Smith Corona was next and, like the Underwood, it was a No. 5 series, though that was all the two typewriters had in common. This one was from the 1950s. It was cute and portable, lots shorter and weighing much less than the clunky Underwood. It had two paper-hold bars in the back that, when extended up, looked like aliens' antennae. If I owned it, I was sure I'd give it the unoriginal name of Bumblebee from Space.

A blue and white 1960s Olympia Traveller was next. It was also a portable typewriter and was in pristine condition. It wasn't as cute as the Smith Corona, but more squared-off and official looking, as though it would give important documents the proper attention. I wondered if it had ever been used.

I hadn't ever seen the other model of Underwood that was on the bench in person. It was a brown and dark grey 1940s Ace, squat with art deco lines along its side. It belonged in a smoke-filled room with Sam Spade uttering words like "dame" and "broad."

The last typewriter was a gray-cased and green-keyed Hermes 3000 that had been built in the 1950s. I'd fixed a few Hermes, and Chester still had one up in his apartment somewhere but I couldn't remember which model he owned. The Hermes was all business, but with its curved lines, I could imagine a young female author greeting it each morning as she placed a contrasting vase of flowers next to it before she got to work.

Other than the Underwood, they were in terrific condition. I fell into some typewriter love with each and every one. It was a hazard of the business I was in.

"These are all from the newspaper, Homer?" I said.

"Well, sort of. I can't remember which ones, but I think a couple were just samples sent to me by salesmen who were trying to sell a bunch to the paper."

"Except for the first Underwood, they're in mint condition."

"Oh, yes. I kept the Underwood strictly for sentimental reasons. I typed a lot of articles on that typewriter when I was first a reporter," he said. "When the others came into fashion, I was an editor, so not so much sentimentality with those."

"Was Mirabelle's new when she bought it?"

"I doubt it. It was probably part of a group of used ones that we sold when we got new models. It must be a workhorse to still be typing."

"It's great," I said.

I started over at the beginning of the line of typewriters, but this time, as I looked at each one, I acted like I was more interested in their inner workings. I looked inside them and gently pushed on the keys. I tried to be inconspicuous about looking at the sides of the key bars. I did not see any scratched-on writing, but not all the key bars on Mirabelle's No. 5 had the scratches; there was a chance I wasn't hitting the correct keys, but I could only look for so long without Homer charging rent.

Suddenly, I had nothing else to keep me there. Well, maybe one thing.

"Homer, the last time I was here, you were mad at Chester. I can't remember why, do you?"

Homer blinked and thought a minute. "Probably the same thing that I get mad at him about every time I see him. That interview he gave to the Salt Lake reporter. He should have granted me the interview, and then I would have gotten the national attention."

"The article about the press he built?"

"That's the one. Chester definitely had his fifteen minutes. So did that reporter. I didn't."

"Had you asked him for an interview?" I said.

"Oh, yes, and I was quite offended when he granted it to the other reporter." Homer laughed. "Silly stuff now, I suppose, but at the time I was mad as a moose on Sunday, and I still like to hassle your grandfather about it."

"Did he tell you why he chose the Salt Lake reporter?"

"Never did."

I nodded. I didn't even know about the article until Olive had mentioned it. Talking about it with two different people today was either a coincidence or the universe wanting me to pay attention. I wondered why Chester hadn't given the interview to Homer. Chester Henry was all about Star City. It would have been unlike him to choose someone from Salt Lake over someone from Star City — ever, for anything.

I needed to track down the article and ask Chester about it.

"Thanks, Homer. I'm really sorry to have come by without notice, but I appreciate your time and the chance to look at your typewriters. You have a great collection."

He followed me to the front door, but the dog led the way again.

"Homer," I said once we were at the door. "Have any of your grandkids visited recently?"

"No," he said, but I could see the lie. He'd both answered too sharply and hesitated for the most miniscule of seconds. The hesitation filled the air with millions more questions, but I didn't know how to ask them without being pushy and rude. Jodie would have known what to do, and she wouldn't have cared about being pushy and rude.

"Well, I hope they do soon. It's always good to have family visit," I said, even though I knew that wasn't always true either. Sometimes even the closest of family members weren't welcome visitors.

"I agree, dear. Thank you for coming by, and give my regards to Chester."

"Will do," I said, the door shutting before I got the two words all the way out.

17

"I've cooked us dinner," Seth said as I stepped out of the front door of Little Blue and joined him on the porch. "I hope that's okay."

"At your place?"

Seth laughed. "As it is. I cleaned up a little, but I still haven't unpacked all the way. However, you'll probably understand me better the second you see it. It will either scare you away or keep you curious. I've been told I have weird stuff. Yeah, I just wanted the chance to talk without interruption this time. My phone never rings so, other than a little music — traditional classical or rock, you choose — we should have some quiet."

"Sounds good," I said as I pushed up my glasses. I'd taken longer than I thought I would with Homer, so I'd gotten ready in a flurry, and my hair, makeup, and glasses hadn't had a chance to settle yet.

I wasn't so sure I should be going to a stranger's home when they were still such a stranger. But I decided I'd roll with it until I felt even an inkling of discomfort.

"Well, since I live right across the street, you can run away screaming if you're not having any fun, and you'll be home in record time," Seth said as if he were reading my mind.

The temperature was cool, and I'd thrown a thin white sweater over the light green summer dress I'd donned. It seemed almost everyone in Star City had at least a few thin jackets and sweaters for summer evenings. As we crossed the street, we took a moment to enjoy our perch and the view it gave us.

As it began to set, the sun sent a yellow-orange half halo up behind a dark mountain peak to our left. Baskerville would be on the east shelves by now. The town extended down the hill and across a wide valley. Where there weren't homes or businesses, trees filled the spaces, their leaves still green, the fall color change not beginning for another month or so. Down there, many of the homes and neighborhoods were new and modern, but here in the part of town that was original, most of the homes were older, typically smaller, many of them chalet-style like mine. Around the valley and high on the mountainsides were the giant rich-people homes. Movie stars, some popular authors, and CEOs lived in these. There were lots of famous people with homes in town, lots more who simply traveled through.

"Beautiful place," Seth said.

"You'll never get tired of it," I said.

"I believe that."

Seth looked very nice. He wore clean, untorn jeans and a yellow button-up shirt. The shirt was wrinkled, but like the tinge of time on the older houses and buildings around us, there was something charming about the wrinkles. His hair was brushed, and he'd run his fingers through it a couple times just since picking me up at my door. I thought he might be nervous, which only made him cuter. He didn't have his glasses on, and since he was much taller than my five feet, six inches, I found myself looking up to inspect his eyes. Was that a natural color blue or were contacts involved? They'd been that color even with the glasses on, I thought.

We walked slowly across the street, but no matter how slow the pace, it was a short trip. Seth lived in an apartment above a gift shop. Star City Stars had been around for as long as I could remember. It was a small place owned by Elizabeth Owl. She sat in a big cushioned chair in the back of her shop and called out greetings to customers as they came in. As far as I knew, she never got out of the chair to personally say hello. She always wore long, flowy things and giant round glasses that made her look just like her last name.

The shop specialized in charms, stones, and crystals that were supposed to give off particular energies. Her business had been going strong for over thirty years, but I always wondered if it was because she rented the apartment above the store and had the extra income.

The glass entry door to the apartment was located to the side of the shop. As we passed by the shop, I peered in through the front window to see if Elizabeth was in her chair. She was, and she was reading one of the oversized astrology books she often quoted from. She didn't look up to see me looking in.

I'd never known anyone who lived in the apartment, but I'd seen it once when it was empty and in between renters. It was an appealing space, and I was interested to see what Seth had done with it.

Seth unlocked the glass door and then let me go up the stairs first. I noticed that he gave me a moment to get far enough ahead that he wouldn't be following too closely behind. I liked that.

As we stood on a small landing at the top of the stairs, he unlocked a solid door made with thick dark wood that had been worn smooth and shiny around the brass door-knob.

"It's purely coincidence that I'm living above a shop that sells rocks," he said with a laugh. "Honestly, I don't think I could have planned something like that even if I'd wanted to."

I stepped into the apartment and under-stood the coincidence. His place was one giant rock shop. Above a rock shop.

"Oh my," I said, meaning it in a "wow" way, not a "yikes" way.

"Yeah, I know. I'll leave the door open a little if that would make you more comfort-able."

I looked at him. I wasn't sure if he was still joking or not. Had women really run away from him because his house was full of rocks?

"I'm fine," I said with a smile.

"Good," he said as he pushed the door closed with a quiet click. "Come along and I'll show you my collection." He winked.

The layout of the apartment was similar

to Chester's except there were walls separating Seth's back bedroom from the rest of the large one-room space — living area in the front, dining table in the middle, and kitchen in the back. The sidewalls were lined with dark-wood-framed windows, the wood of the floor matching the window frames. The space was slightly smaller than Chester's, making it cozier and more comfortable.

Well, I could envision it being comfortable and cozy at some point. Currently, it was kind of a mess, and very full of rocks.

I laughed. "Oh my goodness."

"I know. It won't be so bad when I can get organized and get stuff on the shelves, but everything's everywhere right now. I straightened up the dining table — wow, you should have seen all the stuff I had on it — and the couch so we could watch a movie or something later if you want."

I saw a little red come into Seth's cheeks.

"Sounds great!" I said, hoping to move past any innuendo he thought he'd accidently backed into. "So tell me about all this stuff," I said.

It wasn't easy to keep track of the details, but he showed me things like icy-white sharp quartz crystals that must have come from Superman's training cave; pink quartz aptly named Rose, some smooth, some sharp; peacock copper, which was also true to its name and very colorful. My favorite item wasn't even a rock or a mineral. It was something called Orthocera, which was a fossil of an animal that had lived about three hundred million years ago and was a relative of squid.

"There's too much here to go into all the details on only our second date, so I'll save some for later, but this is the geode," he said as he high-stepped his way over to the other side of the couch.

"Is that real?" I said when I'd joined him.

It looked like a two-foot-in-diameter rock had been cut in half and the inside had been loaded up with purple crystals.

"Not only real, but nature-made," Seth said.

"It's beautiful," I said.

"I thought you'd like it."

"I do." I studied the geode's crystals and decided that Superman should get purple crystals too.

"Sorry, if this was all overwhelming. I can't help myself sometimes, but after you get to know me better, I won't be so obnoxious. Or at least I'll try not to be."

"I don't think you're obnoxious," I said.

"That's a great start," he said. "Usually

by now, I've scared off regular girls. Girls like you wouldn't have stayed once they stepped inside and saw my crazy obsession."

"Girls like me?"

"Yeah — knockout beautiful."

I laughed. "Well, thank you."

"My pleasure, believe me. Now, tell me you like lasagna."

"I love it."

"I make the best you've ever tasted. Even better than your mother's, but I'll gladly bow out of any competition she might be a part of."

"My mom's not much of a cook," I said as we moved toward the kitchen table, bringing the cubby hole of a kitchen into better view. The appliances were all white, smaller than normal, and old but in a charming, antique way. "I thought I smelled oregano and garlic. Yum."

We talked easily while we ate. I thought Seth had a way of making rock and mineral stories interesting. He was a geologist, but he'd also obtained training and experience in explosives. It was actually *really* interesting to hear about some of the mines he'd worked on and what his tasks had been.

"Do you mind if I ask about this morning?" he said when we both had finished every single thing on our plates. "Everything okay with the police?"

"Fine, I think. Just procedure. No one seems to have any answers regarding who the victim was or who murdered him." I thought about telling Seth about the license plate, but I wasn't sure if I was supposed to or not. I'd ask Jodie before I started spreading the news.

"So strange. Have you figured out why anyone might have wanted that specific typewriter?"

"No," I said. I looked at Seth a long moment and decided it wouldn't hurt to give him a little more information. Lots of people already knew about this part. I reached into my pocket, pulling out the paper I was still carrying around. "I found these numbers and letters on the key bars. The police know."

He took the paper and looked at it less than five seconds before he said, "Longitude and latitude."

"What?"

"I suspect these are longitude and latitude measurements. Put together properly, they signify a location on our planet, perhaps a location important to the murder."

"Really? What makes you think so?"

He shrugged. "I work with that sort of stuff all the time. The 'N' and the 'W' give it away, but the amount of numbers works too."

I took the paper back from him and looked at it. "How should it go together?"

"That's the hard part," he said. "As they are, they could be put together millions of ways, I suppose. Most of the combinations would lead somewhere."

"That's amazing."

"Not really, but I'm okay if you want to think so."

"Any suggestions on how I should begin? Well, how the police should begin to pare the locations down?"

"Let me make a copy of everything, and I'll do some deductive reasoning. Were these numbers in some sort of order?"

"Yes, they were scratched on the key bars, left to right, top row to bottom row."

"I'll try that order first. If that doesn't lead to something, I'll play around with it a bit. I love number puzzles and mysteries." He looked up from the paper and at me. "I bet that doesn't surprise you."

"It's a good non-surprise."

"How was dinner?"

"Best I've had in a long time."

Seth smiled.

Suddenly I sensed a great make-out session in my near future. I felt like a silly teenager, but I hoped it didn't show. It had been so long since I'd felt such a connection, and it was delightful. It was like all my senses were turned up a notch. I wondered if it was the Superman quartz or something else nature-made.

We didn't watch a movie and we didn't make out, though we both probably wanted to. Seth cleaned off the dinner dishes, served some homemade apple pie a la mode for dessert (we ate every last bite of that too), and we just talked. About everything. The world, our families, even a little politics and religion. It wasn't a requirement for a future date, but I thought we were both pleased that we leaned toward the same political party and our religious upbringing was similar.

The time flew and I realized it was not only the best date I'd had in a long time, it was maybe the best date ever, but that might have just been me dissing the memory of my time with the cheater Creighton.

We were crowded close together on the small landing outside his apartment when we exited a few hours later. The good-night kiss I got on that landing curled my toes and made me think it was probably a good thing we'd kept our distance from each other inside. Who knows what regretful thing might have happened. Okay, so it might not have ended up being regretful, but it wasn't worth the risk quite yet. Then it turned out to be an extra-good thing that we got the kiss in because a big kink got put in the evening as soon as we exited the glass door at the bottom of the stairs.

When we'd walked over from my house, the street had been filled with parked cars. That was pretty normal for Star City. But as the weekday evening wore on, most of the cars left, their drivers taking them back to Salt Lake City or other close towns. I hadn't paid any attention to the vehicles earlier, and I had no idea yet exactly what Seth drove, but now I noticed a motorcycle parked a short way farther up the hill. And inspecting the motorcycle was the person I was just dissing in my head a few moments earlier. Creighton.

All I could do was hope he wouldn't notice Seth and me, but that would have been nearly impossible, even if Creighton wasn't an observant police officer, because Seth saw him too and walked directly to him.

"Hi, Officer, something wrong?" Seth asked.

"Is this your — Clare?" Creighton cleared his throat, and I muttered something that sounded like a confused but overly firm hello before he looked at Seth again. "Sir, is this your motorcycle?"

"Yes. Well, it's my brother's. I'm watching it for him. Long story, but he flew out of the Salt Lake airport."

"I see. And are you aware that it's missing the back license plate?" Creighton said.

"No," Seth said as he stepped around to the back of the bike and next to Creighton.

Two distinct thoughts ran through my mind at the same time. One was, of course, oh crap! There was a motorcycle license plate found today where a dead body had recently been.

The second thought, however, was inappropriate considering everything else, murder included. Other than their height, Seth and Creighton were so different. Seth's tall, thin frame and tousled hair were completely opposite to Creighton's buzzed hair and bulky, squared frame.

This was not important at the moment, and I mentally shoved away the thought and went back to the one about the license plate being found where the dead body had been.

"I'm sorry, Officer, I had no idea," Seth said.

"You from Wyoming?" Creighton asked.

"No, my brother is though," Seth said.

"Your name?"

"Seth Cassidy."

"I need you to come with me, Seth. I need to ask you some questions."

Seth blinked and looked at Creighton. "Of course, Officer. I'd be happy to go with you."

He hadn't missed a beat and seemed genuinely surprised by the missing plate. I wanted to be angry at Creighton for ruining the end to my perfect date, even if he hadn't meant to. I wanted to ask Seth some of my own questions. One being had I just had dinner with someone somehow involved in a murder? For some reason, I just didn't think so.

"Do you want me to call you an attorney?" I said to Seth.

"Not at all," he said. "I'll call you if I need bail money though." He winked at me and I smiled at him.

There were no handcuffs as Creighton opened the front passenger door of his police car for Seth. Once inside, Seth smiled again and waved at me. He was putting on a brave face, but I could see a pinch of concern in his features. It was impossible not to be nervous about the police wanting to talk to you. Even if you were innocent and one of the officers was your best friend, apparently.

I watched Creighton's car disappear down the hill. The night was not young. It was late and I was tired, but I was also wired.

"Shoot!" I said aloud as I thought about the numbers and letters that Seth had perhaps understood, or at least partially. I hoped he didn't tell Creighton what he'd deduced. I wanted to tell Jodie first.

But it didn't matter. Ultimately, the police needed to know no matter who told them. There were so many unanswered questions that even contemplating the idea that Seth knew what the letters and numbers were for because he was somehow involved in the murder felt like a giant stretch. I'd tell Jodie everything, though, and hope for the best.

I should have gone home. I should have gone to bed. I had plenty of work to do tomorrow, and I functioned better if I wasn't tired. But instead of going back to Little Blue, I walked down the hill toward Bygone Alley. Most of the Main Street storefronts were dark. Noise rumbled through the closed theater doors behind which Hollywood's next greatest indie film would be crowned in January at the Star City Film Festival. A very drunk woman exited a tiny bar, stumbling dangerously. I had the urge to grab her arm and make sure she didn't drive anywhere, but she went from the sidewalk to flopping into the backseat of a cab; the cabbie smiled tiredly at me before he pulled away from the curb.

I turned onto Bygone, and while staying across the street from The Rescued Word, I walked slowly, peering into more mostly dark windows. The diner was bright, its shiny chrome counter gleaming under the few fluorescents left on after closing time.

I looked toward The Rescued Word. Its windows were dark and almost foreboding with the glow of a streetlamp only reaching one corner of the front window. There was a light on upstairs. If Chester was there, he was probably alternating between reading and falling asleep in his chair. Though he napped through most evenings, he didn't think it was right to go to bed before midnight. Baskerville would either be on his lap or in the store on a shelf if he was feeling particularly introverted.

The lighted window upstairs gave me an idea. It was sneaky and close to illegal, but I'd try not to step over the line.

I speed walked to get around the corner in a hurry. At the end of Bygone, I glanced toward Mirabelle's house on my left and then turned right, proceeding slowly down that side of the street.

I decided I'd have to cross over to the other side like I'd done when I was following Chester if I wanted a really good look.

I zipped across, dodging a couple of parked cars and a bike rack.

It was dark enough that I was extra careful with my footing. I'd walked up and down that side of the street many times over the years. The downward view was horrifying if you were afraid of heights, but I knew how to stay far enough away from the danger.

I was sure some people must be out on their front porches — the night was too nice not to be. But I didn't see anyone as I stopped in front of the third house.

Lights blazed brightly out of the two large front windows, one on each side of the front door.

I made sure my feet were a safe distance from the back edge and lifted myself up to my toes.

And I saw nothing except the bright light. The house was too high up to even see the top of a lamp.

I lowered back to my heels and plopped my hands on my hips as I thought about a good reason for climbing up the stairs and knocking on the door. Of course there wasn't one. It was late.

But the lights were on.

I looked up and down the street and still didn't see anyone. Lights were on in windows, but all the cars were quiet and dark. I didn't hear the creak of a rocking chair on a porch or the low hum of quiet conversation.

If I climbed the stairs only halfway, I could probably look inside the windows and then jump down and hurry away quickly.

It wasn't a great plan, but it wasn't terrible. I wasn't going to break into the house, and I was only going to take a quick look.

I trotted across the street and began climbing the stairs to the front porch. Once I got halfway up, I stretched my neck again and tried to peer inside. This time I did see the top of a lamp through the right window and what looked like the side view of a piano through the left window.

One more step. Two more. Three more. When I reached the top step, I hesitated. Moving onto the porch seemed so much more intrusive than walking up the stairs.

Nevertheless, I lifted my leg to take that last step.

And the door was flung open.

I had two choices — jump down the stairs and run, or freeze in place and hope they didn't notice me. I froze, even though I didn't truly think I would remain unnoticed.

Once the two people who'd been exiting the house saw me, the woman made a small surprised sound and the man said, "Clare? What are you doing here? Is everything okay?"

"Hi, Chester," I said more sheepishly than I'd ever said anything in my entire life.

"Clare," Chester said again when he probably put together exactly what was going on. Finally, he turned to the woman. "Ramona, this is my granddaughter, Clare Henry. Clare, this is my friend Ramona Bridger."

And then something even more surprising happened. Ramona cackled just like a movie witch, but friendly, not evil.

"Aren't you the silly one?" she said to Chester with the deepest southern accent I'd ever heard. "Friend? After what we just did tonight, I would think we were more than friends."

"Well," Chester said with a smile in her direction but with no sign of being the slightest bit embarrassed. That was okay, I was embarrassed enough for both of them.

"Oh," I said. "I'm sorry to disturb."

"No need to apologize, honey, we're done. For the night," she said. And then she cackled again.

I tried to figure out what to do with my

hands and arms; they suddenly seemed so
foreign. It appeared that my grandfather
had just seen lots more action than I had
that evening.

I didn't know what else to say, so all that
came out was, "Oh dear."

18

"Clare, I am old enough to have a girlfriend," Chester said as he poured coffee into the mug he'd placed in front of me on my worktable. It was too late to be drinking coffee, but that never stopped me.

"Of course you are," I said. "I'm not upset that you're . . . dating someone. I think it's great!"

"You do?"

"Why wouldn't I?"

Chester sat in a chair on the other side and stretched his legs, crossing them at his ankles.

"Because of your grandmother. I don't want you to think I've forgotten her or am disrespecting her memory."

"She's been gone for so long. We've — your family — only wanted you to be happy. If you spent all these years not dating for our sakes . . . well, then, I'm sorry."

Chester shrugged. "Well, I've dated. But

until Ramona I haven't found anyone who tripped my trigger, if you know what I mean."

Briefly, I closed my eyes and shook my head a couple of times. I didn't need to know those sorts of details. I didn't even want to know about those parts of Jodie's relationships. Well, I'd be curious about Mutt. But not so much Chester or Ramona.

"Who have you dated?" I asked. "This is Star City. Everybody knows everybody. I've never heard of you dating anyone."

"Discretion, my dear girl, is the better part of valor. Surely, you've heard that before."

"Of course, but . . ." I sighed. "Chester, I'm not upset, but I wish you would have told me about Ramona. About anyone you've been interested in."

"I hear you. Ramona is special. I wanted to make sure. She's nothing like your grandmother, and I have to admit that's part of the attraction." He laughed. "There's simply no comparison, but your grandmother would have really liked Ramona, in a 'gracious, that woman sure is loud' way."

I smiled. Chester could never stop loving my grandmother. None of us would, and she'd never be forgotten either. If she'd given any thought to the idea that Chester would outlive her by so many years, she

259

would have told him she wanted him to move on and find another love. She might have sought one out for him. In her organized way, she would have made lists of eligible women, noting their pros and cons, and then she would have created color-coded file cards, instructing Chester on the best way to proceed.

"I'd like to get to know Ramona," I said.

"You will. She wants to take you out to lunch tomorrow if you're available. We were talking about you earlier in the evening. I told her she needed to meet the family, beginning with you, and she wanted to meet you right away. I guess you helped her accomplish her task."

"Yeah, I didn't mean to look so sneaky. I saw you go there yesterday and I was curious."

"Ah. I understand."

"Chester, since we're sharing, will you please tell me why you were looking up pancreatic cancer? I don't believe that it was an accident. I think you knew exactly what you were doing."

Chester nodded. "It was not an accident. Ramona's husband died of pancreatic cancer a few years back. A man my age has heard plenty of awful stories about death, but I've never known anyone personally who has died of pancreatic cancer. I wanted to understand what she'd — and he'd — gone though. You have to understand something, sweetheart. When you get to my age and you've had good past relationships and so have others who come into your life, those people we've loved and lost become a part of our new relationships. They are there with us and show up, sometimes when we least expect them. But they're welcome in, Clare. There's no jealousy. We welcome our dead and we still love them. There's just no other way. Can you understand that?"

"Of course I can. I wish you'd just told me. I was worried, very worried. I didn't need to be."

"I'm healthy as a duck during elk season."

"I've never heard that one before." I laughed.

"Now, tell me about your tall young man. Seth? Is that correct?"

"Yes, he fixed me dinner this evening, and then afterward was detained by the police regarding the murder of leather man. Creighton picked him up."

"No! Goodness, that's not happy news. However, I would bet that Seth is innocent and that Creighton was just trying to get under your skin, Clare."

"That's not it. It was kind of coincidental.

I don't think Creighton knew I was with Seth when he came upon the motorcycle Seth said was his brother's. One of the Wyoming license plates was missing. Jodie found one out back today, and she and Omar wonder if it's tied to the murder, maybe pointing to a motorcycle group who helped with some goat relocations."

"A Wyoming plate?"

"Yes."

"That most certainly throws up some doubt, but let's wait for the answers before we jump to any conclusions." Chester sounded as if he was trying to convince himself. He sat up a little straighter. "Well, how was dinner?"

"Delicious."

"Just think, Clare, you could end up being the first Henry to date a murderer. No, wait, I think my great-great-grandfather had some trouble with the law."

"I honestly don't think Seth is a killer. I might just like him too much to see him clearly, but he's too intrigued by his job to be concerned about killing men in leather who pine away for specific typewriters. I think I'm reading that right. I hope."

"You like him *too much*? Well, I haven't heard that in a while."

"I do, Chester. It's early yet, but he's a

sweet man and there's something about his attentiveness. It's like he notches it up when I'm around, like he's particularly interested in me and my mundane parts. I got the impression he'd listen closely even if I read him my grocery list. And I was interested in everything about him. I think I was as attentive. I hope so."

"I'll be. If he isn't a killer, perhaps I'll have lunch with him soon."

"He's very tall," I said, moving the conversation forward.

"I'm tall. I know the feeling. You're more in the height-challenged range, but that can be forgiven."

"I'm five-six, Chester. That's not height challenged."

"You're on the verge."

"All right."

I didn't let Chester walk me all the way home, but he did see me to the end of Bygone and watched me as I made my way up the hill. It was late enough that the only other people I saw were the few customers left in the small bar as I passed by it again.

I felt much better about Chester and his health but became concerned again about Seth when I walked past Elizabeth Owl's shop and Seth's dark windows above. I checked my phone but he hadn't called or texted. It was late though. He didn't know I'd stayed out after he'd been detained.

The motorcycle was still parked next to the curb. That was a good sign, or so I assumed. I walked past it and then crossed the street. I thought Seth had mentioned that he had a car too. There was an old Honda a short way down from the motorcycle. I wondered if it was his. I hurried across the street, turned around, and waved at Chester, who was still watching me from the end of Bygone, then took my porch stairs a couple at a time.

"Clare," a voice said.

It was a wonder I didn't break my neck or a kneecap or something.

"Jodie! Have you lost your mind?" I said to my friend on the porch as I grabbed the railing and reestablished my footing.

"Sorry," Jodie said.

"Holy heart jump. You okay?"

"Fine. Sorry," she said again.

Jodie moved to the edge of the porch and sat on the top step, and then patted the space next to her.

"You want to come in?" I said.

"No, it's too nice out here. Have a minute to chat?"

"Of course," I said. I took the spot next to her, still feeling my heart beat fast in my throat. I glanced quickly down the hill. There was no sign of Chester. Either he hadn't seen me practically kill myself on my porch stairs, or he'd seen Jodie so he knew I was in good enough hands. "What's up?"

"I stopped by for a couple reasons. One, to check on you, but you weren't here so I felt the need to wait. And two, to tell you that I had a great time on my date with a guy named Mutt."

"That's wonderful!" I said. I looked at her. Never once in all the years that I'd known Jodie had she said she had a great time with someone — this included good old what's-his-name. She'd dated a little after the divorce, but most of the time those dates weren't worth more than a shrug when I asked her how they'd gone.

"I don't have time for a boyfriend, Clare. And do you have any idea how my father and my brothers will react to him? Let's not even talk about my mother since she will become a non-issue quickly and die the second I tell her that Mutt is his real name."

"First of all, everyone has time for a boyfriend or a girlfriend or whatever. It's just a matter of finding a match that can work with your availability. Is Mutt willing to be flexible with your schedule?"

"We'll see, I suppose. He seems to be, but

it's early. All I really know at this point is that the only other person who I've ever had so much fun with is you, and since we're not lesbians — no matter about that rumor in high school — I have to keep my options open. Mutt told me he likes me too and wants to see me again. Tomorrow."

"That's great. And you're underestimating your family," I said. "They want you to be happy." I thought about the conversation I'd just had with Chester, and though Jodie's family adored her, she might have a point. They might have a problem with Mutt, but their love for her would win out, once her mother regained consciousness at least. It wouldn't kill her all the way.

"We'll see," she said.

"You seem sad."

"I'm just surprised. I'm almost thirty, and I realized tonight that I might have finally met my match and it could potentially upset everyone."

"Let's not worry about that yet," I said. "One day at a time."

"Right. How was your evening with the nerdy but cute geologist, who may or may not have a criminal record? Have you looked at the papers yet?"

"I have not. He lives over there, above Elizabeth Owl's. My date was really great

266

too until Creighton took him into the station for questioning."

"What?"

I told Jodie what had happened, and she pulled out her cell phone. It was when I saw her grab it from the bag she carried that I realized she looked really nice, dressed in girl clothes and carrying a purse, which was unusual. She was more the backpack or pockets-only type.

I was under the impression that she spoke directly to Creighton. She asked questions and answered back with abrupt and impatient noises. Only a moment later, she ended the call and looked at me.

"He's been released, but Creighton told him not to leave town, which is standard procedure. I didn't get many details, but just from Creighton's tone, I don't think he thought Seth was guilty. Creighton did ask me if you and Seth were dating. I didn't give much of an answer."

I looked over at the dark windows. "Any idea when he was released?"

"Didn't get that."

He must have just gone to bed. I couldn't help but be a little disappointed he hadn't called or texted me first.

"Jodie, I showed him the numbers and letters that were on the key bars. He had a hunch that they were for longitude and latitude measurements, and that if put together correctly, they might give a pertinent location."

"Pertinent to the typewriter?" Jodie asked.

I shrugged. "That seems weird, but I don't really know. Pertinent to something leather man was looking for maybe, so potentially pertinent to his murder."

"That's interesting. And might be very helpful," she said hesitantly.

"Hey, thanks for calling Creighton," I said.

"My pleasure," Jodie said. She stood and swung her purse over her shoulder with too much force, thwacking herself in the back, but she didn't seem to notice. She wiped the bottom of her nice dress pants and stepped down the stairs, glancing over at the windows I'd been looking at.

"You should read the background report I gave you, Clare. Just do it."

"I might." I meant it.

"Good. I'll be in touch tomorrow. You have plans in the morning?"

"Work, but Chester might be able to watch the store. What do you have in mind?" I had lots of work to do, but I didn't want to miss out on any more police outings, even if I was always unofficial.

"Not sure yet, but I'll give you a call." She

turned and walked toward the Bronco that she'd parked on the street a couple houses up. "It would have been easier if we'd been lesbians, you know that, don't you?"

"Then you could have cheated on me instead of your brother," I said.

Jodie turned, and even in the dark I could see her smile as she waved. "Later, Clare."

"Later, Jodie."

19

It had been a few years since I was a teenager, but I still couldn't help the small teenage-girlish squeal of happy surprise when I woke the next morning and found a text on my phone from Seth.

It said:

Great time last night. Sorry to have cut it short by becoming a potential suspect in a murder case, but stuff happens. Kidding. I've been cleared. Well, mostly. At least I had an airtight alibi, but they talked about an ankle bracelet. Kidding again. I look forward to date 3.

I texted back that I'd had a great time too and was also looking forward to seeing him again. Neither of us was playing hard to get. How refreshing.

I wouldn't say I danced through my morning routine, but there was much less heel-dragging than normal as I slowly awakened. I mellowed a bit by the time I was ready to leave the house, but I was still a touch happier than I should have been. My good mood wasn't ruined immediately, but it was severely jolted when I opened my front door.

"Creighton? Kelly?" I said to my surprise visitors.

"Clare, do you have just a minute?" Creighton said.

"Do I need to go back to the station again?" I said as I swung one hand up to a hip and tried to look bothered.

"No. I promise we'll be brief," Creighton said.

Both he and Kelly were in their uniforms, official and stern. I knew that Creighton worked a lot, but he didn't look as if he'd been up late the evening before. He never had needed much sleep.

"Sure." I opened the door and stepped back. Creighton stepped through without looking at me, but Kelly gave me a quick smile and nod, which was strange for someone who was never friendly to me.

They both sat on the couch, making me think they were going to be longer than they'd said. I'd hoped for a stand-up conversation. I took a seat on the chair.

"What's up?" I said.

Creighton sat forward. "We talked to your friend last night, and he mentioned the numbers and letters you found on the key bars could potentially be made into longitude and latitude coordinates."

"Yes, that's right," I said. I wondered how their conversation had managed to get to that point and if Creighton had talked to Jodie since last night. I didn't ask.

"Right. Well, we wondered what you thought about that theory," Creighton said.

"I guess I thought it was as good as any," I said. "That's a strange question, Creighton. Why would what I think matter?"

Creighton and Kelly looked at each other. Kelly seemed to understand it was his turn to talk, so he sat forward, duplicating Creighton's elbows-on-knees pose.

"Clare, how well do you know Mr. Cassidy?" Kelly said.

"We just met a few days ago. Why?" I looked at Creighton as I asked the question. Was this a sneaky way for him to get in the middle of my personal life?

Kelly cleared his throat, perhaps to pull my attention back his direction.

"Clare, this is a bit awkward considering your past with Creighton," he said.

"Really? We're going there?" I said.

Kelly held his hands out as if to ask me to

hang on a second. Creighton remained quiet and oddly stoic and unreadable.

"Clare. Look, we could have sent other officers up to talk to you. Creighton and I discussed this, but we didn't think you wanted the entire force to know what we found. This wasn't an easy decision, but I hope you realize that it was done with your feelings in mind, in a good way." Kelly sighed. "We didn't even tell Jodie. We thought that should be your choice."

I took a deep breath and silently told myself to calm down.

"All right," I said. "What is it?"

"Mr. Cassidy has a criminal hiccup in his past, Clare," Kelly continued after being prompted with an almost imperceptible nod from Creighton.

"Go on."

"He was arrested for theft from public lands. He was accused of stealing something . . . something called a geode. His case went to trial, but the geode in question disappeared mid-trial and so the case was dismissed."

"He wasn't convicted?" I asked as I thought about the rock-and-mineral tour from the evening before, and the stunning geode that Seth kept out in the open for anyone to see. At least it had been out in the open yesterday.

"No, when the evidence disappeared from the evidence room, there was no reason to continue the trial. Charges and the case were dismissed."

"Where was this?" I asked.

"Wyoming," Creighton inserted. "Where his brother lives and where the motorcycle license plate that Jodie found in the walkway is from."

"You think this might somehow make Seth a killer?" I said.

"No, we don't," Kelly said. "We're pretty certain that Mr. Cassidy isn't the killer. His alibi checked out quickly and easily. It's just that . . . well, this is an unusual situation and we wanted to let you know. Evidence is key, but coincidences make us curious."

I looked at Kelly and Creighton. It was impossible to know if they'd given me the information just to mess with my personal life or if they had some real concerns about Seth they were sharing only cryptically. I decided to keep it simple. "Thank you," I said.

"You're welcome," Kelly said. He looked at Creighton and then back at me. "Look, Clare, it might seem like we're interfering in your personal life, and we probably are, but our intentions are good. Please remember that Mr. Cassidy wasn't convicted of anything, and even if he had been, it wasn't like it was murder."

Creighton's mouth pinched briefly.

"I got it. Thank you again," I said as I stood up.

Creighton and Kelly followed my lead and stood too. I opened the door for them, and we all politely but without eye contact wished each other good days as they exited. I closed the door behind them and gave them a few moments to be on their way so my walk to work wouldn't require me to talk to them further.

I grabbed my bag, peered out the front windows to confirm they were gone, and opened the door again.

Then, changing my mind, I closed it.

I set the bag on the table and opened the side pocket. There it was, the tri-folded elephant in the room.

"Jeez, just get it over with," I said as I grabbed and then unfolded the papers.

I was immediately struck by two things — one, this was, without a doubt, a terribly intrusive and wrong thing to do. And, two, it was pretty interesting.

His name was Seth James Cassidy. We hadn't even asked each other our ages, but he was three years older than me, his birthday in October. He'd been born in Beaver Dam, Wisconsin, and had attended the Universities of Wisconsin, Alaska, and Southern California. He was very well educated, with a PhD, though so far he hadn't referred to himself as "doctor."

His background report was marred only by the arrest for stealing from public lands. The report didn't mention anything about the case's outcome — there was no conviction listed. Just the arrest, that was all. I wondered how Creighton and Kelly had known the detail about the evidence being removed from the evidence room. Had they made that part up or had they made some calls?

Obviously, the only way to understand what had really happened was to get the truth from Seth. Ask him. Kelly was correct though; his crime wasn't heinous, or so it seemed. I knew that stealing from public lands was serious, but the only other case I'd heard about was the theft of some ancient artifacts in southern Utah. Geodes weren't considered ancient artifacts, were they? And what did the ancient artifact designation matter? I didn't know, and at the moment I didn't much care.

I did not see how I could ask Seth outright about the charges. Telling him that my police officer best friend and police officer ex-boyfriend were concerned enough about me and my dating decisions that they pried into Seth's past made them look like bullies and me look much weaker than I hoped I truly was.

"Ugh," I said as I folded the report and dropped it on the table. At this point, I didn't even want to have it with me. I felt like I'd cheated on Seth already, and we hadn't even had our first real make-out session.

The coast was totally clear when I opened the door again. I glanced up at Seth's dark windows but thought he might be at work already. He'd mentioned that he got up early, and the text had come in at about five a.m.

I was glad to finally set out on the walk down the hill toward work. I decided that I would push all the bad thoughts away, at least for the time being.

It was going to be another great summer day in Star City, and the pedestrian traffic was already starting to build. I smiled at everyone and they smiled back. Good vibes were being spread and shared.

By the time I turned onto Bygone, I'd convinced myself that there wasn't any need to worry about anything, that everything would work out. I didn't see Jodie's Bronco, so I thought I might be able to get a little work done before she called or stopped by.

My mood had lifted almost all the way back up to cheery as I pulled open the door to The Rescued Word.

Chester was sitting in a chair in front of the counter, his long legs extended out; the same pose he'd adopted the night before. Along the counter was a crowded gathering of old typewriters. Another person was sitting in a chair facing Chester: Homer Mayfair. When I registered his presence, I realized that the typewriters were the same ones I'd looked at the day before, the ones that had been sitting on the ledge in his office.

"Homer, hi!" I said.

He stood and came forward to greet me with a handshake. He moved easily, his limp not terrible, but again I wondered why he had stuck with the wooden prosthetic. There were so many more realistic and helpful ones now. As we shook though, it occurred to me that the toast given throughout the bars the night before the ski season opened would be much less enthusiastic if glasses were raised in honor of Homer's prosthesis instead of his peg. Perhaps he liked the tradition enough to keep the inconvenience.

"Clare, hello again," he said.

"Homer said you paid him a visit," Chester said.

I nodded his direction and then turned back to Homer. "You brought in the typewriters?"

"I did. I thought they could all use some attention. Can you tune them all up?"

"Of course," I said. "Have you decided to start using them again?"

"Except for the battered No. 5 I just might, but even if I don't, I think they should be better taken care of," Homer said.

"Yes," Chester said. His tone with that one word was so suspicious that I looked at him with raised eyebrows. He continued, "Homer was hoping to also have a look at the old Underwood that he sold to Mirabelle. He said that he'd love to 'take a trip down memory lane.' "

"Oh," I said. Hadn't I told Homer that the police still had Mirabelle's typewriter?

"I, however, told him it was unavailable," Chester said.

"Right," Homer said. "With the police? Still?" he added with a "hopefully not" tone.

"Right," I said, but that was a lie I could get easily caught in. I decided I needed to add more, which was never the right decision, but brazenly I continued on. "Actually, I had to send it to another repair person just last night, someone with more experience."

Chester's eyebrows went higher, but I couldn't be sure if they were on the rise in question or with admiration.

Baskerville jumped up and onto the counter, fitting himself onto the tiny corner space that was still available. He was unhappy about all the typewriters in his way. He looked at me and then sent distasteful glances and snapping tail tips toward Homer. Homer didn't seem to notice.

"You did? Someone in Salt Lake City?" Homer said.

"No, no. I had to send it to Bulgaria," I said.

Homer blinked. Chester stood. His bushy eyebrows about flew off his forehead, and a high-pitched sound escaped his throat. Baskerville meowed doubtfully, or was that disappointedly?

"Really?" Homer said.

"Yes," I said. "But how about these? Anything specific you want done?" I stepped around Homer and moved next to the counter, placing my hand on top of the old Hermes. Baskerville watched me.

"Just whatever you think needs to be done to get them shipshape."

"I can do that."

We all — Chester, Baskerville, and I — looked at Homer expectantly, as if we were waiting for him to say something else. Or perhaps no one could top my Bulgaria mention.

"Well, all right, then," Homer said as he patted his pockets as if he was searching for his phone or his keys, but he didn't retrieve anything. "I guess I'll be on my way. Just call me when they're ready."

"Thanks for stopping by, Homer," Chester said. "It was great to talk to you."

"You too, Chester. We need to do it again soon."

"I'm always here," Chester said.

"I'll wait for your call, Clare," Homer said.

I nodded and smiled.

As Homer left the building, Baskerville meowed.

"He's a perfectly nice man," Chester said to the cat.

Baskerville hopped off the counter and then over to his high west side perch.

"And Bulgaria?" Chester said with a laugh as he looked at me. "That was stunning."

"I know. I wanted something that he couldn't even fathom checking out. I don't know why. I didn't want him talking to the police. And I didn't want him to bother

Mirabelle either. Maybe I'm being too weird about it, but I find his curiosity today kind of strange."

"I do too. I probably would have said Cincinnati though. That might have been good enough."

"What did the two of you talk about?" I said.

"First I helped him unload the typewriters, and then he wanted to talk about the mining company. In fact, we only spent a little time talking about his typewriters or Mirabelle's. After I told him hers was unavailable, he asked if he could wait for you. I told him he could, and he jumped right into questions about the mining company."

"What specifically did he want to know?"

"Historical stuff, like when they went out of business and if there were any items from them left in the building."

"What did you say?"

"I told him that I found a huge chunk of silver in the back but that I sold it years ago, long before silver was worth what it's worth today. And that the mining company went out of business in 1958."

"You found silver?"

"Of course not. My stories are to entertain, Clare. How bored would he have been if I'd told him I found a useless pickax, a couple mining helmets, and a bunch of dust?"

"What about when the mining company went out of business? Was it really 1958?"

"Yes, the building was empty for two years before I purchased it."

"Weren't you two good friends at one time?"

"Yes, that was many years ago though. I started The Rescued Word about the time he was promoted to editor. He, Mirabelle, and I skied," he said. I thought I heard regret.

"What happened to the friendship?"

Chester shrugged. "Time moves on."

I waited a beat for him to say more, but he wasn't going to.

"Do you remember the newspaper article about you and the press you built?" I asked.

"Ah, I see. Homer brought that up yester-day."

"Not really. I did. I remembered you and he being testy with each other when we went out there when I was a teenager. I asked him if he remembered what it was about. He guessed the newspaper article."

"Good guess. He's been mad at me for years about that, and I suppose that had something to do with our friendship fading."

"The article was a pretty big deal, huh?"

"Oh, I don't know."

"Olive knew about it. She told me you were famous for a short time. So was the reporter."

Chester waved away the notion of fame. "Not really."

"So why didn't you want Homer to write the article? You and he were pretty good friends."

"We were." Chester looked down at the ground and ran his knuckle over his mustache. Whatever he was remembering or thinking about, it wasn't pleasant.

"Chester?" I said.

He looked up, surprised, as if he'd gone so far into the past for a moment that he'd forgotten I was in the room.

"Mirabelle asked me to talk to the Salt Lake reporter, not to Homer," he said sadly.

"Why?" Mirabelle was like Chester when it came to Star City. She loved her home and wanted the best for it, above all other places. Always.

"She wouldn't ever tell me, Clare. I quit asking a long time ago. But I did as she requested. How could I not have — it wouldn't have been gentlemanly of me to go against her wishes."

"That makes me very curious."

"Me too."

"Do you care if I ask her?"

"Only if you share the answer with me if she gives you one." Chester looked at the typewriters, touched a key on the Underwood Ace, and said, "Excuse me a minute."

I watched him walk to the back, wondering what sorts of nerves I'd touched and how it was possible that all these years later they were still so tender.

I took a closer look at the typewriters that I wished I'd been able to take at Homer's house. There were no numbers or letters scratched onto the key bars, nothing unusual about any of them except for the fact that all but the old Underwood were in amazing condition, probably wouldn't even need tune-ups. Why had Homer *really* brought them in? He could have just brought one in if he wanted to talk to me or Chester, or to inquire again about Mirabelle's No. 5. He could have just stopped by without any typewriters in tow. What was going on?

And what was the deal with his curiosity about Mirabelle's typewriter? If he knew about the scratches on the key bars, did he know what they meant? Did he put them there, forget about them, and I'd jogged his memory? If that was it, why didn't he just say so?

When the front door opened again, I expected it to be Jodie, but it was Seth. He was dressed as though he had a day of dirty work ahead of him. He wore overalls and boots that had seen better days.

"Hi," I said.

He stood by the front door and said, "Hi. I don't want to risk tracking any muck I've got on me through your store. Do you have a minute to talk outside?"

"Sure," I said.

"I'm so sorry about last night," Seth said when we were both on the sidewalk.

"Did it go okay?" I asked.

"It went fine. I wasn't even in town when the man was killed. I have plenty of witnesses. I was in southern Utah — just got back in town when I came in to pick up my book from you. So I'm off the hook."

"That's good," I said, but even I heard my lack of enthusiasm. I smiled big to try to cover it up.

Seth blinked and cocked his head slightly. "What's up?"

I sighed. It was no use. I could not have a secret about him and be expected to keep it to myself. I was sure that both Jodie and

286

Creighton knew about this fault in my personality, my inability to be friends with someone while knowing something about them they might not want me to know. Their intentions were probably only good, but at the moment I was not happy with the Wentworth family.

"Seth, you know that I'm pretty good friends with the police, right?"

"Sure, your blond friend scares me more than the guy from last night. She's not someone to be messed with."

I tried not to smile, but the corner of my mouth twitched. "Anyway, Jodie, the blond woman, and I have been best friends for a long time, and, well, since you're new to town and all . . . and probably because there was a murder . . . well, Jodie did a background check on you."

Seth's eyes squinted and all hints of humor disappeared from his face.

"And she gave it to me, and I read it," I finished. I pulled in a deep lung full of air and then released it through puffed-out cheeks. "I had to tell you, Seth. It didn't seem fair that I knew what I knew without you knowing that I knew."

"I see. And what's your verdict based upon the background check?" He asked the question, but his icy tone told me that he didn't really care, that this was probably our very last conversation. My future was about to be filled with glances out my front windows, watching him go in and out of his apartment with other women for the rock-and-mineral tour and the best lasagna in the world. I would be very, very jealous of them all.

"I like you," I said with a shrug. "If I didn't like you, I wouldn't have told you."

For an instant his anger was gone and I saw the friendly, inquiring eyes I'd first thought were so attractive, but they didn't stick around long.

He looked at his watch. "I've got to get to work, Clare. Thank you for the lovely evening last night."

I nodded and wanted to say something else, but nothing came out of my mouth before he turned and walked down Bygone toward Main Street.

"Well, that was fun," I muttered to myself quietly, finally finding my words.

As if on cue, Jodie and her noisy Bronco turned the corner and pulled up to the curb in front of the store. She rolled down her window.

"Did I just see your boyfriend walking that direction?"

"I don't think I want to talk to you about

that today," I said.

She squinted. "All right. I'm sorry?"

I sighed and put my hands on my hips. "What's up?"

"Do you want to come with me out to talk to the motorcycle gang again?"

No, I didn't want to go anywhere with Jodie. I wanted to puncture her tires and break the windshield on that damn Bronco. Nevertheless, I also really wanted to see what she might uncover next. "Yes. Let me tell Chester I'm leaving. I'll be right back."

20

I told myself to shape up. There was no reason for me to feel such an immediate sense of loss.

When I'd gone to talk to Chester, he'd seen right through me.

"I'm going with Jodie for a bit," I told him.

"What's wrong?" he said.

"Nothing."

"Something's wrong," Chester said.

"No. Well, I just told Seth that Jodie pulled a background check on him and I read it."

"Why on earth did you tell him that?" Chester said.

"Seemed like the right thing to do."

Chester had been sitting on the corner of my worktable reading from a magazine. He stood and frowned and walked to me, placing his hands on my arms.

"Well, those Wentworths are far too intrusive in your life, Clare, but they do mean well, in their police, bossy ways. And I understand why you told Mr. Cassidy what you told him."

"But you think I shouldn't have?"

"Was he steamed?" Chester asked.

I liked it when he used words and phrases that weren't quite from this time period.

"Boiling, I think," I said.

Chester looked up to the ceiling a moment and then back at me. "I make up my stories, but have I ever lied to you, Clare?"

"Never, even when it might have been a good idea." I smiled.

"Right. Well, give him a little time. He just reacted, perhaps. I do think that if he likes you enough, he'll come back around. Probably not today though, so don't get your hopes up too high that you'll see him in the next twenty-four hours or so."

"Thanks, Chester." I hugged him.

"Love you more than ink on paper, Clare," he said as he hugged me back.

"Love you more than books," I said when we disengaged.

"Oh. Well, that's tough to beat. Go with Jodie. Try to enjoy yourself, but don't get shot or anything."

"I'll be back in a couple hours. I do have work to get done."

"See you then." Chester waved me away.

I felt a million times better by the time I

exited The Rescued Word, but that empty void of loss was still there in the background.

"Coffee?" Jodie said hesitantly as she nodded to the mug she'd already put into the cup holder on my side.

"Thanks, that's perfect," I said.

We didn't talk much as she drove us back to Purple Springs Valley. Jodie hummed with the radio a little, but we'd had enough of these sorts of moments together that we both knew that silence for a short time was best.

Our friendship was too strong not to get through an occasional bump in the road.

"There aren't nearly as many motorcycles," I said, speaking the first almost-complete sentence of the trip as we pulled into the valley. I didn't mention that I'd seen no motorcycles the day before. I didn't want to explain my visit to Homer.

"No, most are gone. Most of the goats have been transported too. Mutt's here to finish things up. He said a few others will be too — some of the organizers of the project. They had gathered names of those who would be participating. I got the list and it didn't yield any Mayfairs, but in-person visits can sometimes bring good surprises."

"Oh, Jodie! I totally forgot to look again for the cards with the names I'd written. I'm sorry."

"It's okay. We'll check later."

I swallowed the guilt I felt and told myself to make the card search a priority.

Mutt spotted the truck, separated himself from the small crowd of people, and walked over to greet us.

"Clare, good to see you again," he said as he extended his hand to me first. "Jodie, always a pleasure."

They didn't shake hands but they didn't hug either. They looked at each other briefly in that way that told me they weren't quite sure how they should go about their physical greetings at this stage in their relationship. I wasn't jealous, I didn't think, but I had to stop my eyes from rolling.

"Thanks, Mutt. Did you let them know we were coming?" Jodie said.

"Nope. I thought it best just to let you show up. If anyone knows anything, they didn't have the chance to think about rearranging the facts."

"Thanks," Jodie said, all business now. She'd turned off the flirtation and somehow made her shoulders seem bigger. I could never quite figure out how she did that. The smile was gone, and when she sniffed once and rubbed her finger under her nose, I knew she'd transformed into full police-officer mode. "Let's have a chat or two."

"This way," Mutt said.

There were eleven people left from Angels for Animals. Of the eleven, it was clear that eight of them had nothing to contribute regarding the Mayfair name or it in conjunction with someone who'd attended the goat relocation project.

They were "dismissed." Jodie firmly told them so, and they didn't need to be told twice to go find something else to do.

Mutt was one of the remaining three, but whatever he knew he'd already shared with Jodie. The other two actually proved to have more information, though tying it all back to the man who was killed behind The Rescued Word would be difficult at best.

Lillian Thurman was in her midforties but looked closer to sixty than to fifty. There was no mystery as to the reason for her gruff, gravely voice; she chain-smoked, literally. While we were there, I never once saw her pull out a lighter or a match. When she was close to the end of one cigarette, she'd pull out another one and use the stub to light the new one. Watching her smoke was, to me, almost hypnotic, a choreography of puffs and smoke and fire. It was most definitely a nasty habit, but at least she did it with style.

She had no time for fixing her hair or donning makeup. She probably saw a barber for the short cut she sported, and the thick field of tiny hairs over her top lip made me wonder if she shaved. If she did, she'd neglected that part of her grooming routine for at least a couple of days.

When Jodie brought up the name Mayfair, Lillian made a quick noise in the back of her gravelly throat and waved her hand, the one with a cigarette between her two fingers, and said, "Here, right here. I almost talked to someone with that name."

Along with Lillian, another Angels for Animals member seemed to potentially have some information regarding Mayfair. Duncan Bates was a small man with narrow shoulders; short, black, greasy hair; thick glasses; and a sickly skin tone, ghostlike and gray. He wore a leather vest with no sleeves, and I wondered how he wasn't tanned or sunburned.

"Yeah, I know a Mayfair from southern Utah," he'd said.

Jodie looked at me. It took me a second to understand the question in her eyes, but I responded with, "Yes, at least some of Homer's kids and grandkids live in southern

Utah, I think."

"All right. Lillian, tell me about the Mayfair you talked to here," Jodie said as she turned back to the woman.

"There was more than one." Lillian blew out smoke and then took more in, which was how she rolled apparently — constant in and out even amidst conversation. "There were two men, I think. One of them had Mayfair on the back of his jacket."

"What did they look like?" Jodie said.

For a long, thoughtful, smoke-filled moment, Lillian slowly shook her head. "I don't remember at all. The only reason I remember the name is because the first time I saw it, my eyes played tricks on me and I thought it said Mayflower, which I thought was interesting."

Jodie pulled a picture out of her back pocket and showed it to Lillian only, purposefully keeping it out of Duncan's line of sight.

"Do you recognize the man in this picture?" Jodie said.

Lillian blinked and frowned. "Not a great picture."

"No, but it's all we've got," she said.

"No, I don't recognize him," Lillian said.

"All right." She put the picture back in her pocket. "Anything else? How do you know there were two of them?"

"I assumed they were brothers, I suppose. When I saw the name, I was standing pretty close to them. We were waiting to begin the relocation. I was going to say something to the one with the name on his back — you know, 'Hey, dude, thought you were a Mayflower at first' — something like that. Small talk to pass the time. Mutt said that as those in charge of the event, we should talk to people, get to know them, said it was good for the group, good for everyone. Anyway, as I got a little closer, I heard the Mayfair vest say to the other one, 'The old man will never go for it. He's a blankity-blank idiot.' I'll leave out the expletives. So I stepped back. Sounded like a brotherly conversation about their dad or something, but I could be guessing wrong, I suppose. And there was something about his tone, meanlike, maybe. I don't know, but something in my gut told me to step away, so I did."

"I see," Jodie said. "You keep saying the one with Mayfair on the back of his jacket. How come not everyone is required to have their name on them?"

Lillian shrugged. "We ask them to, but someone made such a big stink about it once that we had to make it a suggestion instead of a requirement. Right, Mutt?"

"Right," he said.

"Anything else you can remember? More about the clothes, hair, accent in the voice?" Jodie said.

"No, nothing."

"Thanks, Lillian. If you remember any-thing else, anything at all, give me a call." Jodie handed Lillian a card.

"Will do." Lillian looked at the card in the palm of her hand. She didn't strike me as the type who would hold on to it for very long. But one glance at Mutt's stern face probably told her she should keep this one. She put it in her back pocket and patted it once as if to punctuate that she would do as she was told.

Jodie turned to Duncan. "Mr. Bates, you know some Mayfairs?"

"No, I don't know them really, I just know of them," he said.

I got the impression that Mr. Bates didn't like talking to the police. He held his arms crossed tightly in front of his chest, and he glared at Jodie. He wasn't much taller than her, but he was puffing, as if to make himself seem bigger. Jodie didn't appear to notice.

"Tell me what you know *of* them," she said.

"Just that they're a pretty quiet group, keep to themselves mostly. They aren't like some of the crazies who live out in the boonies and bring out their rifles whenever someone drives up their road. But they do live out of town a bit, have a few houses. Don't know a thing about any guns though. Don't think so."

"A few houses? All Mayfairs?"

"I think so."

Jodie looked at me again, but I had no idea if those Mayfairs were Homer's family or not. I shrugged and pushed up my glasses.

"I see. You're sure you didn't see or talk to any Mayfairs here?"

"Pretty sure. I don't ask everyone's name, but still . . . I think I know who I talked to."

"What do the Mayfairs you know look like?" She pulled out the picture again.

"Nothing in particular."

"Any chance this guy looks familiar?" She held the picture out for the man to look at.

"Criminently, that's a dead man!" he said.

Jodie nodded but didn't pull the picture away.

"No, I don't know. How would I know?" Duncan said, but even I noticed that he never truly looked at the picture.

"All right. Call me with anything else."

Jodie handed him her card too. He was much less interested in putting on a show of keeping it as he absently stuffed it into his front jeans pocket.

"That all?" he asked.

"For now," Jodie said. She didn't thank him as he turned to leave.

"Not much of anything useful. I'm sorry about that," Mutt said.

"Do you think they were both being honest?" Jodie said.

"I do. I can't think of any reason either of them would lie. They've both had a couple run-ins with the law but nothing dangerous. Duncan's not interested in talking to the police, obviously, but he could have just said he had no information if he'd wanted to. Lillian's your best bet. It'd be great if she remembered more," Mutt said.

As he spoke to Jodie, I inspected him. He spoke well and had bright, intelligent eyes. But he looked like a thug, or a potential thug at least. I was disappointed in myself for the observations. I knew better. But still, I decided to ask Jodie what Mutt's background report said about him.

Suddenly, Mutt looked at me, his bright, intelligent eyes now full of question.

"Clare?" Jodie said.

"What? Oh, sorry, I was off in my own

world. Did you ask me a question?"

"How many children, exactly, does Homer have?" Jodie said.

"I think he has two sons and one daughter, but I'm not sure how many kids each of them have."

"You know some of Homer's family is in southern Utah. Do you know who?"

"No idea. Sorry."

"No problem," Jodie said. She turned back to Mutt. "Just let me know."

"Will do. We still on for tonight?" he said.

I took an unconscious step backward, but Jodie kept it simple. "Tonight would be fine."

Mutt smiled. "Very good. See you then. Excuse me, ladies. Duty calls," he said before he turned and walked away.

"I need to track down some Mayfairs. See what they look like, see if anyone from their family has gone missing," Jodie said.

"Seems like a pretty weak connection," I said, realizing I now needed to tell her about Homer and his typewriters.

"It is, but it's all we've got." Jodie allowed her eyes to watch Mutt a moment longer before she turned back to me and said, "Let's go."

21

As Jodie — with Baskerville's curious assistance — hunched over Homer's typewriters to inspect them for clues, I excused myself to my office, which had the computer, so I could work on Olive's research.

A simple Internet search confirmed that my memories about the book were correct. There had been three states — in laymen's terms, versions — of the *Tarzan of the Apes* first edition published June 6, 1914. It was Edgar Rice Burroughs's first novel to be published in hardcover. All of the three states had been bound in maroon cloth. The condition of the cloth over Olive's book was extraordinary. No matter how much care a book is given, one as old as Olive's most always shows some wear, or at least partially bent and frayed corners. This one had been as close to pristine as I'd ever seen, its corners only beginning to bend slightly.

My biggest question and the part I'd been

most unsure of was which state Olive's book was. My research indicated it was the second state for a couple reasons. The publisher, A. C. McClurg & Co., was printed on the bottom of the spines of all three states, but an acorn had also been included on the second state. It was placed between the "A" and the "C" of the publisher's moniker. Olive's book had an acorn. I remembered seeing it, but I also confirmed my memory by finding the specific acorn picture on my phone.

And though the acorn was a sure determination, there were a couple of other features I confirmed. On the copyright page the words "W. F. Hall Printing Co., Chicago" were there in an Old English font, which was a characteristic of the first *and* second state.

Inside the third state, the words "W. F. Hall Printing Co., Chicago" were printed on its copyright page using a Gothic font.

I knew there were other variances that had come into play for different markets, such as the Canadian market, but Olive's was unquestionably an American first edition, in its second state.

I also confirmed the existence of a mystery surrounding another state of *Tarzan,* but that was for my own curiosity only. In a

1964 book by Henry Hardy-Heins, *A Golden Anniversary Bibliography of Edgar Rice Burroughs,* Mr. Hardy-Heins claimed that a fourth state of the first edition of *Tarzan* had also been printed and was identical to the third state, though it was bound in orange or green cloth. Finding any of those orange- or green-bound books has, as far as I could find, been an impossible task, even though Mr. Hardy-Heins claimed to have spoken personally to some owners of the fourth state.

One of my favorite parts of the *Tarzan* mystery has to do with the book that Mr. Hardy-Heins wrote. Originally, *A Golden Anniversary Bibliography of Edgar Rice Burroughs* was something similar to a magazine that Hardy-Heins created because he was so enamored with Edgar Rice Burroughs. When a man named Donald Grant used Hardy-Heins's book to launch his own publishing company, the initial printing sold out quickly — those books from that initial printing are pretty valuable too. The book is still available in subsequent editions, though it's expensive to acquire. I'd restored a later printing a few years earlier.

Once I'd taken enough notes and printed out a few Internet pages to give to Olive, I closed the browser and took my own moment to remember the other part of the story, the best part and the good memory Chester had referred to when we'd talked about the book.

I had a special spot in my heart for Mr. Burroughs and a personal story about him, in a distant way of course. When he began writing fiction, he was also a pencil-sharpener salesman. It was a story Chester told me when I was a little girl (true to our earlier conversation, he never lied or embellished the stories he told me) and we read *Tarzan of the Apes* together. The book and the wild character of Tarzan spoke to the tomboy in me, the little girl who loved to climb trees and run through the mountainous woods around Star City or race my grandfather down the slopes on our skis. But the story about the author being a pencil-sharpener salesman was even more fascinating to me for some reason; perhaps it made him more real, more human in my mind as he stood next to his wild fictional character. One day, not long after Chester and I had read the book, a paper salesman came into the store when both Chester and I were there. The salesman pulled an electric pencil sharpener out of his bag and tried to get Chester to stock them in the store. I was probably eight or nine, and I still remember tapping on Chester's arm to get his attention.

"Is that the writer who wrote about the wild man in the jungle?" I said, pointing at the salesman when I saw the sharpener on the counter.

"No, that was a different kind of sharpener. I'll show you one of those later."

I looked at the salesman, who looked back at me with obvious question in his eyes. I authoritatively and snottily said, "Edgar Rice Burroughs sold pencil sharpeners, dummy. You should know that."

Chester wasn't sure whether to laugh or reprimand, but he was closer to laughing. And fortunately the salesman had a good sense of humor. He smiled and said, "I did not know that, and you are correct, I should have. Thank you for telling me."

Later, Chester, still with a glimmer of humor in his eye, did tell me I probably shouldn't call anyone a dummy, salespeople included.

Just as I was getting up from my desk to rejoin Jodie, she appeared at my office door. "Nothing funny that I can find on those typewriters, Clare. I'm outta here for now. I'm going to stop by Mirabelle's and make sure all is well there and that Homer hasn't bothered her. You need anything else from me?"

"I'm good. Let me know about Mirabelle," I said.

I'd planned a speech, or maybe it was a lecture, about wanting her to never, ever again butt into my private life by pulling a background report on someone I was interested in dating. Part of the fun of dating someone new was getting to know them, criminal record included, particularly if the criminal record was nonviolent. Most particularly if the crime was about a stolen geode.

But I didn't recite the lecture aloud. I'd talk to her later, when I was less irritated about the whole thing, or when Seth someday moved out of the apartment directly across from my house and I didn't have to see him escorting his dates upstairs for rock tours and lasagna dinners every now and then, and be reminded of the life I could have had.

"Will do," Jodie said before she pulled her head back and disappeared, leaving Baskerville in her wake. He stood in the doorway and looked at me as if to ask what in the world I was doing in the office I rarely visited.

"Working," was all I said to him. I gathered him in my arms as I exited the infrequently visited space and together we found Chester at the front counter. It was his turn to examine the typewriters.

"Clare," he said, "do you have any idea when your brother's going to quit being so worried about Marion? I think we're fine here, and we sure could use her help. I just got another stationery order over the phone. I also know the little vixen likes to make money, and I have it on good authority — a text from her — that she'd like to come back and make more of that money."

"Vixen?" I said.

"I meant it as a term of endearment. She looks like you, but you were pretty clueless when you were her age. She knows the power her beauty wields."

I shook my head, deciding that it would be better to ignore most of what Chester had just said.

I was less concerned about our safety than I had been a day earlier. Perhaps the passing of twenty-four hours or so with no horrible incidents was not enough, but I felt much better about Marion coming back into the store. "I have no idea, but call Jimmy. Let him know we're good and we miss her. I'm sure she's driving him crazy too. And when did you learn how to text?"

"I'm so much more than just a pretty face, Clare."

"Hello y'all!" Ramona said as she came through the door.

"Oh, Ramona and I are going out for coffee," Chester said.

"Hi, Ramona!" I said.

Chester didn't say anything as I handed him the cat and then walked past him.

"Ramona," I said as we met in the middle of the store, just this side of the holiday shelves and next to what I called the Skittles shelves, a rainbow of brightly colored paper and card stock. "Good to see you again."

"You too!"

"I hear you and Chester have coffee plans," I said.

"We do, and we would love for you to join us," she said, her drawl so appealing that I had the sense that if I moved closer to her, I'd smell southern things, like lilacs and sweet tea. "Or maybe just you and I could go to lunch?"

"I don't want to intrude on coffee and I have a bunch to do through lunch, but I'd love to invite you to dinner. Tonight even? Are you available? Chester, you can come too." I looked at him.

"I would love to join you for dinner," Ramona said, sending Chester a smirk that made me wonder if she was letting him know that he hadn't needed to be so weird about her not meeting his family.

"I would too," Chester said.

I had to give him credit. He was properly chastised and humbled by Ramona's smirk. He must really like her. Maybe I'd ask Jodie to do a background check on her.

"Excellent. Be at my place at seven. I just live up Main, Ramona. Small blue chalet. There's a sign by the mailbox: Little Blue."

"I'll pick you up," Chester said to her.

"See you both then," I said.

"Thank you, Clare," Ramona said, the sincerity somehow more real with her thick accent.

"I look forward to it."

I watched the two of them, arm in arm, leave and meander to the diner across the street. I continued to spy on them as they sat down in a booth and, facing each other, started to smile, laugh, and talk. Interrupting my covert surveillance from around a pillar, Baskerville batted my ankles with his head.

"Hey," I said.

He blinked up at me as if to ask if I was paying attention.

"I am," I said.

He took the familiar route up to his high

310

sunny perch, but once there, he didn't go into repose mode, but looked down at me and meowed instead.

"Okay?" I said.

He started walking along the top of the ledge, stopping every few steps, and meowing down at me.

From the ground level, I matched his path. "I don't know what you're trying to tell me."

Baskerville looked at me like I was hopeless and then walked back to his favorite spot in front. He sat and looked at me again, meowing one more time.

I did not think he could communicate based upon what he'd learned from human conversation, but I thought he was a very in-tune cat. I didn't know if what he was trying to tell me was what I suddenly seemed to "get," but *something* became clear as I looked where the cat had brought my eyes.

I pulled my phone out of my pocket and hit Jodie's contact.

"Hey, what'd you forget?" she said when she answered.

"Nothing. You know the pictures that were on leather man's camera?" I said.

"Yes."

"Any chance I can take a look at them

again?" I said.

"I'm not sure I'm supposed to pull them out of evidence, but it sounds like you really want to."

"I do."

"Want to meet me at the station?"

I looked at Chester and Ramona across the street. They were still smiling. "Actually, I'd like it if you could bring them up to The Rescued Word. Any chance that can happen?"

"See you in half an hour?"

"Deal."

22

Chester had been correct. Marion *was* champing at the bit to get back to work. She enjoyed the job and was unquestionably our best personalization expert. She also really liked to earn money. While I waited for Jodie, I convinced Jimmy that I would never want his daughter back in the store unless I was one hundred percent sure she was safe, and that was true. I didn't think she was in any danger. In fact, the only person I thought was dangerous was the man who had been killed in the walkway on the day he came in wanting Mirabelle's typewriter. I didn't think his killer was interested in harming any of the rest of us. I hoped not.

Though she said she would bring the pictures, Jodie wasn't the officer to show up. Instead her partner, Omar, in full uniform, came through the front door with a laptop under his arm.

"Jodie got busy. She told me I was supposed to show you these pictures, but we aren't supposed to let anyone else on the force — no, let's see, she said that we weren't allowed to let anyone else in the entire 'expletive' universe know that I showed them to you."

"Secret's safe with me," I said.

"And me," Marion said from behind the counter where she'd eagerly gotten to work only a few seconds after driving her Jeep to the store. Her father finally released her "from her abominable parental prison."

"I didn't think I'd need to convince either of you," Omar said as he set his laptop on the counter.

"Thirsty? Can I get you something?" I said.

"Nope. Gotta get back to the station toot sweet. Here we are." Omar turned the laptop so we could both see the screen. Marion was curious enough to come around to the other side and observe too, from behind my shoulder. "There were twelve pictures total."

"But the only ones of just me are when I'm at my kitchen sink and when I'm leaving my house, right?"

"Yes, the rest are of you and Mirabelle and Marion in the store."

"But is that what they really are?" I said as I turned Omar's laptop my direction.

"I think so," he said.

I scrolled through the other nine pictures, and it was true that in some combination Mirabelle, Marion, and I were in them, but we weren't necessarily the focal points. If we had been, then the photographer didn't know how to take a very good picture. We were oddly off center and strangely angled, almost giving the pictures a fish-eye effect.

"Omar," I began. "I can't explain the three pictures of just me, but the others look like leather man was trying to take pictures of the inside of the store, not of us."

"I don't get what you mean."

"Look at the shelves, the ones with the carved doors." I pointed around the big room.

"Okay."

"I think he was trying to get pictures of the doors," I said.

"Why in the world would he do that?"

"I have no idea," I said. But I did have a little bit of an idea; I just wasn't ready to share it yet.

"That's very interesting, Aunt Clare," Marion said.

"Excuse me?" Omar said.

"You're not from here, Omar, but you

know this building used to be a mining company's offices, right?" I said.

"Sure. You can still kind of see the company's name above the front windows."

"Right," I said. "The shelves with the doors were put there by the mining company. Come on, let's take a look around."

Baskerville, who'd been at my ankles since I'd called Jodie, stayed proudly there as we began at the front of the store. Maybe the cat really had figured out something the rest of us were just catching on to. It didn't seem likely, but Baskerville *was* Arial's offspring, and she had unquestionably been the greatest cat ever.

"Look." I pointed at the first carved door.

"It's a mountain and a creek," Omar said. "Lots of both of those around here."

"Yes, but maybe it's more," I said.

"More than what?"

"Maybe the doors tell a story, a real one. Maybe the doors illustrate some important location."

"Important how?" Omar asked.

"Well, that part I'm not sure of quite yet. But what if there's something here that ties in with the latitude and longitude measurements from the key bars?"

Omar nodded a little as he looked more closely at the first carved door. "Okay, but where is all this? It could be anywhere."

"Don't know that yet either, but maybe we can figure it out."

There seemed to be a connection — other than the fact that they were all outdoor, mountainous scenes — between the carvings on the doors. Perhaps there was some sort of theme carrying us from one to the next. But the connection wasn't as clear as all that. The only color on any of the doors was the dark stained wood, but the scenes took place in the summer, or so we deduced. There was a general sense of bright sunny days with green grasses blowing in light breezes.

"No snow, but no evergreens or pines either," Omar said.

"Right. Actually, no trees," I added. "Maybe a valley, maybe the mountains are supposed to be more in the distance so we can't see the trees? It's difficult to know. They're not abstract, but they just don't have much dimension."

"So why wouldn't leather man just come in and take the pictures while standing in the store? People do that, right?" Omar said as we moved to the last door on the west wall.

"They do. I don't know why he didn't. Didn't want to be obvious, maybe?" I said.

"What's going on?" Chester said as he came in the front door without Ramona.

I greeted him by grabbing his hand and taking him back to Omar's laptop. I showed him the pictures, leaving out the three of just me and explained my idea to him.

"I tell people stories all the time about these doors," Chester said when I finished. "Usually I say something like trolls live among those mountains and they don't like to be bothered, that these doors are a warning to all, but there's something behind my made-up story. There was a legend that the mining company perpetuated about their mines that was similar to that. Silly and fun, but sort of scary too. It's been so many years and I've torn the story apart so much that I don't remember the original version. However, I always assumed these carvings were representations of locations where the mining company was going to mine or wanted to mine or maybe had already put a mine, and these were the 'before' pictures. Perhaps they're tied to the mining company's legend somehow. Darn it, I can't remember the details."

"Do we have locations of all their mines?" I asked.

"I don't. I'm sure there are records somewhere though," Chester said.

Omar and Marion had made their way down both walls when Omar stepped away from Marion and joined Chester and me at the counter. Marion continued to look at the last carving at the front of the store, her head cocked to one side and her finger tapping her lips. I thought she might recognize something, but I didn't want to disturb her thoughts until they seemed to have fully solidified.

"I don't know, Clare, Chester. I'll have someone research the mine locations, but I'm just not sure it ties together." Omar shrugged. "But sometimes you start looking and things appear and start to make sense, so I appreciate the ideas. Jodie will too. I need to get back to the station if that's all." Omar closed the laptop and gathered it from the counter.

I walked him out of the store and then stopped next to Marion when I came back in.

"Recognize it?" I said.

"There's something about it," she said. "I've never paid a bit of attention to these doors, Clare, but, yes, there's something familiar about this one."

"Just this one?" I said as I looked at the door. Actually, it was one of the least appealing scenes, with low peaks that were

319

more like hills, and an uninteresting, cloudless sky.

"Yeah, I think so."

"It'd be great if you could remember where you might have seen it."

"I'll work on it."

"Clare!" Chester called from the back of the building. "Help me with this dagburn computer thing, please."

I petted Baskerville's head and told him he was amazing and then left him at the front of the store with Marion.

Chester wanted me to help him set up his very first e-mail address. We accomplished the task quickly, securing for him the moniker HotSkier1357, which made him smile cheerily before he shooed me out of my own office so he could send his first e-mail to Ramona. I didn't mind being sent away. I had a dinner to prepare for, after all.

23

Marion was my date, and I decided she was the second best date I'd had this week, though always by far the best niece.

Even though she wanted to work late and catch up on her stationery orders, I knew Jimmy would bust an artery if he thought she was left in the store alone, so on the way out I told her to be at Little Blue approximately thirty minutes after I left to help me "prepare." Chester would be leaving shortly thereafter to pick up Ramona.

She'd arrived on time and ready to help.

"Lasagna and salad?" Marion said as she joined me in the kitchen. "Yum."

"I picked it up from Tony's." Despite the repeat in dinner menus, Tony also made great lasagna. Picking it up on the way home made it a perfect choice for a dinner I hadn't even thought about until earlier this morning.

Tony's Italian Ristorante and Bistro was

one of the better Italian restaurants in the entire state. Tony came to Star City directly from Ravello, Italy, a beautiful village on a hill next to the ocean, according to the pictures I found on the Internet. Tony was the blondest Italian I'd ever seen and had a way with anything pasta that made people close their eyes, lean their head back, and savor each and every bite. I'd heard people say they actually ate more slowly when they were at Tony's, just so the meal could last longer.

"I love Tony's," Marion said. "What can I do to help?"

"Get the table set." I nodded toward the dining room, where the window wall currently displayed a green mountainside and some white puffy clouds slipping slowly across a sharp blue sky. It was too bad I wasn't a painter.

Two of us made the job of getting ready much easier. Besides, it was always good to have Marion around. She was a much less flippant teenage niece than teenage daughter. I remembered being her age, though, so I tried to persuade Jimmy to cut her a little slack regarding her tone sometimes. Jimmy wasn't interested in parenting advice from his younger, childless sister. It was hard to blame him.

"I'll get it!" Marion said gleefully when the familiar three-rap knock sounded from the front door.

"Marion, my dear," Chester said. "Ramona, this is my stunning great-granddaughter, Marion Henry."

"Oh, aren't you lovely," Ramona said as she pulled Marion into a friendly hug.

I knew Marion wasn't into hugs, but she didn't stiffen too much.

"Come on in," I said. "I don't mean to be abrupt, but dinner is ready. I picked it up from Tony's, and I decided I could either keep it warm in the oven and risk doing something bad to it or we could just sit and eat."

"I for one am as hungry as a pretty girl prepping for a pageant," Ramona said. "Let's eat."

Dinner was easy and enjoyable. Ramona and Chester liked each other, a bunch it seemed. Ramona shared the story of her former husband's disease and death and how much it had affected her. They'd spent forty years together, and when he died, she spent a whole year just crying. One day she woke up without tears so she packed up a few belongings from her Georgia home and took off to some place where she wouldn't be reminded of her husband all the time.

The two of them had never been west of the Mississippi, and the idea of skiing or snow was foreign. Ramona hoped her husband's spirit was laughing at her choice of a house on the side of a mountain in an old ski town.

"Where I come from," Ramona said at one point, "there's a tendency for widows and widowers to live the rest of their lives alone after their spouse dies, never to date anyone again, but this handsome man made a couple dates too tempting." She smiled at Chester.

"That's a good thing," I said.

Ramona looked at Marion and then at me. "I'm not going to try skiing, just so y'all know. It still seems ridiculous, up there on slidey things in the snow. No thanks."

"What about snowboarding? I can teach you," Marion said.

"Aren't you the sweetest thing ever created, but no, I don't think so. Thank you though," Ramona said with a big flourish of her hand. "I would, however, like to ride up and down the thing on the big wires."

"The lift?" I said.

"Yes, I believe that's what it's called."

"We'll have to take you up on one of them, or a tram. Those are enclosed and run during the summer too," I said. "That would be fun."

I looked at Chester. Never would I have imagined that he would become smitten with someone who had no interest in skiing, someone with red nail polish and soft but sweet perfume. But he was smitten. In a big way.

I had loved my grandmother, deeply in fact. Even though she'd died when I was young, she had been a huge influence on my life, teaching me compassion on a level that, though my family was full of pretty good people, no one else I'd since known had been gifted with.

But she would be fine with Chester finding happiness with someone new. I just knew she would.

As Ramona was showing Marion a diamond bracelet around her wrist, the doorbell rang.

"Excuse me," I said as I stood.

The only person who ever stopped by my house was Jodie, but she usually called my cell phone first — it was currently in my bag, being ignored through dinner, and I hadn't had a landline in a couple years.

I didn't need to make it all the way to the front to know that the person on the porch was tall, with brown, unruly hair. I could see that much through the window at the top of the door.

I was suddenly anxious. Now was not a good time, but I didn't want Seth to think I didn't want to talk to him. In fact, I really wanted to talk to him.

I opened the door and immediately said, "I'm sorry."

He said the same thing at the same time.

We both laughed and then smiled at each other in that goofy way that single people hate. I know, I can relate. I was single just a few days ago and still might be.

"Let me be ungentlemanly and go first," Seth said, but he was stopped short by a rise of laughter from the dining room. "Oh, you have company."

"I do," I said. "Want to join us? There's plenty."

"No, no. I'll talk to you later," he said.

"Don't be silly, young man, come inside," Chester said from over my shoulder. "We'd love to have you join us."

Seth smiled and blinked.

"Give us one second, Chester. I bet I can talk him into coming inside," I said.

"Good. Please know you're welcome," Chester said before he turned and made his way back to the dining table.

"It's me; Chester; his new girlfriend, Ramona; and my niece, Marion," I said.

"Please come in. There's lasagna from Tony's, and you'll love it, even if it isn't as good as yours. I'm sorry about the background report — see, I slipped that in there. Sneaky, huh?"

"Clare," he said with a smile and a sigh. "I'm sorry I behaved like a child who needed to have a temper tantrum. I was caught off-guard, but you don't know me, and your best friend is a police officer. I get it. And I would like to explain the stolen geode accusation to you — some day, but not right away, if that's okay."

"It's very okay," I said.

"Start over?" he said.

"Sure, if our first kiss can be like the last first kiss," I said.

"I'm not sure I can duplicate. How about I try for even better?"

"Deal." I opened the door a little wider.

Seth stepped inside and then stopped. We looked at each other a brief moment, but it wasn't the right time for anything romantic. We shared a shrug of disappointment.

I closed the door. "Follow me."

Chester had already grabbed another chair and a table setting. He was putting the fork in place just as we rounded the wall.

"Well, hello there," Ramona said as all eyes turned toward Seth.

I introduced everyone, and we sat down as Seth filled his plate with lasagna and salad, and we were all entertained by Ramona's stories about growing up in the Deep South.

"Why, that brother of mine picked us up in a garbage truck. It was his job, driving the truck and picking up the garbage. We climbed aboard and rode to the baseball game we were fixing to play, and we all stunk like garbage."

"You played baseball, not softball?" Marion, the athlete of the family, said.

"I did. I loved baseball when I was a kid. I could hit and I could pitch, but no one was as good of a pitcher as Billy Bean Johnson. He could throw strikes like they were lightning shooting right out of his glove, but that was only after he quit hitting everyone. It took a few hitters to let him get adjusted. He was" — she looked around the table, making sure we were all listening — "he was blind as a bat on a cloudy summer night."

"Blind?" Chester said.

"As in, couldn't see?" I said.

"Yes, he pitched based upon voice instructions. The catcher would guide him, and Billy Bean would strike almost everyone out. But the catcher would always let Billy hit a few kids first. It worked to our advantage."

"Was this an organized league?" I said.

Ramona laughed. "No, nothing was organized back then. We all just played outside. Some of us played baseball; some of us played other things. Most of the girls didn't play the way I played. They were more interested in pretty dresses and finding a husband. I just wanted to hit and throw baseballs. Funny thing is, that's where I met my husband. We were sixteen and we both played. Met each other when I struck him out." Ramona laughed. "It's a good memory, and I became all girly shortly thereafter."

"Sixteen?" Seth said. "That's not little league. Throwing strikes and getting hits are harder."

Ramona leaned over the table toward Seth sitting on the other side and said, "I was really good."

"I bet you were," he responded with a knowing smile.

"You played?" Ramona asked.

"I did, through college actually, but I wasn't all that good. Well, nowadays good has to be great to get very far. I was a first baseman. I played all of high school but stayed in the dugout for most of college.

Got some playing time my senior year."

I tried to envision Seth as an athlete. He hadn't struck me as physically awkward — nerdy maybe but not awkward.

"Batting average?" Ramona asked.

"Senior year was .333."

"Very good."

"Just okay compared to the others."

Chester and I smiled across the table at each other. Not that we were worried or would have cared that much, but it was obvious that Seth and Ramona were going to get along just fine.

Interrupting what I thought was turning into one of the most interesting conversations regarding a sport I'd never paid any attention to, the doorbell rang again.

"You want me to get it?" Marion asked.

"No, I got it," I said.

I hurried to the front door again and saw only the very top of Jodie's blond head through the window.

"This should be everyone," I muttered to myself before opening the door.

"Hey, Clare," she said as she walked in and directly past me. "Omar told me about your ideas regarding the doors on the shelves. Can you explain better?"

Again, before I could speak, the buzz of

conversation reached us from the dining room.

"Oh, I'm sorry. I'm interrupting," Jodie said. "Who's here?"

I smiled. "You want some lasagna?"

"No, I ate."

"Come on back anyway," I said.

"Jodie! Come on in. There's plenty. Want some dinner?" Chester said.

Once Jodie was seated and after she made sure that I knew she was pleased about Seth's appearance (she did this with an obvious eyebrow lift my direction — everyone else saw it and Seth smiled too), I repeated the ideas I'd shared with Omar.

"Maybe another piece of the puzzle, but I don't know how it all fits together," Jodie said. "We're getting a list of the old mine locations, and we'll see if the number combinations work with any of them. What do you think, there's a mine out there waiting to be mined? Full of silver or something?" Jodie gave in and spooned a serving of lasagna onto a plate.

"And someone killed for the location?" Marion said.

Everyone was looking at me. "I really don't know, but it sure seems like something to be explored."

As if we'd all been cast in a black-and-white comedy film from the last century, the doorbell rang again.

"I have never been so popular," I said as I stood and excused myself once more.

As with Seth and Jodie, I recognized the person on the other side of the door by the small part of them that I saw through the window. Creighton's uniform-clad shoulder told me that the dinner party was about to become too crowded.

"Hi," I said as I opened the door.

"Hi, Clare. Is Jodie here?"

"Yeah, you want to come in?"

"No," he said. I was sure he heard the noises from the other room too. "I just wonder if you could send Jodie out here."

"Sure. One second."

I gathered Jodie and sent her to the front porch. I closed the door behind her, leaving them alone, but I didn't want to. Something was up. Creighton could have called Jodie. He came and got her. It seemed like a sign of a big deal.

I could hear their voices but couldn't distinguish their words. There was no laughter, just seriousness. Just as I turned away from the door to give up trying to eavesdrop, Jodie swung it open and stuck her head through.

"Gotta go," she said.

"What's up?" I said.

"Something out at Homer Mayfair's. I'll have to give you more details later."

She shut the door again before I could comment. I hurried to the front window and watched as both she and Creighton got into his police car. The second the engine started, Creighton also turned on the flashing lights atop the roof and the siren. He made a quick, tire-squealing turn and then zipped down the hill, I assumed toward Purple Springs Valley and Homer's house.

"What's going on?" Chester said from behind me.

"Creighton was here to pick up Jodie. There's something going on at Homer Mayfair's."

Chester's eyebrows came together. "They rushed out of here?"

"Yes."

"That's worrisome."

"I agree."

Chester said, "I don't think I should call Homer and ask what's up. Until this morning when he came in, he and I hadn't talked in quite some time. It might be more intrusive than friendly to make that kind of call now."

"I'm sure we'll know what's going on soon enough. Come on, let's have dessert. I have enough even if a few more people stop by," I said, trying to add a little levity to a suddenly serious moment.

"Excellent," Chester said. He looked over his shoulder to confirm no one was behind him before he continued in an exaggerated whisper, "He's back, I see. Told you. And before twenty-four hours were even up."

I smiled and led the way back to the pleasantly crowded table.

24

Dessert was just as good as dinner. Tony's chocolate chip bread pudding rendered us all blissfully silent as we chewed and swallowed. I asked Ramona if bread pudding was a southern dish. She said that it was and that Tony had figured out how to make even his American dishes sweet, creamy, and delicious.

Shortly after dessert and coffee, Chester, Ramona, and Marion all seemed to become very tired. Marion performed an exaggerated stretch and yawn to punctuate her sheer exhaustion.

"They weren't too obvious, were they?" I said as I closed the door behind them.

"Not at all," Seth said.

"Coffee on the porch? It's a great night."

"That sounds perfect. What can I do to help?"

"Go on out. I'll be right there."

Only a few moments later, we were on the

front porch, sitting side by side in the same spot Jodie and I had sat the night before, sipping from freshly filled mugs. It was another perfectly cool summer evening, and I'd put on the same sweater I'd worn to Seth's apartment.

"Even with the lights from the town, the stars here are stunning," Seth said.

"I know, I have a great spot," I said.

"You do," he said as he peered up from under the porch roof at the sky.

"Hey, Seth, I'm so sorry about . . ."

"No need to apologize again. Let's just move forward, Clare. We can start by you telling me if you have any sort of criminal record so I can hold it against you someday when we're having a big fight."

I laughed. "I'm clean. Way clean. So boring that I'm sure my high school teachers thought I was just one big act. I did what I was supposed to do. I even did all the extra credit."

Seth looked at me. "I was that way too, except I wasn't a pretty blonde."

"Glasses back then too?"

"More back then than now. I only need them now after my eyes get tired and I want to see small things close up. Back then I needed them for everything, and I even had tape holding them together over the nose.

Lasik, it's a great thing."

"I'm too chicken," I said as I looked his direction and pushed my glasses back up my nose.

For a long moment, we looked at each other, me staring at Seth's face in the mostly dark. Him staring back. I wondered what he was thinking, but I guessed he was also wondering what I was thinking. We probably weren't all that complicated.

Just as we both leaned in toward each other, hopefully for another shot at that first kiss, my phone buzzed, vibrated, and played the *Star Wars* Stormtrooper theme. Jodie had programmed the ringtone into my phone to announce that she was calling.

"Sorry," I said as I reached for the phone I'd placed on the side table.

Seth smiled.

"Jodie, what's up?"

"Hate to bother you, Clare, but could you meet me at the station? Right away?" Jodie said.

"Uhm. Sure," I said. There really was nothing else I could say, even if I was in trouble again.

No matter if Jodie was calling as a police officer or as my best friend, she wouldn't want me to meet her if it wasn't important.

Leaving the mugs on the porch as I shut

the front door, I explained to Seth what I was doing.

"You sure you don't want me to go with you?" he said as we stood next to my car.

"No, it'll be okay. Hey, I might have a record after tonight."

"And we'll have so much more in common," Seth said.

The typically awkward good-bye moment wasn't all that awkward. I was in a hurry and Seth knew it.

"Call me when you're done," he said as I got into the car.

"It might be late," I said out the open car window.

"Doesn't matter," he said.

I told him I would call, and then I turned the car around almost as well as Creighton had turned his, and headed down the hill.

25

"I don't understand," I said as I sat, my knees weakening with the news. It was a good thing there was a chair behind me.

"I'm sorry, Clare," Jodie said.

"He's unconscious? They don't know if he'll make it?" I said.

"Yes, we found him in his office."

"Oh, no. I'm so sorry. I saw him just this morning, Jodie. Just this morning. And yesterday, I sat in his house and we chatted. What happened?"

Jodie had taken me into the same interrogation room I'd visited recently. She'd met me at the front door of the station, immediately took my arm, and guided me toward the room. We'd passed Creighton, Omar, and Kelly, all of them with concerned frowns below too-bright, anxious eyes. I'd seen that they were all upset about something.

Jodie shook her head. "Head injury, but

you don't need those details. I brought you here for a couple reasons, Clare. Bear with me, okay?"

I blinked at her tone. "Okay."

"Look, Homer was found in his office, left for dead. The office had been torn apart, a really big mess."

I nodded.

"And, well, there was a note on his desk. We think it was written by Homer himself, but of course we can't be sure. We're having a handwriting expert look at it, but we can't know for sure at the moment."

"You said that twice — that you can't be sure. I hear you."

"Right. Well, the note mentions you. It says . . . It's like a journal entry, actually, in a notebook that we think he used as a journal. He has a number of them. Does that make sense?"

"Come on, Jodie, just tell me what it says."

"Specifically, it says, 'Clare Henry, type-writers, dangerous.' "

"Well, that could just be a note that I stopped by, that we talked about the type-writers. I have no idea what 'dangerous' means. Do you think it has something to do with me or with whoever hurt him?" My voice was pitched too high, my breath a little shorter than normal, and I felt like I might start to cry.

"There's a little more."

"Go on."

"It looks like the item that they hit him with was left behind, and again I hate to go into too much detail, but it was an old Underwood. We think it was Mirabelle's."

"What?" I couldn't understand how Mirabelle's typewriter got to Homer's office, let alone the fact that it might have been used to try to kill Homer. "Oh no, are you going to tell me something happened to Mirabelle?"

Jodie took a deep breath and then put her hands over mine on my lap. "We can't find her, Clare. She's not at her house."

My thoughts went into high gear, and I spoke even more quickly, not making complete sense. "Happens. She goes places. Salt Lake City? Happens. Her car, the Subaru?"

"Right. Her car's not at her house. She doesn't have a cell phone. But, and this is good news, there's no indication that anyone broke into her house or that any violence occurred there."

"You brought me here to tell me all of this?" I said as I stood. I wanted to search for Mirabelle, but that would have been impossible, of course. I would have gone to her house and found a way in, but after that

341

I wouldn't have had any idea what to do. I also wanted to make sure Chester and Marion had made it home okay. Marion. Maybe Marion *wasn't* out of danger. I was suddenly concerned about my entire family.

"I need to check on people," I said.

"I know. Chester's fine. Marion's fine too. We even made sure Seth is fine. We've got that covered. I asked you here, of course, because I wanted to give you all the news in person, but I also didn't want us to be interrupted so you can give me some information I need."

"Anything," I said, but I still didn't want to sit back down.

"I need you to tell me about Homer and Chester's friendship from all those years ago, whatever you can tell me. And I also need — really need — you to tell me about your building. Is there anything more about the carved doors that you remember?"

I sat slowly.

"I don't know much about their friendship, except that I know they were friends at one time," I said. "But that was way before *my* time. You'll have to ask my dad maybe." I looked at Jodie. "What's going on? Why do you need this?"

"We're trying to solve a murder and an attempted murder. Homer, Chester, Mirabelle — they were friends back in the day, right?" she said, though I didn't think she'd answered my question of why she needed the information in the first place.

"Chester and Mirabelle have always been friends," I said. "But I don't know anything more than that. Mirabelle got the typewriter from Homer back when he was the editor of the paper, but that was a long time ago and no one remembers the details."

"Were Chester and Mirabelle or Homer and Mirabelle ever more than just friends?"

"No! I mean, no for Chester and Mirabelle. Chester was with my grandmother forever, since they were thirteen, I think. When Homer and I were talking, he mentioned how much he admired Mirabelle, but I didn't get any sense that hearts had been broken, if that's what you're asking. I have no idea who Homer was married to, but he's been a widower for as far back as I can remember." I thought back to what Homer had said about the newspaper article and how he was angry at Chester for talking to the Salt Lake City reporter. Had that really been the reason for his irritation? But I had no doubt that Chester and Mirabelle hadn't been more than friends. It just wasn't possible. I didn't quite know what I didn't know, and my imagination was beginning to get carried away. "There was a newspaper article about the press that Chester built. He did the interview with the Salt Lake paper instead of Homer. Homer's been angry about it for years, but they seem to tease each other now. Ask Chester."

"Okay, we will," Jodie said.

"Okay."

"Now, is there anything else you can tell me about those doors?" Jodie said.

"No, nothing. The stories that Chester tells people are just silly things he makes up. He mentioned that the mining company made up stories too, but he wasn't sure about any of those other than they were pretty fanciful, trolls and things. Marion might be able to tell you something. She might have recognized a real place attached to one of the doors. I don't know. You'll have to ask her. Why do you care about that?"

Again, Jodie didn't answer my question directly. "Do you know if any of the owners of the mining company are still alive and around Star City?"

"I have no idea, but Chester might know. Wait, Jodie, I never asked you if you tracked down Brian O'Malley or if you confirmed if he was the one who broke into the empty store. Please don't dodge my question again. Did you?"

"Yes, I tracked him down. Yes, I talked to him, but he denied breaking in. There are so many fingerprints there that we've only started with the ones on and around the back door. No match to Brian O'Malley yet."

"Thank you for answering," I said. "Now what, Jodie? What do we do next?"

"*We* do nothing. You go home, and I start searching other avenues. We have an advantage. I doubt anyone could have predicted that we'd visit Homer today, but we did simply because you showed me the typewriters he brought in, and the notion that he brought in five typewriters that mostly only needed a little dusting just kept bothering me. You helped, Clare, by letting me know about them. It's too bad we didn't get to his house sooner, but that's on us. His attacker probably thought no one would find him for a long time. If he wakes up, we'll learn more, but with Mirabelle unaccounted for . . . well, we just have to keep at it."

"Jodie, what about any Mayfairs at the goat relocation? Did you find them?"

"Mutt confirmed that there were no Mayfairs on his list of attendees. It means that none were truly there or that they snuck in. We're still trying to put it all together."

"Oh, Jodie, I still haven't looked for the cards."

"It's okay. We're operating on the idea that they were there."

"I'm sorry."

"You're helping, Clare. I promise you are. Look, I'm going to get you home. Try to rest. I'll call you the second we find Mirabelle, and I have no doubt that we'll find her, safe and sound."

"There's nothing else I can do? Come with you? Wait here?"

"No. I'm sorry I had to call you back in, but it was important. Thank you."

Jodie escorted me back through the station. I didn't pay attention to any other faces as we marched through, but there were no sounds of cheerfulness.

"Go directly home, Clare," Jodie said as she closed my car door. "We'll be checking on you."

"You think I'm in danger?"

"No, but it's always good to be careful."

"You *are* worried about me."

"I'm always worried about you, Clare. You're kind of a nutty girl, but just . . . well, just be safe." Jodie tried to smile, but it looked more like a pained squint.

As I drove back up the hill, I took deep, cleansing breaths, but I still didn't feel better. Homer was attacked and nearly killed? Mirabelle was missing? And there was nothing I could do about either of those situations. My stomach hurt and I shivered.

I'd been so deep in my thoughts that I didn't notice Seth crossing the street until he met me as I got out of my car.

"Hi," I said.

"Everything okay?"

"Not great, but I'm fine."

"Can I walk you in?" Seth said.

"That would be nice," I said.

Once inside and without my prompting, Seth walked around and looked in all the nooks and crannies of Little Blue. When he was done, he joined me on the couch in the front room.

"Why did you do that?" I asked.

"I'm not totally sure, but with everything going on it seemed prudent to make sure there were no surprises waiting. Can you tell me what happened with the police?"

"There was an attempted murder — Homer Mayfair, the town's old newspaper editor and the person Mirabelle bought her typewriter from a long time ago. I'm worried about Mirabelle and sad and scared about Homer. He might wake up, he might not."

"Why are you worried about Mirabelle?"

Seth asked.

"She's not at her house, and she doesn't carry a cell phone, and her old No. 5 was found with Homer. No one knows where she is at the moment. She doesn't check in with anyone."

"The typewriter with the numbers scratched on the key bars?"

"Yes."

"Hang on. Homer who?"

"Mayfair. Why?"

"Something sounds familiar. Like I've read that name recently. I can't quite place it." He looked toward the front door or perhaps beyond.

"Go ahead. If you think you should check it out, I'm fine. Call me if you find anything. Please," I said.

Seth nodded. "I think I should."

I didn't think I would be able to fall asleep. I thought I would toss and turn with images of Mirabelle and Homer in my head. But after I locked all the doors and windows in Little Blue, I climbed into my bed under the stars. I made sure my phone was close enough to hear if Seth, or anyone, called or texted, and then fell into an oblivious sleep.

Only to be awakened by pounding on the front door.

I rolled over to see that it was almost eight

o'clock. I'd either missed my seven a.m. alarm or turned it off at some point.

The list of people who could be at the door was too long to speculate, but the bright light woke me to attention.

I quickly slipped on my glasses and grabbed a sweatshirt and jeans and threw them on over my pajamas. Through the glass, I saw it was Seth.

"Hi," I said as I flung the door open, bed hair and pillow face creases and all.

"Hi," he said. "You weren't at the store."

"I overslept. Did you call?"

Seth laughed. "No, I didn't even think about it. I wanted to talk to you in person so I went there first."

"Come on in. What's up?"

"I have some interesting news," he said as he held up a manila folder.

We moved to the couch again as he placed the folder on the coffee table and began.

"At first, I couldn't place where I'd read the name Mayfair, but I knew I had, recently. There was something about it that stuck with me. It isn't a particularly unusual name, but finally I remembered these." He pointed at the short stack of papers. "They're mining permits."

"They look old."

"They are. Very old. Anyway, I won't go

into too much detail. These are permits that were granted to miners to mine. They're all expired now, but the man who was hurt, Homer Mayfair, was listed on some of them."

Seth fanned a few of the permits over the coffee table and pointed.

I leaned forward, readjusted my glasses, and inspected the papers. They all had Homer's name and signature.

"I don't understand," I said as I sat up. "Homer wasn't into mining. He was a newspaperman. Are these part of the Star City Silver Mining Company? Was Homer somehow part of that company?"

Seth shrugged. "Not that I could find. Hang on, though. Most of these permits are for mines that weren't really mined. Again, I know you're smart enough to understand all this stuff, but to keep it quick, I'm going to give you a summarized version."

I nodded.

"When you mine, you have to get rid of the water that's in the way. It's not an easy thing to do, and it can be very expensive, prohibitively so sometimes, so there are places where items could be mined that never get mined because in the long run getting rid of the water turns out to be too expensive considering the value of what could, in fact, be extracted. Homer owned rights to some smaller potentially mineable areas and some small actual mines. I have no idea how or why he got the rights. Perhaps he could see value where other individuals couldn't back then. Perhaps his family had the rights before him, but I didn't take the time to search historical documents beyond these — which happened to be in my new office in a junk drawer and why the Mayfair name sounded familiar. I'd come across them while I was getting situated."

"All right, so Homer was into mining, but how did that almost get him killed?"

"Still not exactly sure, but I played with the numbers from the typewriter key bars and came up with something. Put together in a certain way, they signify the location of what might have been a potential mine — a very small one." He pointed at one of the permits. "So small, in fact, that I couldn't even find it on any of my lists of possible reclamations, Clare. It seems that this might actually be a forgotten location."

"Forgotten?"

"Well, as in no one, at least in an official capacity — someone like me or someone from the United States or Utah Geological Survey, for instance — has done anything with, or perhaps even seen, the mine. It could be a danger, or it could be so out of the way that it's just been there, not causing any harm at all, so it was forgotten."

"Where is it?" I asked.

"About a mile past an area called Purple Springs Valley. It's up a bit, probably not easy to get to and not well traveled because it's not part of any groomed land."

"Over past the goat relocation?" I said.

"You did mention some goats, but I never got the details," Seth said.

It was too much to explain. "I need to call Jodie."

"Okay."

Jodie was at my house only seven minutes later. Seth recounted what he'd told me. She listened with her cop intensity.

"I'll take a drive out that way and have a look," she said when Seth finished.

"Can I . . ." I looked at Seth. "Can we come with you?"

Jodie gave me her "I don't think so" squint, but then she seemed to rethink. "It's daytime and we can keep a decent distance. You really want to?"

"I do." I looked at Seth.

"From a geologist's standpoint — well, you might want me there to evaluate possible safety concerns anyway," he said.

Jodie blinked as if she wasn't sure if he was serious or not, but when she realized he was, she said, "All right, let's go."

I climbed into the passenger seat and Seth took the back. As we steered out of town and toward Purple Spring Valley again, Jodie radioed in our destination, explaining that she had two civilian passengers with her and telling dispatch that she would call for backup if anything seemed suspicious.

The woman at the other end of the radio actually hesitated when Jodie said she didn't need backup quite yet. I thought that was a bad sign, but I didn't point it out for fear she'd rethink my going along. Seth must have noticed the hesitation too. He and I glanced briefly at each other but kept quiet.

"All right, once I'm over the pass on the other side of the valley, we'll have to go off-road, right?" she said to Seth in her rearview mirror.

"Yes, I think so. There might be some old access roads over there, but I'm pretty sure I haven't noticed any on any maps."

"All right," Jodie said.

We rode mostly in silence. Jodie didn't want to answer any of my questions now, but I wasn't sure if that was because Seth was along or if she was just deep in her thoughts, trying to sort through facts and details. Our task at hand didn't make any of us think small talk was in order, but before long we were through the valley. The compound and monastery were quiet, and my heart ached when I glanced toward Homer's house.

"Homer has a dog," I said. "Did you get him?"

"Yes, he's at Omar's house right now," Jodie said. "I'm sure he and Star are getting along great."

When we reached the bottom of the pass, Jodie stopped the truck and looked out the windshield and up the steep, rocky slope.

"It's only about twenty feet up. It's flat up on top, right?" she asked Seth in the rear-view mirror.

"According to the maps I looked at, yes, it's flat."

"All right. Hang on," Jodie said as she put the Bronco into four-wheel drive and steered us over the rocks, the tires slipping a little but not much, not enough to make my stomach drop like some of the Jeep rides I'd taken with Marion on the slick rock in Moab.

It didn't take long before we were over and on top of an expanse of fairly flat but untamed land.

Jodie stopped the Bronco again. "Look,

right there is an old road. It won't be easy, but it will get us over to the other side better than if I just drove over all the rocks and brush. Seth, from there do you think we'll only be a hundred feet or so from the mine location?"

Seth concentrated out the side window a long moment and then said, "I do."

"Hang on tight." Jodie turned the steering wheel hard and forced the Bronco over some thick brush and in between lots of rocks. Bumpy, jarring, stomach-clenching might be good descriptions of what the ride felt like. It was all those things. Once she hit the old road, which had been mostly covered by encroaching organic matter, the ride was a little better, but not much.

As we moved, I looked ahead. We were traveling toward two small peaks that were more like mounds.

"Stop!" I said.

Jodie slammed on the brakes, and though we weren't moving too quickly, we all were caught by our seatbelts.

"That's the scene." I pointed out the front window. "That's the scene on the last door, the one Marion inspected."

Jodie and Seth both leaned forward and looked out of the front window.

"What does that mean?" Jodie asked.

"I have no idea," I said, "but maybe it's something important."

"Good to know." Jodie stepped gently on the gas again.

We had trudged along another fifty feet or so when the space between the small mounds suddenly came into view.

"No, no, no," I said as I reached to my seatbelt.

I knew Jodie was strong, but I'd never truly seen her combine her strength with her quickness. Before my fingers hit the button for the belt, she'd sprung out of her seat and tackled me against mine.

"Don't even think about it, Clare," she said in my ear.

"What's going on?" Seth asked.

"That's Marion's Jeep," Jodie said.

"Uh, okay. Whose dirt bike?"

There was a bike parked right next to the Jeep. It wasn't a motorcycle, but a dirt bike, something made for off-road travel only.

"I don't know," Jodie said. "Listen, Clare, I'm going to call for backup, and then I'm going to go see what's up with Marion. You are going to stay here. I have a gun. You don't. Seth, you will sit on her if you have to. Got it?"

"Of course," Seth said.

"Oh, Jodie, what if she's . . . hurt or

worse?" I whimpered.

"I'm going to find out," Jodie said. "Remember, I have the gun. I can help her. Seth, is that mound the location listed on the permit? Or the entrance to it, whatever?"

"I'm pretty sure it is, but if there's an entrance, it's grown over."

"How deep will it go?" Jodie asked as she was still on top of me.

"I wish I could be sure, but I don't know."

"Damn. All right. Now, I'm getting off you, Clare. Seth, grab her arm and break it before you let her get out of this truck, okay?"

Seth's fingers wound tightly around my arm. "Got it."

Jodie picked up the handset to the radio and talked into it. She asked for immediate backup.

"Repeat your location," the dispatch officer said.

Jodie repeated.

"Please do not approach any suspicious activity. We will have other officers on scene as soon as possible. Repeat, do not approach."

Jodie looked out toward Marion's Jeep and the dirt bike, she looked at the mound, and then she looked at me. "Negative. I have no choice. Civilians might be in harm's way. I will approach."

"Negative. Do not approach."

Jodie replaced the handset and looked at Seth and me one more time. "Stay here."

I took a deep, shaky breath as she got out of the Bronco.

"She's a good cop, Clare. She'll take care of your niece," Seth said.

I nodded but was afraid to say anything else.

The noise was out of place — a small boom, some sort of brief whistle, and then a ping. Inside the truck, all the sounds were muted, but still very real.

I watched Jodie go down, as if she was a puppet whose strings were cut.

"Jodie!" I said as I got away from Seth and flew out of the truck.

Without any logical thought at all, I ran to her and went on my knees. Seth was right beside me.

"I told you to break her arm first," Jodie said. "Get down!"

In tandem, Seth and I flopped and flattened ourselves next to her.

"You were shot?" I said.

"I'm fine. It barely grazed my arm." She had her right hand over the top of her left arm, but she removed it with an intake of breath through clenched teeth. She swung herself up to a standing position and pulled out her gun and yelled, "Police, come out now! With your hands up!"

I lifted my head and looked toward the mound. My glasses had tilted on my nose. When I straightened them, I could distinguish the hole that looked like a cave opening.

"Put your head down, Clare," Seth said.

I lowered it a little.

"Jodie!" It was Marion's voice.

"Marion," I said to Seth. He nodded and put his hand on my shoulder.

"Marion, come out," Jodie said.

"He'll only release me if you release him," Marion said.

"Who?"

"I don't know."

"Tell him to show himself and we'll talk about it," Jodie said.

An eternity passed before two people came out from behind the overgrowth that covered the opening.

A man had my niece, one arm around her neck and one arm holding a gun forward. Marion looked fine — a little dusty, but totally unharmed.

"Brian O'Malley!" I said with a loud whisper.

"Let her go," Jodie yelled.

"Let me go first," he said.

"What's your name?" Jodie said.

"That's Brian O'Malley," I said, recognizing the man who'd broken into the empty shop.

"That's not Brian O'Malley, Clare. Hush," Jodie said.

I was perplexed. That wasn't Brian O'Malley? I was certain that was the man I'd seen break into the shop. Jodie said she'd talked to Brian and that he'd had an alibi though.

I hadn't see him in a long time, five or six years at least, and this man, the one I thought was Brian, was maybe the same age as the younger Brian that I'd know those years ago. They looked alike.

Didn't they?

Maybe not.

Was it possible that I'd identified the wrong person because I subconsciously thought Brian was a bad enough guy to be involved in these heinous crimes and his father happened to have sold typewriters years ago? That, plus I hadn't wanted to date him. And now this man had my niece. Guilt churned in my gut.

I lifted my head a tiny bit more and looked at the man, and I suddenly realized that he truly wasn't Brian O'Malley, that he didn't really look much like him at all, that he just had the same build and the same hair color the younger Brian O'Malley had sported years earlier.

"That's not Brian," I said.

"No. Hush. Tell me who you are and what you want," Jodie yelled.

"I just want what's rightfully mine: this land and whatever is on it or in it."

"If it's rightfully yours, you can have it," Jodie said. "No one will fight you for it."

"No one would have if you'd all just left it alone, given my brother the stupid type-writer."

Jodie paused a beat or two. "Who are you?"

"Doesn't matter. Just let me go. Let me get what's in there and go."

"He wants to get what's in the mine?" Seth said. "It's not that easy. Jodie, ask if he's a Mayfair, if he's related to Homer. That might help."

"Or not!" I said. "What if that scares him?"

"That's a Mayfair mine," Jodie yelled. "It's yours if you're a Mayfair. You a Mayfair?"

"That's right."

"Then release the girl and I'll let you go. It's your mine. I mean it. I'm all about you getting what's yours here, I promise."

"Uh-oh," I said. Jodie didn't believe in

making promises. It was one of her few life rules, along with never again drinking tequila after that incident a few years back.

Seth's hand pushed on my shoulder a little more.

Jodie slowly lowered her weapon. "Let her go, man. We'll call it good."

Another eternity came upon us as we watched the man think about what to do next. Marion didn't squirm, but her blue eyes were big and her face was sickly gray. I wanted to run to her so much. I wanted to tackle the Mayfair man. Actually, I wanted to kill him.

Seth pushed even harder.

"All right. I'm going to let her go and then I'm going to ride out of here. I'll come back later for my belongings. Everything in there is mine. I know what's in every bag. If one piece is missing, I'll sue."

"Bag?" Seth said, more to himself than to me.

"I like that plan. Go, get out of here," Jodie said.

"Put the gun on the ground. Throw it out in front of you."

"Let her go, then I'll throw it; that's the best I can do."

A moment later, he pushed Marion away from him and aimed the gun at Jodie. "Put it down."

"You got it."

Jodie was a good cop. She wasn't the best — she sometimes let her personal feelings get in the way — but she was a good cop. She was an even better shot.

She swung her arm back and then forward as if she was going to throw the gun, but like some fancy old gunslinger she brought the gun up instead and managed to aim and then shoot the man as he stood by the opening, all before he could even register what she was doing.

There were some interesting and colorful words used in her next commands, but in summary she told Marion, Seth, and me to get in the Bronco before she ran directly to her victim.

26

Everything happened so quickly. Jodie managed to wound the Mayfair man, but it was enough to subdue him and keep him from hurting anyone else and also keep him talking to Jodie and Creighton when he showed up.

I looked Marion over from top to toe, confirming that she hadn't been hurt. There was a small scratch on her arm, but it was nothing to worry about. She got tired of my inspection, and her skin regained its normal color. I was grateful for her resiliency.

Seth, Marion, and I sat in the Bronco and watched as other officers and a couple EMTs arrived. There was no way to get an ambulance up over the terrain we'd traveled, but the EMTs had come up with Creighton in another truck. Jodie had wrapped something around Leonard Mayfair's arm, but he walked just fine even with his hands cuffed behind him and Jodie's forceful assistance. Once she spent a little time with him, she handed him off to her brother and the EMTs and then stopped back by the Bronco.

I was sitting in the front passenger seat. She stood next to the door and looked in the open window.

"You should have stayed in the Bronco," she said.

"You got hit. I thought you needed help," I said.

"Doesn't matter. You should have done as I told you to do. I'm fine." Her arm was wrapped too, but I didn't see any blood.

"I'm sorry," I said. I was, but that was only because in her eyes I saw more than her words could have ever said. She'd been worried about my safety. Probably Seth's too, but mostly mine. Who knows what would have happened if she'd really been hurt or worse. But she was correct, I should have listened to her order.

"Apology accepted. All right. The guy is Leonard Mayfair, grandson of Homer Mayfair. He and his brother — aka leather man — had come to town from St. George to find their grandfather's hidden fortune. Don't know all the details yet, but bottom line, Leonard got greedy and ended up killing his brother and trying to kill his grandfather. Creighton just told me that Mirabelle is fine, but I don't know how her typewriter got to Homer's yet. I might after Creighton talks to him. Thankfully, Homer's going to be fine, we're pretty sure. For now, apparently this wasn't an active mine, but just some land where Homer hid a fortune in silver he stole from the Star City Mining Company back when he was still a reporter and long before he became editor, I believe. I'll get more on that from Homer too." She looked toward the backseat. "We're going to make sure there aren't any surprises in there, but I thought since you're a geologist and everything, you could take us in after that if you deem it safe."

"Be happy to," Seth said.

"All right. You okay?" Jodie said to Seth.

"Totally fine."

"Marion, you okay, sweetheart?" She looked at Marion, who was sitting next to Seth.

"Fine, Jodie. Thank you for saving my life."

Anger pinched at the corner of Jodie's eyes as she nodded. The fact that Marion had been put in harm's way would bother her for a long time.

I turned in the seat and looked at Marion. "What were you doing up here? You drove apparently."

"I did. I just wondered if this was the scene on the door I recognized. I didn't think it would hurt to drive up and look. The guy on the dirt bike surprised me, and when he heard the Bronco coming, he freaked."

"When in the world have you ever seen this place?" I said.

"Look over there." Marion pointed out the side window where one of the groomed but currently green ski runs was in perfect view. "I snowboard down that hill all the time. I'm good enough to look around while I'm on the board. I always thought this was a cute little valley and wanted to check it out. I've seen it with snow on it. The carving didn't have snow. I couldn't tell for sure without looking."

"Leonard follow you up, you think?" Jodie asked.

"I don't know. He just found me here. I saw the inside of the cave — or mine or whatever. He shoved me in there when he heard someone coming. There are like ten big burlap bags of silver. It's crazy."

"Well, we'll see. For now, give us some time to clear everything," Jodie said.

As we waited more and watched the official people do official things, Seth told us about the land before our time. He told us we were on what was once part of an ocean floor, and how our peaks and valleys had been carved out by glaciers from all the ice ages. He mentioned that ice ages were pretty frequent on our planet. When Marion and I both looked at him with big concerned eyes, he clarified. "Well, every ten thousand years or so. We've got some time."

It was all very interesting, and I wondered if maybe Seth had ignited an interest in geology in my niece. Mostly, though, I was grateful for his easy tone and the fact that before long none of us were thinking about trigger-happy bad guys with their arms around Marion's neck.

Creighton was the one to gather us from the Bronco and escort us to the cave — the police did quickly determine that it was just a cave, void of any other people or surprise holes from any previous mining. I suspected that Seth wondered about the mining permit for the spot that was in Homer's name and if, maybe, there were things in there that could be extracted. I was sure he'd discuss it with the proper authorities.

"All right, it seems okay for us to go in there and gather the bags, but we'd appreciate your opinion regarding the safety," Creighton said to Seth. In a friendly tone.

"Sure." Seth disappeared into the opening with Kelly by his side holding a light and guiding the way.

"Leonard's brother — leather man — his name was Robbie," Jodie said as she sidled up next to me.

"Leonard killed his brother and tried to kill his grandfather? Wow," I said.

"Yeah, years ago the brothers found one of Homer's old journals in one of those stacks of stuff at Homer's house. Homer had a bunch of journals; we picked up quite a few when we found him last night. We didn't see the one that mentions that he stole and then hid a bunch of silver, marking the spot by carving the longitude and latitude letters and numbers into a typewriter's key bars, but the boys did when they were little, and remembered it recently."

"But he sold the typewriter to Mirabelle. That seems like he was pretty casual about it all."

Jodie shrugged. "I don't know, Clare. Homer knew where it was hidden, and I wouldn't be surprised if he sold the typewriter to Mirabelle just so she could find the treasure. Maybe he didn't want his family to have it. Considering what they did to try to get it, maybe he didn't like them even back then. Maybe his kids were as bad as his grandkids. It happens. He was enamored by Mirabelle's writing, apparently. He loved her stories so much, her way with words, that his feelings for her writing turned into a bona fide crush on her. Saw that in a journal. As the years went by and she didn't notice the type bars, maybe he just quit thinking about it or still hoped she'd figure it out someday. I saw something else in a later journal that mentioned him hinting to Mirabelle that he'd stolen the silver and she'd become so angry that he couldn't bring himself to tell her about the secret code on the typebars."

I thought a moment. "Do you remember the date of that journal?"

"Hmm. Maybe the mid-1960s," Jodie said.

There'd be time later to tell Jodie about the article and Mirabelle's request that Chester give the interview to the Salt Lake reporter, but I was pretty sure I now understood the reason.

"Where had Mirabelle been, and how did her typewriter get to Homer's?" I said.

"She was in Salt Lake City. And she doesn't lock her front door. But here's a surprise. It was Homer that went in and got the typewriter. At least that's what Leonard told us."

"Homer?" I thought about my earlier tale

of sending it to Bulgaria, a story that would have been difficult to believe. I should have said Cincinnati.

"Yeah, we think he got it from her to hide it from his grandsons, keep them from trying to take it from her. Didn't work," she said sadly.

"Why were they at the goat relocation? They were there, right?"

"Yep. The journal mentioned Purple Springs Valley, but just generally. They thought they could blend in with the biker group and also search the valley. When that didn't work, they decided to go after Mirabelle's typewriter. Imagine their surprise when, as they were going to knock on her door, she came out of her house carrying that ridiculous machine, put it in her car, and then took it to you."

"But the pictures of the doors in the building? Why were they after those? Because of the scene on the last door?"

"Nope. According to Leonard, those pictures were all about you and Mirabelle and the typewriter and had nothing to do with the store or the carved doors. Bad photographers, I guess. They'd staked out the place because of the whole typewriter connection, and Robbie thought you were pretty cute and followed you home. He took all those pictures."

"Creepy. So the carving on the door is only a coincidence?"

"Something tells me it isn't. Something tells me that it has something to do with the fact that Homer stole all that silver from the mining company, but for the life of me, I can't figure that one out. I hope I get to ask Homer."

"Maybe it's in the journals."

"Yeah, maybe."

"How did he steal all the silver?" I said.

"I think he was doing a story on one of their plants, refineries, whatever they're called, saw it, and figured out how to get in to steal it. Maybe the journals will give us more there too. That's just my speculation. Leonard didn't know."

"Seth's brother's motorcycle plate?" I said.

"Ah, yeah, Leonard broke into the building next door to The Rescued Word when he thought the typewriter might be in there. He was trying to find a way through. He was planning on trying to steal a motorcycle and needed a different plate. Apparently Seth's bike was too out in the open to steal the whole thing but sandwiched between cars enough that he could swipe the plate. It fell out of his jacket when he was either breaking into the building or running back out of it."

"I can't believe I thought he was Brian O'Malley," I said.

"False IDs happen all the time, Clare. It's one of the reasons we like to bring people into the station to talk to them. In that atmosphere, they can focus better."

"Hey! It seemed like you and Officer Streed were pretty interested in questioning Chester. How come you didn't?"

"We did. His girlfriend alibied him. We didn't need to grill him." She looked at me like she was surprised I didn't know that part.

"Wait." I thought about the sequence of events. "So, you knew about his girlfriend before I did?"

Jodie simply shrugged and then said she had to go do something, though I didn't catch the specifics.

"Get the details?" Marion nudged me in my side.

"Some."

"Will you share with me?"

"Probably. Eventually."

"Thanks. Hey, I really like your new boyfriend."

"He's not my . . . Thank you. I think I do too."

Seth led the way out of the cave. He and

Kelly each carried three of the burlap bags. Seth's eyes searched his surroundings when he was free of overgrowth. They landed happily on mine. He smiled and winked my direction before setting the bags down and going back in with Kelly for the rest of them. He was in his element.

I helped load up the bags of silver into the Bronco. I noticed that Creighton was focused and serious but truly didn't seem upset about Seth and me. Jodie was serious too, but at some point she started joking around with Seth, the two of them sharing a laugh or two over things I didn't quite catch. Marion was wide-eyed and enthusiastic about the idea of finding a hidden treasure right in her own back yard. And Seth was always searching for my eyes with his, no matter what else was going on around us.

Once the bags of silver were properly processed and loaded into a police car that hadn't quite made it over the pass — Jodie took us and the silver back down to it in the Bronco — I realized I wished Chester had been there to see everything that had happened. Mirabelle too.

But as I had those thoughts, I began to wonder how much the two of them knew, if anything. I couldn't figure out exactly why, but I thought they knew more than they were telling or ever would tell.

Then I realized it didn't really matter all that much that they'd missed this adventure. They were still strong and healthy. They had a bunch of adventures in their past, and if my instincts were correct, there'd be lots more adventures ahead for all of us.

HOMER MAYFAIR, JOURNAL ENTRY, NOVEMBER 20, 1957

I can't believe I pulled it off, but those fools had no idea. I couldn't help myself. I had to do it. They owed me. Their mine took my leg when I was a kid; it was time to make them pay or at least suffer.

They didn't even recognize me in my overalls and conductor cap. I put a cushion over the end of the peg they caused me to wear and then rigged a shoe there. I limped, but no one even looked at me funny, let alone stared. I just went in there and told the gal at the desk that I was there to replace that door. She didn't understand what was wrong with the one that was already there, but she didn't seem to be in any mood to argue. When I showed her the new door, she didn't even look at it. She waved me away and told me to get it finished quickly, that she had to leave right at five o'clock that evening.

It was too easy. Now, right under their noses, I've told those greedy bastards where I put their silver. They'll never find it. No one will find it in my lifetime, probably. No matter. It was fun to take it and cause them some problems, even if they'll never compare to the problems they caused me.

I hope Mirabelle figures it out, but I don't think she will. That doesn't matter either. I love her stories so much. A little silver's the least I could do for all the enjoyment she's given me, all the words. Her words rescue people from their sadness, their bad days, but I'm not sure I'll ever know how to explain that to her. I do hope she figures it out.

Time will tell, I suppose. It always does.

FROM *NEW YORK TIMES*
BESTSELLING AUTHOR
PAIGE SHELTON

COUNTRY COOKING SCHOOL MYSTERIES

If Onions Could Spring Leeks
If Catfish Had Nine Lives
If Bread Could Rise to the Occasion
If Mashed Potatoes Could Dance
If Fried Chicken Could Fly
  INCLUDES DELICIOUS RECIPES!

FARMERS' MARKET MYSTERIES

Bushel Full of Murder
Merry Market Murder
A Killer Maize
Crops and Robbers
Fruit of all Evil
Farm Fresh Murder
          Includes recipes!

ABOUT THE AUTHOR

Paige Shelton is the *New York Times* bestselling author of the Farmers' Market Mysteries, including *Bushel Full of Murder, Merry Market Murder,* and *A Killer Maize,* as well as the Country Cooking School Mysteries, including *If Onions Could Spring Leeks, If Catfish Had Nine Lives,* and *If Bread Could Rise to the Occasion.* She has lived in a bunch of places but currently resides in Arizona with her husband. For more information, visit her website: paigeshelton.com.

The employees of Thorndike Press hope you have enjoyed this Large Print book. All our Thorndike, Wheeler, and Kennebec Large Print titles are designed for easy reading, and all our books are made to last. Other Thorndike Press Large Print books are available at your library, through selected bookstores, or directly from us.

For information about titles, please call:
 (800) 223-1244

or visit our Web site at:
 http://gale.cengage.com/thorndike

To share your comments, please write:
 Publisher
 Thorndike Press
 10 Water St., Suite 310
 Waterville, ME 04901